IT TAKES A VILLAIN

A Political Fable

How I Learned to Stop Worrying and Love the Negative Political Ad

By

Dick Doran

For Fred and Ré -
I Hope the minutes don't
Pass like hours.
All Best
Dick
1-8-04

This book is a work of fiction.

ISBN: 1-4107-8072-4 (e-book)
ISBN: 1-4107-8071-6 (Paperback)

Library of Congress Control Number: 2003095855

This book is printed on acid free paper.

Printed in the United States of America
Bloomington, IN

1stBooks – rev. 12/02/03

"Villain…a deliberate scoundrel"

Webster's Dictionary

"Meet it is I set it down: that one may smile and smile and be a villain."

Hamlet
Act 1, Scene V

For Mary, Richard, Patrick, Laura, Ella, and Cleo

CHAPTER 1

BIG TIME VILLAIN

I am a hired gun. I am the most villainous political operator of my time. I robotize candidates for office, turn them into money raising automatons, defame the opposition, obfuscate the issues, fill the airways with negative political ads, spread rotten rumors, destroy reputations, manipulate the media and win.

The Wall Street Journal has profiled me. I have run up eight straight victories. I am a favorite guest of political talk shows like Curveball and Backfire.

I, Charlie Coons, am a player…big time.

I know nothing about the so-called "issues." To me, politics is a game of money and technology, polls, ads and focus groups. What candidates do when they get elected is of no interest to me. A year ago, however, I stepped back from the front lines and arranged with my mentor to be comfortably ensconced in a cushy think tank where I pontificate with other so-called experts on the direction of our political system.

But recently, I was watching, with considerable amusement, the morning after election reports of a victory in the state of Vermont by an independent woman candidate in a special election to fill a vacancy in the United States Senate. I have been living in this comfortable bachelor apartment in Georgetown since my wife left me a few years ago. She hated politics. Said it was dirty. She lost her patience with the long nights, the boozing, the golf outings and the overpowering preoccupation which gripped my mind. So she left. "I talk to you," she would say, "and all you do is stare blankly at the wall like I'm not even in the room. Where are you? What are you thinking?"

So I would stop staring at the wall and stare at her, lost for words as I mentally calculated and endlessly re-calculated the latest poll results from a recent campaign in Idaho. She was questioning my way of life. And so I stopped staring at her altogether. Then she departed.

The name of the woman in Vermont was Josephine Stephenson. Forty something. Mother. Two kids. Lawyer husband. Not particularly identifiable as liberal or conservative. Just "Independent."

How interesting. How amusing. No money, no media, no polls, no focus groups, no opponent destruction. Knowing how this must be, to say the least, unsettling to the political fraternity, I called my sidekick, Ronald West, President of Common Good, a novel new advocacy group. Common Good was a shameless front for a variety of special interests. Behind the back of its principal organizer, Dr. Ludwig Controller, we all called it Common Greed. Under its cover, Ronnie orchestrated political campaigns throughout the nation, charged with insuring victories for candidates favored by his boss.

"Ron," I said. "Its Charlie."

"Come on over," he replied, knowing without saying what I wanted to talk about.

Before I could take my seat, he started. "The Doctor just called. Wanted to know about the woman from Vermont. Coffee?"

"Black, after last night."

"So he started to give me a lot of shit. Went ballistic. But I warned him, Charlie. I warned him weeks ago. I told him Charlie. I really did. Urged him to get another million into the Republican campaign because she was moving up in the polls. But of course he doesn't remember. Convenient memory like always. Right Charlie?"

"She could be trouble, Ron. Big time." I wanted to rub it in. I offered to run that campaign for either of her opponents, the Democrat or the Republican. It didn't matter to me. And they overlooked me. Now they can wallow in the political horse shit they allowed to happen.

"Trouble? Of course she's trouble!" Ronnie became agitated and irritable. "Big time. You're right. And all because of 41% of the vote in the kookiest state in the Union. Look at this, Charlie, look at this." He tossed the returns at me. "The robot Republican got 39%. But the brain dead Democrat only got 20! Maybe we should have fed him the dough, gotten his vote up and take some of the whacko liberals away from her."

"Too late, Ron," I observed, calmly sipping my coffee. Not my campaign. "What's Controller proposing?"

3

"Oh he's just great. LaLa Land. He's so out of it he suggested we invite her to his New Members Annual Golf Outing. Can you believe it? The woman is up there acting like a combination of Joan of Arc and Eleanor Roosevelt and he thinks he can buy her with a golf outing." Rolling his eyes, he kicked the wastebasket.

"It's third world stuff up there, Charlie. The People's Republic of Vermont. The place is absolutely cuckoo. Christ, they started debating secession from the goddam union in the last session of the Legislature."

I was more than casually intrigued by the implications of Stephenson's election. But I was even more curious about what Dr. Ludwig Controller would do. Controller was what his name, real or not, implied: a control freak and a villainous one at that. He was the founder of Common Gr, uh, Good. As such, Ronald's boss and, by extension, mine. He didn't take lightly to the unpredictable. I had experienced his wrath in reaction to adversity. Menacing. More intense and determined than any other political operator inside the Beltway. Or elsewhere for that matter.

"Still, it's only a special election," I cautioned. "You'll have to start right away to beat her in two years."

"That may be true. But I sense it's bigger than that. Charlie, Charlie, hear me," Ronald implored. "We're dealing here with a potential precedent that could have long term implications for our operation. And on the other side, we're dealing with a maniac."

At that moment, almost on cue, the maniac walked in the door.

CHAPTER 2

BIGGEST VILLAIN

The odious countenance and familiar voice of Doctor Ludwig Controller were unwelcome reminders of all those villainous things I once did to keep this man happy and in a position of influence and power.

He was not especially tall nor imposing but seemed to be. He had presence. Ageless but apparently in his early sixties, a gray thinning crewcut, bags under the eyes, a mouth that sank at both extremities and a cold, empty stare were the principal characteristics of his countenance. Very self composed. Neatly turned out in three piece suit, manicured and smelling of after shave lotion. His hands were clawlike, as if they would grab you by the neck unpredictably, in an impulsive fit of fury. This man did not like to be crossed.

It was a source of some surprise to me that he was referred to as charming and gracious on the Georgetown dinner party circuit. Apparently, bejewelled ladies adored him. And apparently Ludwig Controller gave them reason. The less I knew about his private life the better. And I certainly didn't want to know about what he intended to do about this latest affront to himself and the system to which he belonged. But there I was, trapped. And predictably, he would assume I was there to help. So that's what I got for poking my nose into this business. But couldn't avoid it. Couldn't resist.

He first stared contemptuously at Ronald. Then he turned to me.

"Nice to see you Charlie. Here to help for a change?" Thus did he begin in his usual accusatory unemotional monotone designed to remind me once again of my ingratitude in staying clear of him.

He then turned back to Ronald, continuing: "especially since Mr. West here has fucked things up."

Ronald squirmed uneasily. What was there to say? Nothing, actually.

"We'd better be careful about this one," Controller continued as he sat down. "Let me remind you both of something you may find it too convenient sometimes to forget. We in the political establishment are sitting on top of the greatest racket in the world. The Mafia marvels at our organization. Asians are impressed by our bottom line. Aging Nazis envy our discipline and order. Neo Fascists try to steal our techniques. Terrorists are puzzled. We have fashioned an industry of pollsters, consultants, political operatives and technology manipulators that would be on the Fortune 500 if we ever sold any stock. Never has a band of happy warriors come so close to controlling the politics of the greatest nation in the world for its own ends. We have gotten where we are through creativity, dedication, manipulation and what amounts to outright mind control of this nation's electorate and elected."

He paused. For effect. He had given this tedious speech before. He now looked directly at

Ronald and said: "and it won't be threatened by the unpredictable presence of some woman from Vermont."

Ronald had to interrupt, had to say something and sink deeper. "A lot of incumbents were defeated yesterday. It's the age of anti-incumbency. A lot of people ran on independent platforms."

Controller looked away for a moment with the contempt reserved by superiors for those they especially wish to put down.

"I'm not worried about the others," he said, as if not in reply to Ron's comment. "All those other incumbent defeating newcomers will soon be incumbents themselves because, when you get right down to it, they will need the money, the power, the campaign support and the influence. What did you used to say, Charlie? They're all the same guy, wasn't that it? Yes, they're all the same guy."

I nodded, as if I wanted him to believe that I shared a bond of loyalty.

"But this one bothers me for some reason," he went on. "I can sense it. I know that she will never be one of us. I just know it. And I also know that she will cause trouble. I looked at her last night on television and it was as if she were addressing herself to me when she talked about the system, and reform, and the corruption of Washington. It bothers me, Ronald and I want it taken care of."

"But what can we do?" asked Ron in exasperation. "She was elected in a state that doesn't mean a damn thing, with 41% of the vote, and she's

8

going to be in the United States Senate for exactly two years. What's to do?"

"Shoot her," Controller calmly replied.

Ron, at a loss for words, said: "what? What was that, sir?"

"Shoot her," Controller reiterated calmly and coldly. "Kill her. Cement her. Contract it out. Whatever it takes. I want her eliminated. We are not the gang that couldn't shoot straight. We are not stupid. There are ways. And there are means. Find them."

"Doctor," Ronald managed to reply, dry in the throat, "I'm going to pretend I didn't hear that and if I'm ever asked I'm going to deny I ever heard it. I'll just say I don't recall it. You just reminded us that we have the greatest racket in the world. And all it takes to blow it is something really..."

I could tell Ron was about to say "insane," but judiciously settled for "unwise."

"You may get someone to send some two bit hack from New York or Philadelphia down in a plane crash and have them blame it on the mob," he continued. "But this one would be the shot heard round the world."

Controller stared impassively and replied: "I'm not so sure about that. The authorities seem to be having a great deal of trouble solving murders recently, especially when they involve, shall we say, adventurous women."

But I could tell, from long experience, that he was re-thinking his impulsive suggestion. In his mind's eye he was staring at the far wall of his own office where a magnificently appointed armoire displayed his twenty honorary degrees from the nation's finest and most opportunistic universities. No, I could see, it wasn't worth losing. He was coming around and turned around.

"Well, what do you suggest?" he asked.

And so, Ronnie jumped into it.

"Five other people come into play in the Stephenson scenario," he began. "The first is her husband, a lawyer with a firm that does a lot of government work in New England, bond counseling, that sort of thing."

"I didn't know that," Controller acknowledged. "If we can't get her, let's get him on the golf outing."

Him and those goddam golf outings, I thought.

"Yes, yes, we may do that, Doctor. But later," Ronnie insisted. "The point is we have a pressure point we can use. Our boys in New England can influence a helluva lot of legal business and the Stephensons may soon be looking at overflowing pocketbooks. Then there's the two kids, Raymond who's twenty and Henry, fifteen. Henry seems like just a normal kid but our contacts think there's definitely something weird about Raymond. He's at UCLA but before he went out something went wrong at home. We can't pin it down but the gossip is that the kid tried to commit suicide."

"Scandal?" Controller mused. "Possible blackmail? Maybe some threats and intimidation? As Charlie here used to say, get them with the family. That's where it hurts."

Thank you Doctor, I said to myself.

"Yes, yes, we may do that," Ronnie rushed on, obviously counting the limited minutes of concentration his boss had for any subject except money. "But I haven't told you about the other players in this little saga. They're two former classmates of Stephenson's at the Wharton School."

"Male or female?" Controller interrupted.

"Both male sir," Ronnie replied.

"Sex," Controller observed.

What a traditionalist, I thought. You old bastard, what's the difference anymore?

"Well, maybe," Ronnie replied. "But it's even more interesting. One is already a member of Congress from California and the other was just elected from Pennsylvania."

"Ours?" Controller again asked without noticeable interest.

"Well, the one from California is. And the other will be after we get him on that golf outing. You have to meet this guy. Frankie Phillips. PAC fiend. Practically kissed the ass of our regional Common Greed, uh, Good, coordinator in public. And get this…"

"Get what?" Controller asked impatiently.

"He was her boy friend in college," Ronnie announced triumphantly.

"What makes you think there's still a connection?" Controller asked.

"Oh, they keep in touch my sources tell me. Plan to celebrate their joint victories with a trip to New York next week. Spouses along, of course. But you never know."

Controller filed it away and asked:"who's the other one?"

"You know him slightly. It's R. Wentworth Brewster from California. 'Rick' to his constituents. Fifth term. Appropriations, Defense Subcommittee. Thinking of running for Governor."

Controller turned to me, knowing I would be amused by what he was about to say. "Rick, Jimmy, Bill. What's with these diminutives, Charlie? Do these guys really think they can cozy up to average people with their silly nicknames when everybody knows them for what they are? Tell me Charlie. What ever happened to Richard, James, William and Thomas? What happened Charlie? Tell me."

What a needler he is, I thought. Every once in a while, the Doctor got to the core of the cynicism that permeated the political climate.

"And now," I said pointedly, "we have Jo for Josephine."

Controller chortled, the first real sign of life in him since he walked in the room. But Ronnie was not about to let the thing drift.

"Alright, Charlie, let's stick with the subject," he admonished.

As if I had started it. He wouldn't say that to his boss.

"Brewster's reliable, Doctor," Ronnie pushed on. "Returned my call last week and said all the right things. I asked him to the golf outing and then he asked me to hold a fund raiser. Just like that. Seems he has a quarter of a million campaign deficit. Nothing like a little cash to get them back in line. My plan is to get the former boyfriend and the old acquaintance to double team her, monitor what she's doing. Time may come when more drastic action may be needed but right now I think we have a possible containment strategy that may work. Considering the options, of course."

"Can we get our people on her staff?" Controller inquired. "No Burlington Commies, Green Mountain Boys. How about Charlie here?"

"Oh no, Doc, really, been there. Done that," I flubbered. "But I'll help in any way I can. You know that Doc."

Controller just stared at me for a long moment, then said, "guess not. What a waste that would be."

To my everlasting relief, he was finally bored and changed the subject. "Ronald, for tomorrow night's annual meeting of our little Beltway fraternity, I want to motivate these gentlemen for next year. So I'm going to emphasize two principles. First is the No Position Principle. It states that we will maximize profits and political control only if we continue to take no positions whatever on national issues while seeing to it that our little elected automata take so many opposing positions that nothing gets done. Some call that partisan gridlock but I prefer ideological stalemate. It's cleaner. Second is my new Ethical Confusion Corollary, whereby we keep matters such as conflicts of interest so confusing that nobody knows right from wrong. Does that sound satisfactory to you?"

"Sounds good to me, boss," Ronnie instantly replied.

"Charlie, you'll be there?" Controller asked.

"Well, I wasn't planning to. I have a prior engagement."

"Disengage. Be there," he ordered. "You're our inspiration, Charlie Coons. You're family. One of us. Our Cousin Charlie. We need you."

Then turning, and staring at Ronnie, he said, "I'm not sure. I'm just not sure. But for the time being, see what you can do with this Mrs. Stephenson…Jo."

"You won't be disappointed," replied a relieved Ronnie.

"I better not be," Controller concluded.

CHAPTER 3

VILLAINS ALL

I would have preferred not to go to The Mayflower that night. In the first place, I really did have a date that I had to cancel, thereby causing understandable unhappiness for the new Secretary to the Speaker of the House. Should I have told her honestly that I was still a slave to the system? I mean, as if she weren't one too. But I was trying to distance myself as much as possible by spending the bulk of my time at the think tank and she had been impressed with my aura of masculine independence. So I just made up some lame business excuse and headed down Connecticut Avenue.

Six P.M. As usual, my former consulting firm, White, Pinafore and Rock had reserved the ballroom for what they called a public interest dinner. But few were fooled about the real purpose. Every insider knew that this was the most significant night of the year for the Beltway crowd, our own Oscar night, our insiders' tribute to ourselves, our closed door chance to pat ourselves on the back, revel in our power, mock the assholes whose campaigns we had run and whose careers we now controlled, and compare notes on how many bucks we had raked in during the prior election year.

In earlier days, when I first arrived in Washington, such a display of mockery and greed would have been reserved for more staid and traditional surroundings, with two martini lunches or late night boozing at the Playboy. But in the general indifference and carelessness that pervaded the current atmosphere, nobody really seemed that concerned. If the principal racketeers wanted to celebrate their achievements, it didn't matter much. Only the respectable name of White, Pinafore and Rock on the callboard of the gracious old hotel provided a flimsy veneer for the arcane rituals of my colleagues.

Controller loved this event. It suited his sense of the perversity of things. He had flowers removed from the tables and replaced with large green dollar signs that glowed in the dark. In all, three hundred members of the political fraternity would show up, many of them leading candidates for the annual awards he would present.

When I walked in, several were already at the bar. Villains all. They were the ones who came early and left late, the drinkers Controller sarcastically referred to as members of Alcoholics Unanimous. They, and the others who would arrive, were card carrying members of the nation's preeminent political fraternity, a group informally known as The New GOP, the band of brothers who went straight for the jugular of the body politic. Although its label sounded like some reactionary reincarnation of the Republican Party, its initials really stood for the "Get Ours Party." Its symbol was neither jackass nor elephant. It cared not for ideology nor did it exhibit more than a minimal interest in substantive issues. Its sole concern was for the maintenance, enhancement and perpetuation of an insider money driven political system. Through that system, trusted team player pols fed the needs of the consultants, lawyers, pollsters, commentators, lobbyists and assorted other middlemen who virtually controlled the system. They, in turn, fed the campaign coffers and personal perk requirements of the public officials who were also elected to play the insider game. And so it went.

It was this fraternity of the Beltway Brotherhood, as we became known in the subculture of the political world, who peopled consulting firms and campaign groups and who, by extension, placed trusted lieutenants in sensitive governmental posts and key private sector lobbying and policy making positions. These were the ones who were "ours," as Ludwig Controller was fond of saying. I was one. Indeed one of the very best. Not everyone was permitted in, however. Like most private fraternities, it wasn't easy to be included among the truly elite, the ones who would be present on this evening. But once you had arrived, your Beltway Brotherhood took care of you. And yours. Big time. You have no idea – or maybe you do – of how many cousins, uncles, aunts, sisters, brothers and former girlfriends of the mighty find their way into cushy spots on the payrolls of political survivors.

"Another martini on the rocks for Tim here," I ordered the bartender. "With a twist," Tim added.

"And a double Dewar's for Georgie," I added. "With a splash," shouted Georgie, the splash being a sure sign of alcoholic predilection. Who's he kidding?

"Drinkers all, alcoholics unanimous!" I shouted for all to hear. Laughter erupted, glasses clinked and conversation accelerated.

"Timmie baby," I asked Tim O'Connor, preeminent lobbyist, "how much access did you provide this week?"

"Three CEOs in the White House and two Executive Vice Presidents with the Speaker," he proudly replied.

"Get anywhere?" I inquired.

"Yeah, big time. Got their ample asses into five separate upholstered sofas," Tim chuckled. "Did they get anything? Schmoozing. Did they get what they wanted? Who knows? Who gives a shit. They think I'm the greatest thing since sliced bread."

"Tired cliche," I thought. But this whole scene was getting tired. Tim had a point. Nothing may have gotten done but the fees were enormous, the reach into the corridors of power wide and deep and the clients overwhelmed.

Just like me, most of these guys had come to Washington to do good and ended up staying to do well. They got into the Beltway business as others in their college classes joined Wall Street. It didn't take long for them to realize that the ticker tape of the stock exchange could be duplicated by the line item of the federal budget.

So, they left the government while their friends were still in power, slamming their weight around as influential consultants and piling up the bucks. Then one day, their friends would be gone from power and that's when they would meet Dr. Ludwig Controller.

Here was a genius of continuity, a man beneath party, an operator to whom issues meant nothing, a survivor of administrations, immune to the deaths and retirements of powerful Congressmen. He became their godfather and patron. No more interruptions in the predictable flow of consulting and lobbying dollars, speaking honoraria, legal fees and business relationships due to changes of party or administration. By allying themselves with the Doctor, they could have it all. After all, they deserved it, didn't they? And didn't they have a right to it after all those years of public service?

The moment had come. The Doctor never entered a room with a flair. Rather, he just suddenly appeared. I looked down from the bar and there he was, slightly off to the side, chatting casually with Dickie White and Paul Pinafore. But all of us knew that it was time to take our seats.

Nothing ever gets accomplished in Washington unless it's over a full course meal, paid for in plastic and chalked up to business. Thus it was that night at The Mayflower. A six course dinner accompanied by Chardonnay and Bordeaux progressed to coffee, cordials and cigars. With much camaraderie and revelry, a surfeit of dirty jokes and tall tales of fees and contracts, the assembled invitees almost forgot why they were there.

Until the Doctor took the microphone. And so it began.

"I have a preliminary announcement to make," Controller stated matter of factly, instantly getting attention. "No longer will I begin our annual gatherings with the word 'gentlemen.' Tonight, for the first time, it is my honor to welcome three women to our celebration."

Scattered applause and a few boos greeted the announcement.

"Ladies – or should I say women – please stand up and take a bow as I announce your names. First, the toughest talking competitor I've seen in a long while, that sometime girlfriend of our founding member, Tommy Ragin, Sarah Symington."

Sarah, frizzy hair flowing over her shoulders, wide grin of triumph on her face, stood boldly and acknowledged the cheers of the crowd, led by her very own Tommy.

"Next," said the Doctor, smiling for just a split second, "a living testament to survival. This woman has been around here for the past twenty five years and never missed a fee or a government paycheck. Looking back, it's frankly amazing to me that she's not been a formal member of this club before now. But Democrat or Republican, House, Senate, White House, cabinet department or regulatory body, this lady has held forth with authority, recognition and staying power that's the envy of the entire Beltway. So much so that everyone wants to quote her. This woman can even keep her husband on the payroll. And I'm talking of none other than Maria Axelrod."

More demure and ladylike than Sarah, but poised and polished, tinge of gray adding authority to her presence, Maria rose slowly from her seat, savoring the moment of her ultimate recognition as one of the Beltway fraternity. She was greeted with the kind of warm applause reserved for elder stateswomen.

"And finally," concluded the Doctor, "a woman who hasn't been here that long but who has made an undeniable impact on our political landscape. She used to work under the President, as you all know. But much to her surprise and our satisfaction, having been missed in the job cut over at the White House, she's turned miraculously into one of the most successful consultant-lobbyists in town. She has, indeed, brought new meaning to the word 'access.' I am, of course, referring to that fresh young face from Oklahoma, the President's own Mary Lou Waters."

"Stand up, you idiot," Timmie said to me as the applause began. "Her boyfriend will be over at 1600 Pennsylvania Avenue for at least the next two years and we need to be on her good side." I stared, adopted my cynical, world weary pose and slightly rose from my seat as the applause died down.

Now the Doctor really got into it. It was at moments like this that his crude and instinctive vulgarity showed forth among his own in a way that would have astonished his Georgetown friends, his celebrity clients and grantors of his honorary degrees.

"Gentlemen – and Ladies," he began, "gathered in this room is the greatest concentration of political talent in the annals of the Republic. Fortunately, for you and me, we are also the most acquisitive band of power players and money seekers this land of the free and home of the brave has ever produced. I make no apologies for that. We've managed to conduct ourselves like professionals, sometimes crude, frequently vicious. But we are the winners and that's what counts. And we have managed, through our celebrity, to gain access to the best clubs, entree to corporate board rooms, attendance at black tie dinners at the National Gallery, and horseback riding in the Virginia countryside. We are lawyers, MBAs, media specialists, technology wizards and just plain gunslingers. And Dickie White here is even a Rhodes scholar."

Majoring in manipulation, I murmured.

"In this year alone, six of our members have addressed the National Press Club. The Wall Street Journal has profiled four of our most successful campaign consultants. There is not a single sage in this room who has not been sought out by talk shows, media analysts and cabinet members. What I am saying is nothing less than this: we have arrived. We control the country. We are the gurus of its elected officials."

Gurus no less, I thought. Where did he get that?

"Yet, the nature of our business is such that we must continue to maintain a relatively low profile. Unfortunately, the people of this country can never really know the extent of our power. Mind control and the influence of media technology are not saleable commodities to the masses. The people out there must continue to think that our clients exercise their independent judgment. They must continue to believe that the people they elect will be responsive primarily to their needs. We've got to keep them feeling that, while they may distrust the system, their own elected officials are trustworthy. The cynicism that is abroad in the electorate is bad enough without us telling too much of our story."

How thoughtful of him to deplore cynicism.

"So, this annual event will be the only opportunity we have to honor our own. And honor them we will. Big time.

"So, let the awards begin. As you know, we give out citations each year for excellence in various sectors of our profession. Now I know that some of you are uncomfortable with the award itself. It's hardly something you would display in the waiting room of your consulting group. But let me tell you, it's the one testimony to reality that we indulge in, the one symbol of our careers that faces the truth. And, as such, it is truly cathartic. I have had past recipients call me and say that they sometimes wake up in the middle of the night, distraught by some tactic or falsehood they have spread and they look across the bedroom and there, shining in all its glory, is The Finger. And they are resuscitated by gazing upon that gold plated fist and that defiant middle finger and it keeps them going. And for those who receive it tonight, it will keep you going too, on to another victory, another fee and another deal.

"Without further ado, then, let's move on to the first, and most popular category, the selection of the Rottenest Negative Political Television Ad of the year. This award is given to that campaign consultant who best advanced the cause of fear and cowardice in elected officials by producing the commercial most likely to intimidate the aforesaid elected officials, thereby enhancing their determination to duck issues, play it safe, obfuscate and place their fates even further into our hands.

"Several outstanding nominations were received and the selection panel, headed by Ronald West, has chosen the firm of Ragin and Dartman for the ad it created for the Governorship Campaign of Chuck Lawrence in Illinois. And here to accept the award is one of the most prominent hired guns in the country today, Tommy 'Six Gun' Ragin."

To the applause of the assembled, Tommy Ragin raced to the platform, obviously overwhelmed with gratitude and feigned humility. Tommy had come a long way in a few short years. I had worked with him when he was just getting into the business, an obscure young Border stater who, because of his celebrity and outrageousness, was now commanding five figures an appearance for speaking engagements where all of his crudity and down home political savvy were alternately shocking and titillating genteel audiences. If you didn't know Tommy, you'd swear he was a serial killer. And in fact he was. Balding, wide eyed and fiercely intense, in his early forties, with the swagger of a Marine drill sergeant, Tommy's weapon wasn't a gun but the power of television plugged into polling data.

"Tell us the story, Thomas," Controller asked as he gave Tommy the Finger.

"Thanks Doc. And thanks to all you guys for your appreciation. You too Sarah. Gosh. It seems like only yesterday I was growin' up in the back country of Kentucky and now here I am recognized and feared in the power center of the world. Talk about makin' it! Shit, there's nothin' like havin' the recognition of your fella gunslingers. Sorry Buddy Dartman couldn't be here. He'd sure be pleased and proud. But I guess all you fellas know he's over the White House right now cookin' up some damage control on the Prez's latest screw up. Well, the story goes like this. Last year we were retained by this guy named Chuck Lawrence who didn't know shit about the game. All he wanted to do was be Governor of Illinois. For starters we thought he was an asshole but he had ten million dollars of his own money to spend so what the hell. He might as well spend it on us."

Cheers of recognition and appreciation came from the crowd. I just stared. Some of the boys took out their calculators to add up the fees and percentages that Tommy banked for his efforts.

"Anyway, we start by takin' a poll and we find out that the incumbent Governor isn't in bad shape at all. He's got a 70% favorable rating, no tax increases, no indictments, done all the right things. And in the matchup, he beats our guy, 62-24, with 14% undecided. Not much goin' for us, right?"

"Yeah, but you'll fuck 'em Tommy," comes a holler from the hired guns contingent.

Tommy let go with a quick chuckle and continues.

"But there's one weakness we see in the polls. Some of the Governor's soft voters and most of the undecideds keep mentioning personal traits about the Governor that make them feel uncomfortable. You know, like his smile, his manner, his demeanor, the way he combs his hair. The important things. Then, a lot of people who do like him don't like some of the people around him and are dead set against his opposition to capital punishment. So we figure maybe this fella's not tough enough to be Governor. Then – you won't believe this – one of his staff guys is rumored to have gotten AIDS. He didn't get Aids but he's real sick and nobody seems to know why. So we start spreadin' the word that one of the aides got Aids and stuff like that and people start wonderin'

"Then we follow the Guv around with our cameras and get some great footage. One day the Guv is walking out of the Capitol with three of his aides and he sees us with the camera. But the stupid shit thinks we're from the public TV station and starts to smile and wave. And then, as he's walkin' away, with all of them in a group, he puts his arm on the shoulder of the aide walking next to him, brings it down casually and it brushes the guy's back. I swear to God Almighty, for just a split second, it looks like he's pattin' him on the ass."

Derisive laughter breaks out.

"When we get this stuff in the studio, we can't believe it. Right away we start makin up the ad. I do the copy and Buddy Dartman supervises the visual. And here's how it came out."

The lights went down in the ballroom, a large screen is unfurled, Tommy Ragin turns on the video machine and the ad begins:

A SCENE AT THE STATE CAPITAL

VOICE OVER: "Some people think everything's just fine in Springfield. But most of us are worried about the future."

SWITCH TO ACTION CLIPS OF DRUG SHOOTINGS ON STREETS OF CHICAGO, NATURAL DISASTERS DOWN STATE.

VOICE OVER: "A lot of Illinois voters are deeply concerned about Governor Billingsley's strength, toughness and determination in dealing with drugs, crime and the other major issues facing our society."

ACTION SHOT OF GOVERNOR AND AIDES COMING OUT OF THE CAPITOL

VOICE OVER: "It's not just the Governor. He seems to mean well but it's the people around him. And in government, it's the people around you who make the difference. Do we really want to put our future – and our children's future – and the well being of our senior citizens – in the hands of strange people we can't trust?"

VIDEO AT THIS POINT HAS GOVERNOR WAVING, SMILING, WALKING AWAY AND SWINGING HIS ARM BEHIND HIS AIDE. AND THEN, THE SPLIT SECOND THE COMMERCIAL IS ALL ABOUT. WHOOPS!

FINAL FRAME; A CONTRASTING PICTURE OF CHUCK LAWRENCE SHAKING HANDS WITH HARD HATS, COAT OFF, TIE LOOSE, SMILING MASCULINELY AT THE WORLD.

VOICE OVER: "You won't have to be concerned about where Chuck Lawrence stands...or who he brings into your government. With crime and drugs overrunning our streets, it's time we had a real man with solid values who talks straight as Governor. LAWRENCE FOR GOVERNOR. HE WON'T HESITATE TO PULL THE SWITCH."

Lights up. Applause died down. Tommy Ragin continues: "Chuck didn't like the ad but who gives a damn what he likes, right? We told him he didn't have a chance without it and showed him the numbers. Christ, Billingsley's negative ratings was only 22% after four years in office. We had to build up the negatives, right? Define him before he defined himself, right? So Chuck, who wants to be Governor so bad he can taste it, folds as we knew he would and tells the press some bullshit about those decisions on negative ads being made by his campaign consultants and he really didn't know all that much about it and won't disavow it because the people should know if it's true, blah, blah, blah.

"Now let me tell you somethin'. In the first fifteen days we ran the ad, Billingsley's negatives went up a point a day. Some people screamed foul but the rank and file didn't one bit like it that their Governor might be a faggot. Billingsley and his people carried on like hell, calling the League of Women Vultures and the editorialists and stuff like that but we figured, screw them, the more attention they draw, the more questions get asked. Billingsley got so rattled, he blew the debate and then, would you believe it, the aide who was sick died and they said it was pneumonia!

"Four days before the election, the polls said we were tied and on election day we pulled out a victory by just 1500 votes out of four million cast. Now we got the Governor of the fifth largest state in the union. I don't know what kind of Governor he's gonna be, because I don't give a shit about government. But I do know I'm good for a nice fat consulting retainer for the next four years. And I know where the bond business, legal fees, jobs and political money are going. Okay you guys? You're all invited to the Inaugural. Just bring your clients' checkbooks!"

Deafening applause and a standing ovation followed Tommy's story.

"Thank you, Tommy," Controller said as Ragin left the podium. "I think you've proven beyond a doubt that there won't be a candidate in the country anymore who won't be so terrified of the thirty second ad that he'll be looking for the kind of dimension you and others like you bring to a campaign.

"And now for our second award, for the Slickest Pollster of the Year. Again, we had a lot of admirable nominees but for the third straight year, for sheer robot-like control of a candidate, the award goes to Hap Mandell. Hap, come up here and get the finger."

Only a smattering of applause greeted Mandell who was clearly not the favorite Beltway Buddy in the room. As they say in the trade, some of them 'hated him with a passion.'

Controller fixed Mandell benignly with his eyes and asked him to tell his story.

"Thank you, Doctor," Mandell intoned. "I also want to thank Ronald West, Common Good (the polished Hap was one of the few members of the Brotherhood who never slipped into Common Greed) and the selection committee for this third straight award. It's a great honor and I'm sure my wife and children will join me in expressing our gratitude."

Where does he think he is, I wondered, the Oscar ceremony? At that moment, somebody at the Hired Guns Table shouted out "what about your girlfriend, Hap baby?" Hap winced but pretended not to notice. Controller stared, cold and impassive.

And then Hap began.

"As many of you know, I have been doing in depth polling on the abortion issue for various church groups over the past few years. In their wisdom, the churches have finally begun to realize that, if you're going to be a player in this highly competitive arena of public opinion, you simply have to adapt to the sophisticated techniques of modern communications. The significant change over past years on the abortion issue was in the depth of feeling. In the past, pro-lifers – excuse me, anti-choicers – invariably said that this issue alone would determine how they voted. They were, as we say, single issue voters.

"But this year, things changed. In addition to simply asking people how they felt, we asked them to hold a little device we call a feely counter in their hands while watching an early debate in the Senate race. During the course of the debate, they would squeeze the little device and we would record their reactions on a scale of one to ten, thereby getting a much better indication of how they were feeling."

At this point, Hap gave a visual demonstration, taking the squeegy little thing out of his pocket, placing it in the palm of his hand and squeezing it as if in reaction to external events.

"Well," he said awkwardly, "it at least gives you some idea of how this revolutionary device works."

I stared in amusement as the same voice from the Hired Guns Table was heard to say, "feely yourself, Hap."

Again ignoring the comment, Hap continued.

"What the feely counter indicated was that, for the first time, pro-choicers were prepared to vote on a single issue basis in greater numbers than ever before. Furthermore, the polls themselves indicated that the 35% in the middle, while leaning to the pro-choice side, had all sorts of reservations about just how far abortion should go. The feely counter didn't exactly measure these nuances so we had to go back to talking to people.

"One obstacle to our strategy was the candidate. Most of you know him but he shall go unnamed because I think we all consider him to be one of the most opportunistic and unprincipled sons of bitches in the business and that's saying a lot. He was a Roman Catholic who, in previous years, repeatedly took the pro-life side.

"Well, it didn't take long for him to see that one could, for the first time, be threatened by pro-choice single issue voters. In a matter of minutes, after consulting of course with his conscience, he found that he was able to shift positions. He enraged the pro-lifers who began stalking him up and down the state, issue threats, and of course he shocked the Catholic hierarchy who, by this time, had their own problems.

"But the truth was in the numbers and the numbers indicated what was really going on. An abortion landslide was in the making! A combination of extreme and moderate attitudes produced 57.2% of the vote. So we formulated the following position which our candidate repeated with mindless regularity as if it had been taped inside his silly brain:

"WHILE I RESPECT THE POSITION OF MY CHURCH AND AS A MORAL ISSUE AM PERSONALLY OPPOSED TO ABORTION, I DON'T BELIEVE THAT MY PERSONAL VIEWS SHOULD BE THE BASIS FOR PUBLIC POLICY ON THE ABORTION ISSUE. THEREFORE I FUNDAMENTALLY SUPPORT THE PRO CHOICE POSITION IN THIS CAMPAIGN. I AM NOT, HOWEVER, FOR ABORTION ON DEMAND OR PARTIAL BIRTH ABORTION. I ALSO BELIEVE THE HUSBAND SHOULD HAVE A SAY IN MAKING THE DECISION. BUT I DON'T THINK WE SHOULD TURN THE CLOCK BACK ON ROE VS. WADE. IT'S SETTLED LAW."

Hap glanced up from the statement and smiled triumphantly.

"On Election Day, our candidate got 57.1% of the vote and I'm still trying to find out what went wrong with that other tenth. I would ascribe it to margin of error but my polls simply don't have a margin of error. We have so refined our system that I can tell at any time exactly how the voters feel about any given issue and I can turn that knowledge precisely into what should be said in order to produce the vote."

The grudging and reluctant applause for Hap outraged Controller. "Show a little respect!" he shouted. "Hap Mandell, more than any other member of this fraternity, has pioneered the use of polling into what amounts to a mind control device over public officials and candidates. That man was the first to turn politics into a technological exercise. He helped get us where we are today and he deserves our respect."

He stopped. And stared. And continued staring until you could hear a pin drop.

As the night wore one, secondary awards in such categories as the Dumbest Piece of Direct Mail, the Most Intimidating Fax Message to Fund Raisers and the Most Fearsome e-mail Warning were given. Then Controller once again took the floor to close the evening.

"Now," he announced, "I want all of you to know that there's a new group affiliating with us this week. For some time we've been concerned about the media's potential for denigrating our efforts. In our search for the proper spin on our activities, I'm creating a new consortium of spin doctors with assistance from an informal association of communications billionaires concerned about ratings, ad lineage and the bottom line. Our goal is to spin commentary on public issues through a group of reliable celebrity politicians whose appearance on all talk shows and public affairs programs will increase ratings while saying nothing you haven't already heard. It will be the ultimate in political commentary, feeding the hungry cameras and entertaining the masses. For public consumption, it will be called the Foundation for Balance in Public Analysis. But privately, just among us boys and girls, I'm calling it the Ass Kissinger Group."

Howls of laughter. Even I thought it was funny.

"We will be particularly interested in having the networks retain has-been politicians with big names, especially ones who have been involved in controversies requiring bureaucratic double talk. We will be interviewing some campaign hired guns fired for dirty tricks and various incompetents from prior administrations."

"Goddamn!" Tommy Ragin hollered, slapping his blue jeaned thigh. "That's fuckin ingenious, Doc."

As the glee calmed down, Controller concluded the evening with a tirade.

"You've heard of exit polls?" he asked in a cold monotone. "Soon we'll be employing entrance polls. We'll have this system so under control that everyone in the country will be told what to think. And we'll use the media to do it. There will be so many numbers on the screen about so many issues that anybody who had one drink during the network news will think he's looking at a computer printout. For those who think television is the new political boss, they better start thinking about who's bossing television. You people will think up so many sound bites that those sound bites will come back to bite all of them in the ass."

By midnight even Controller was tiring. "No more Wilbur Mills," he concluded, reminding us of just how long he'd been around. "I don't want any of you Alcoholics Unanimous members driving into the basin in the middle of the night. So let's all stand now, raise our arms in unison and recite our motto one more time."

All three hundred – yes, even me – stood up and, with arms held high, some with fingers held higher, joined in reciting our motto:

"LET EVERY POLITICIAN KNOW, WHETHER HE WISHES US WELL OR ILL, THAT WE SHALL EXACT ANY PRICE, BILL ANY CLIENT, STOOP TO ANY TACTIC, ELECT ANY FRIEND, DEFEAT ANY FOE, TO ASSURE THE SURVIVAL AND SUCCESS OF OUR COMMON ENTERPRISE. THIS WE PLEDGE – AND MORE."

Every time they recited that low life mockery of the Kennedy Inaugural, it turned my stomach.

As the dazed participants filed out, some doing obscene imitations of Governor Billingsley, Ronnie West grabbed me by the arm. "Doc wants you to go up to Vermont, check out the Stephenson broad," he said abruptly.

"Are you mad?" I asked. "I'm doing some consulting this week for the think tank."

"Fuck the think tank," he replied. "Controller controls it anyway so what's the difference. Vermont tomorrow, Charlie." There was a sense of urgency in Ronnie's voice. "He's preoccupied with her. It's an obsession. And you're elected."

"No choice," I thought. "What next? Is there no escape? I wonder how the skiing is this year at Mad River Glen."

CHAPTER 4

SKI TRAILS ON THE MOUNTAINSIDE

The song kept going through my head. "Warbling of the meadowlark…you and I and moonlight in Vermont." I must admit the notion of spending a week in the snowy north with Dawn Meadows, Secretary to the Speaker of the House, wasn't the worst thing that could have happened to me.

Dawn. No dummy. Daughter of Senator Peter Meadows of Colorado whose brief marriage to television anchor Betty Wilkens had produced this trophy companion. I invited her to join me in part because she was still unhappy that I stood her up the night of the awards dinner.

"I want to stay in Stowe," she insisted.

"We can't," I replied emphatically. "Have to hang around Burlington and check out the woman who was just elected to the Senate."

"Why?" Dawn asked.

"Because we do, that's why," I answered.

"But all my friends are in Stowe," Dawn persisted.

"Then they'll have to stay there," I said flatly. "We're at the Radisson in downtown Burlington and that's it."

She just glared at me, said no more and got on the plane.

"Ski trails on the mountainside…snowlight in Vermont," I kept reiterating in a sort of mumble.

"I love that song," Dawn said as she sipped her martini. "And you know something else, I love you Charlie."

That was reassuring. But it also made me uncomfortable. I had to admit to myself that, as much as I didn't like it, I had a lot more to do than just hang around with Dawn. Even worse, I didn't know where to start. The order from Ronnie filled me with foreboding. I could see myself being inexorably dragged back into Controller's latest obsession. For I was indeed as morally dulled and humanly insensitive as the others. The difference was that I knew it.

After we checked into the hotel, I called the only political operator I knew in the entire state of Vermont, a lawyer-lobbyist type named Willie Welsh. It so happened that Willie was going to ski at Mad River Glen the next day and we made arrangements to meet for lunch in Stowe.

Then, much to my surprise, as I strode through the lobby looking for the newsstand, I glanced at the day's Calendar of Events and noticed that there was going to be a victory celebration for Senator-elect Stephenson in the ballroom that night. Unbelievable! Perfect! I thought I'd just sort of wander in and "try to make sense of this thing" in the hackneyed lingo of the media.

What a crowd, I thought, as Dawn and I casually sauntered into the ballroom after a couple of drinks at the bar. A lot of people with beards who looked like they came down from the mountains for the first time since Ethan Allen led them against the redcoats. And Burlington lefties with long hair. Proper Vermonters who apparently were direct descendants of Calvin Coolidge. And a handful of African Americans wearing Al Sharpton buttons.

"All you have to do is take a look at this crowd and you realize how she got elected," I commented to Dawn.

"I'm not surprised," Dawn replied. "We have people like this in Colorado too."

"Every place has people like this," I said. "Trouble is, we don't get to see them that often. Out little world is rounded by the Beltway." I enjoyed paraphrasing a well known dramatist.

"See that guy over there?" I asked. "The fat one in the business suit looking self important? He's got to be the Campaign Treasurer. And from the stunned look on his face, he's been wondering ever since election day how the hell she pulled it off and why it wasn't him."

"You're too cynical," Dawn observed.

"Oh yeah? Watch." At that, I strolled over to the fat man and introduced myself.

"Hi, my name's Charlie Coons, up here for a ski week. What's going on? What's all the excitement?"

"Victory party for our new Senator," he replied somewhat cautiously. "I was her Campaign Treasurer. Great thing, this election. Yes sir, great thing. Big time. Had no idea we could pull it off."

"Was it the issues or was it her, Mr…eh." I had to get his name.

"Joe Benton," he replied, loosening up. "We're different up here. It wasn't just her. Hell, I could have won this one."

Dawn winced as I darted a smile at her.

"Well, thanks a lot Mr. Benton," I said, attempting to end the conversation, having proved my point.

"Think nothing of it my boy," Benton replied. "Hell, if she screws up, I'm running next time. Most important thing is that she don't forget who put her in there. There's a hundred people in this room who think they elected her and every one of them's now thinking they can do it next time. Or Governor. Or Congress. Politics is a funny business, Mr. Coons."

"You don't say," I replied with a hint of mischief in my voice. "Well, maybe we'll just stick around here and join the celebration," I concluded.

"Make yourselves at home," Benton concluded, eyeing Dawn for the first time. "Have a beer on us. All home brewed Vermont brands. Independent, just like everything else up here."

At that moment, the small rock band broke into a halting and improvised rendition of, of all things, "Hail to the Chief," and, as we looked to the ballroom entrance, a crowd surged around a female figure, some slapping her back, some just smiling and not a few looking envious as hell. You could tell what they were thinking, just like Joe Benton:

"It should have been me."

"If she can make it to the Senate, I can win the other seat."

"If she can make it to the Senate, how about me for Governor?"

And then I saw Benton throwing his weight around, sublimating his envy with a loud "Terrific, Jo! Make way everybody for our new Senator!"

Balloons began to pop. Applause filled the room. Emotions ran high and I was straining to get a look at this political phenomenon who was about to experience the great instant American celebrity treatment. Her appearances with Larry, Oprah and Sally had already been announced. Front page New York Times.

In her pictures, she seemed tall. But in person, like so many other public figures who appear larger than life on television or in photos, she had to be no more than five foot five.

On television, her blonde hair seemed stylish. In person, it was considerably less blonde and even a bit disheveled. The perpetual smile was gone as she walked toward the podium. In person she looked very much like the perplexed heroine and I could tell that a lot of things were on her mind, the type of things that keep politicians up half the night. Immediate family problems. The dislocation of moving to Washington. The vulnerability of celebrity. The irritation of the media. The intrusion on privacy. The instant expectations of supporters for jobs, recognition and favors, most of which were illusory but they would never understand. The second class citizenship of her lawyer husband who followed behind probably for the first time in his life. He didn't look happy. "The Senator's husband" syndrome.

But attractive she was. Nice body, I thought, in that loose at the collar, tight in the rear dress that's halfway between Burlington propriety and Manhattan stylish. Eyes alert. Poised demeanor. Inner strength. I was beginning to see why the Doctor was concerned. He perceived instantly that this was no ordinary fluke. Fluke maybe. But not an ordinary one.

And then the most surprising thing was her performance on the podium. As a measure of the broad coalition that had supported her, the celebration organizers had asked Page Coster, the editor of the University of Vermont newspaper, "The Cynic," to introduce her. Apparently, Stephenson liked the paper and loved its motto, "Pissing People Off for 125 Years."

"One week ago," Coster shouted, "Vermont made history again. We're sending to the United States Senate the first independently elected member in more than half a century!"

Cheers filled the room.

"Over at UVM, we're just as proud of our Senator-elect as you are. We see in her election a sign of things to come. The collapse of the old order! The end of Beltway bullshit! A return of the government to its people! We think Senator Stephenson will start a new revolution in this country."

More cheers, and this time more animated. For just an instant I thought I detected her rolling her eyes.

"I could go on and on and on but you didn't come to hear me. Ladies and gentlemen, without further ado, Vermont's newly elected Senator, Josephine Stephenson."

Nothing modest or demure about this lady. No sir. Took the mike right out of Coster's hand like she was going to belt out a country ballad. Perplexed heroine? Wrong! At least not when the performance began.

"Thank you, thank you," she started, toning down the deafening cheers, whistles and applause. "As all of you may have noticed, this isn't a fund raiser to pay off a campaign debt."

Knowing laughter filled the crowd.

"The Vermont beer is free and the ballroom's donated. Even the band came over from UVM on their own time. Everybody in this room and thousands of people throughout Vermont won this election by the power of ideas in a campaign where we raised and spent just ten thousand dollars!"

Cheers and applause once again filled the room. It had the effect, however, of making Joe Benton look not exactly powerful.

"Do you know what the average amount spent on a Senate race in this country is today, including the state of Vermont?"

"No," the crowd responded, "and we don't want to know."

"Well, I didn't want to know either," she continued. "But I know now and you better know too because it's the kind of thing we're going to put an end to in this country. First of all, each of my opponents spent more than four million dollars in a state with only 400,000 voters. That's at least ten dollars a voter and they couldn't even win six out of ten of them combined!"

Shocked boos filled the ballroom.

"And the average amount spent in this country is more than $8 million to buy a seat in the Senate!"

The decibel level of boos tripled.

"Who do you think's doing the buying and who do you think's being bought? I'll tell you the answer to both. The big boys who really control this country are doing the buying and it's the United States of America that's being bought! Do you know what a professional fund raiser told me when I interviewed him for my campaign? 'A thou gets you access; five thou gets you a piece and ten thou buys the whole ball of wax.' Well, I had a ball of wax for him. Wrapped him in it and sent him right back to Washington!"

Cheered again and, as she was, I watched her intently to see what kind of an act this was. Sincere or insincere? Demagogue or righteous reformer? Her eyes were cold, her demeanor fierce and her stance arrogant with newfound power.

"Thanks to you," she continued, clutching the microphone, "I am going to Washington and we're not going to stop until the rotten system which has tied this country in knots of money and influence is brought down once and for all and replaced with a government of…" She sought a reply.

"The people," they screamed.

"By?" she demanded.

"The people!" they responded.

"And for?" she shouted.

"The people!!!!" came the response, so intense that it seemed the very walls were shaking.

Dawn cringed in the corner but I continued to stare intently at this dangerous creation.

"I'm going to Washington to accomplish three things," she said, adopting a calmer tone. "First is to promote the economic well being of the people of this state." Cheers. "The second is to clean up the rotten politics that pervades our national life and which affects every one of us in Vermont." More cheers. "And the third is to keep the heavy hand of the federal bureaucracy out of our affairs!" Deafening cheers. It seemed to me that points one and three were potentially contradictory but I wasn't about to argue the point.

"And if you don't get them," someone shouted from the back of the room, "we secede from the Union!!!!" With that, pandemonium broke out but the interesting thing was that she heard the secession business clearly but didn't say anything. All she did was smile, stare at the crowd, pause for a moment and say "Thank you all and let's get on with the party."

She passed the microphone back to a mesmerized Page Coster and moved into the crowd, shaking hands, kissing people, being slapped on her shapely back. Around the fringes, the more seasoned political people in the room were subdued. They knew, as I did, that some new, unpredictable and potentially primitive force in the form of this yuppie woman had been unleashed in American politics. Far more scary face to face in a flesh and blood crowd than her more genteel demeanor on television. It seemed to me that she had looked around to be certain that no cameras were in the room. Print reporters maybe but no cameras. The woman had an agenda. It was threatening. And I was about to have my snug skiing week altered and my life profoundly inconvenienced and perhaps permanently affected.

****

"Let's not overdo it," said Willie Welsh sipping his bloody mary. "She's just a yuppie know it all with a loud mouth and an uncanny instinct for the political sound bite."

"I agree," said Dawn, but who asked her?

"You're jealous," I said to her jokingly.

"Jealous of what when I have you, sweetie," she retorted. Goddamn it, she had a way of getting the last word.

I turned my attention back to Willie, dapper in his state of the art ski garb, thirtysomething and perfectly nonchalant. We had met a few years prior when I came to New England for the Presidential primaries. Since then, Willie had made his living very nicely doing bond issues and other legal work for quasi-governmental bodies.

"The husband?" I asked.

"Nice guy, nice guy," Willie responded. "Kooky kid named Raymond out at UCLA. Rumor has it the kid tried to commit suicide a couple of years ago but I don't give it any credence. And the other kid, Henry, is just a regular blue jeaned kid with a basketball in his hands. A basketball."

"Then what's the big deal?" I persisted.

"No big deal. No big deal. Luck. Behind the facade, she probably doesn't know what hit her. Wasn't the candidate of choice of the independent movement. In fact, some of her so-called supporters actually hate her with a passion. But Bernie Sanders was happy in Congress and everybody else thought it was a loser. So she ran to prove a point. To prove a point."

"Where'd she come from?" I asked, somewhat distracted by Willie's insistently repeating himself.

"Moved up here from Pennsylvania after she graduated from Wharton. Got a job teaching history and political science at Vermont. UVM to us. UVM. Married George Stephenson about two years after she got here. Nothing unusual. Just joined the independent movement. Whole thing is a special election fluke. A fluke." Willie shrugged his shoulders and sipped his drink.

"Friends, allies, associations?" I was trying to get a hand on something.

"Not many that I know of," Willie replied. "An activist named Maureen Sullivan is her campaign manager. Probably will go to Washington with her. But other than that, the usual stuff. Nobody special. Could come back to haunt her. Loyalty doesn't seem to be her strong suit."

"Do you know her?" Dawn asked.

"Casually. Casually. Met her a few times at political things. Had me figured out from the first minute. Doesn't trust me at all, I'm sure. One of the bad guys in her book. She pretends to be just folks. Probably at home right now doing the laundry and giving orders to the kid. Down home stuff but it's all a phony. She's a calculating bitch, I think. A bitch." It was difficult to tell whether Willie was being totally objective or just frustrated because he wasn't, for the first time, on the inside with the winner.

"Don't use that term!" Dawn demanded.

Willie was taken aback for a moment. He knew full well he was talking to the daughter of the distinguished Senator from Colorado.

I quickly changed the subject. "Should I try to get to meet her while I'm here?"I asked.

"I doubt it," Willie replied. "The time may come when you may have to in Washington and then she'll think something's suspicious, you being up here and all that."

I stared out at the slopes. There was nothing more to say. No handle. No angle. No way to get at this thing.

"Have a good one," Willie concluded.

"A good what?" I asked.

"A good what?" he asked, astonished. "What do you mean, a good what? A good day, a good run, whatever."

"Oh, okay," I said. "Just thought you could be a little more specific."

We parted, with Willie looking at me as if I had two heads, two heads.

"Let's get back to the mountain," I said finally and before long we were back on the lifts, back on the trails, Dawn skiing superbly. "Mad River Glen: ski it if you can," said the ads and she sure could, performing as only a native Coloradan could. It was a brilliantly sunny day. Lots of snow had fallen in the two weeks before our trip. The mountain, unlike so many that had been ultra modernized in the past few years, seemed out of a 1950s time warp. For a few brief days, we lost ourselves in the green-white mountains of Vermont while, only occasionally, did I think about what I was going to tell Ronnie and Controller.

Four days later, I called Ronnie to tell him we were coming back and that I thought they should be damned concerned about this new Senator but that I just couldn't get to the bottom of it.

"Don't worry about that," Ronnie said. "Controller wants you to come directly to the golf outing in Florida. You can brief him there."

"The golf outing!" I said with exasperation. "But I don't want to go to the golf outing. I hate golf outings. Especially this one. I..."

Before I could finish, Ronnie interrupted me with "dump Dawn off at Reagan. There's a ticket waiting for you – first class – at the Delta counter. See you there." And he hung up.

Muttering all the way to the airport, I ran into Willie again just before we got our flight. "Oh, one more thing, Willie," I said. "What's this secession bullshit?"

"Nothing," he replied. "Nothing. Don't pay any attention to it. A couple of academic kooks and backwoods eccentrics. They have a book out that claims George Washington made a secret deal with Ethan Allen. In return for joining the union, Vermont would have the right to leave whenever things didn't go its way. It's all ridiculous. Folklore. Nonsense. They chuckle in the bars around here. Claim they want the United States to leave Vermont, not the other way around. Pick up a copy of the Vermont Secession Book over there at the news counter. It'll tell you all about it."

Willie smiled; we shook hands. "Have a good one," he said. "A good wha..." Oh forget it Charlie, I said to myself. And then we were winging our way back to the land of the Beltway. And I would be off to the golf outing for newly elected members of the next Congress of the United States.

CHAPTER 5

THE GOLF OUTING

The event would be amusing if it weren't so grim and depressing. Imagine forty five Senators and Congressmen decked out in their proper slacks and pot bellied pullovers, perpetually smiling, straining to overachieve, guffawing at each other's unfunny one liners, trying so hard to schmooze their corporate hosts.

The Boca Raton invitation was irresistible. Fading Hollywood movie stars Ron Johnstown and Burt Westwood added a faint flicker of glamor to the proceedings. With considerable difficulty, Senators remained aloof out of a sense of decorum but Congressmen waited in line to get their autographs ("wait'll my daughter sees this!") As I dragged my own bags, like a peasant, into the stately lobby of the Grand Miradora, Johnstown, the latest "sexiest man alive" according to the TV tabloid "Soft Porn Copy," was boasting to the assembled media and gawking officialdom about the ten days he had just spent in splendid sexual isolation with Hollywood's latest amazon, Caryl Falana ("after two days, we had to send out for food and water"). It never ceases to amaze me how otherwise accomplished individuals melt in the presence of celluloid celebrity. They don't just stare. They gape.

As I was registering, I noticed a commotion, followed by a flurry of security activity. It was none other than the former Vice President of the United States stiffly crossing the floor with a vacant stare heading resolutely toward the revolving door and his limousine. I subsequently found out that he had played nine holes that morning with a few select Senators elect and a handful of important people. I had known him for years. In fact, I had run his first campaign for the Senate ten years ago. Do you think he even noticed me? No. One of these days I'll get him, I thought to myself just as I was rudely brushed aside by one of his aides.

That was nothing, though, compared to what would happen on the following day. None other than the President himself would be stopping by for brunch, necessitating the provision of forty limousines for his official party, food testers, reporters, aides, aides to aides, select cabinet officials, a few hanger on family members, an army of secret service agents and even the obscure man with the apparently obsolete little black box. Except for the little American flags and the absence of floral displays, you would have thought it was a Mafia funeral.

As I turned and headed toward the elevator, the moment I was avoiding arrived. Ludwig Controller himself was standing right there, in the middle of the lobby, staring at me.

"Well, I'm here," I commented. With Controller, there was never any need to say Hi Doc, or Hello, Doctor or some other common form of salutation. He always looked like he was about to say, "dispense with the bullshit."

"You're late, Charlie," he said, without changing expression. "You missed the ex-Vice President. I could have used you since you two are such old acquaintances."

"Well, he just walked out the door without even recognizing me," I stammered. "I doubt I would have been much help. Besides, the President's coming tomorrow and I worked on his first campaign for Governor. Maybe he'll ignore me too."

"The man's a pain in the ass, Charlie," Controller replied impassively. "We get our business done with him or without him. Here today. Gone tomorrow. But enough of that. I have a foursome I want you in tomorrow morning. New Senator from New Hampshire, the Secretary of State and our former House Speaker Tom Righter. I understand our new found friend from New Hampshire knows our new found enemy from Vermont. Perhaps you will learn something you apparently failed to learn on that skiing trip to Vermont."

I sidestepped the Vermont remark and reacted to the former House Speaker. "Isn't it a little risky having Righter here?" I asked. "After all, he was convicted of mail fraud and had to resign."

"Thrown out on appeal," Controller reminded me. "Besides, he needs the money and he's loyal. I'm giving him a fifty grand fee and I just retained his wife as a consultant on the social events for the week. By the way," Controller noted wryly, "he's been completely rehabilitated. Perhaps you didn't notice up there on the ski trail that Righter is becoming a cable commentator and will shortly be holding forth for millions of viewers on the ins and outs of Congressional ethics." He smiled knowingly. I changed the subject.

"Well, I think I'll get upstairs and change," I said. "I'll be ready for the foursome and anything else you need."

"Thank you, Charlie," Controller replied. "And remember, the big dinner is tonight. The Secretary of State is going to tell us everything we already know about the Middle East. Be early for cocktails. You'll need it."

There are other golf outings at which corners are cut. But not this one. No expense was spared. No need left unaccomodated. No comfort neglected. No meal left unprepared. Inside the lap of luxury which was my room, I first rested my eyes on a selection of golf accessories from that master of trendy lifestyles, Rolfe Lawrence, all arranged neatly on the king size bed. Every level surface was filled with fruit basket, fifth of Scotch, ice bucket, cold hors d'oeuvres, personalized writing pad. A Zucci robe adorned the bathroom door and, best of all, a memento from the resort, a silver putter signed by the Silver Fox himself, the all time winningest golfer, Nick Masterson.

I was not unaccustomed to the trappings of luxury and comfort as provided by clients and influential power brokers. In fact, it has become somewhat of a joke within the fraternity that I was labeled "America's Guest," a designation that I happily accepted. But I must admit that this particular event was obscenely lavish and I felt that the Doctor had finally overdone it.

Now is perhaps the time, if indeed there is an appropriate time, to reveal more about Ludwig Controller.

I said I thought he was in his early sixties but he was one of those people who could be fifty or seventy five. He had been a peculiar figure on the Washington scene for at least a decade. Prior to that, no one was quite clear about who he was or where he came from. But since that was true of most Beltwayites, few of whom wanted their own origins discovered, his past never became a subject for serious discussion. He was alleged to have a Yale degree in Biology and an M.D. from Harvard Medical School, followed by extensive studies abroad in psychiatry. But I once secretly checked with both institutions and neither had a record of his attendance. Of course, the name may have changed and maybe the stories were inaccurate from the start. In any event, the past was closed off.

He lived alone on an elaborate estate in McLean, Virginia. He was unmarried as far as anyone knew. He was frequently referred to as a lifelong bachelor in love with his work and that comment elicited the predictable behind-the-back rumors that he was gay. His frequent socializing with young male staff members fueled the suspicions but I never personally experienced or observed any kind of sexual dimension whatever. As far as I could tell, he was neuter.

Controller first achieved Capital notoriety after he allegedly treated successfully the extreme alcoholism of noted media mogul Willa Schramm. Accurate or not, that piece of gossip meant that Ludwig had arrived. He began to show up at Willa's Georgetown dinner parties, usually seated at her right, rubbing shoulders with cabinet members, millionaires, journalists, Senators, casino operators, game show hostesses, fly-ins from Hollywood, Presidential relatives and the various other levels of celebrities that wandered in and out of the nation's nerve center.

After a while, he simply became "the Doctor," or "Doc." His presence at various social events was noted with increasing frequency in the social column of The Washington Post. Initial queries such as "who's that guy," gradually were replaced with knowing references to the fact that one had cocktails with "that fascinating Doctor Controller." Having achieved an undocumented, untraceable and, as far as I could tell, undeserved, reputation for excellence in psychiatry, he began to get referrals from his influential new friends. Fees went up and the Doctor became a man of considerable means, exclusively addressing the psychiatric problems of the well off, the well connected and the wellborn, that American establishment triad. I always felt, deep down, that "the Doctor's" reserve hid the apprehension that he would one day be found out. But by whom? I would ask myself. A lot of other people were also concerned that one day they too would be found out. Thus developed a conspiracy of silence among those with a vested interest in burying their pasts and foreclosing investigation into their own undeserved reputations lest they be found out. No "what goes around comes around" around here.

The thing that really put Controller over the top, however, was the circulation throughout the national political network of a pamphlet he authored called "The Seven Manifestations of Political Illness." The tract was a revelation to the entire fraternity of power and influence seeking ways to deal with severe symptoms of political instability.

Just look at the chapter headings and you will get an idea of how compellingly Controller had touched the nerve ends of the political establishment:

> "1) Enduring Adversity and Embarrassment
> 2) Psychic Methods of Living with Ethical Violations and Investigative Stress
> 3) Feeding Your Ego and Ambition
> 4) No Surrender to Boredom and Burn Out
> 5) Managing Paranoia and Related Symptoms of Envy, Jealousy and Sullen Resentment
> 6) Getting Through the Night with Insecurity and Fear
>
> and
>
> 7) Making Lying and Hypocrisy Credible"

It was said that the Doctor's treatments and dictums, though obscure, had literally begun to transform weak and intimidated power people into happy, secure and stable statesmen. The key to his success was a series of motivational seminars and audiotapes which had the effect of re-programming the subconscious mind to accept, enjoy and turn to advantage each of the alleged problems analyzed; to play to them, not against them; to turn them into positives instead of negatives, thus making the psyche secure and comfortable in evaluating options and making command decisions, the two principal responsibilities of powerful people. Thus the evolution of "Alcoholics Unanimous." "Alcoholics Anonymous? Bull shit!" the Doctor once cried derisively. "If you're going to drink, then drink! Nothing to be ashamed of. Hell, everybody does it!"

The Doctor's prescriptions were enveloped in anecdotes and aphorisms. To deal with adversity, he would quote Disraeli's famous maxim that "there is no education like adversity." For those convicted of or charged with ethical violations of criminal import, he recommended dwelling on the potential for making tons of money as a speaker, author or network commentator once the hard part of investigation, indictment and possible conviction was over and celebrity name recognition enhanced. "Public morality is a passing thing," he wrote in his book, "but private enrichment can go on forever." The social structure of the Beltway is a floating phenomenon, he would say. Ostracized today, welcomed back tomorrow. People forget easily because they want their own foibles forgotten.

One of his interesting distinctions was between ego and ambition. Ambition, he said, was the fire in the belly that causes you to go for it, make it, get it all. Ego, on the other hand, was the condition one achieved after having arrived. His prescription? Feed on them both. Seek the next highest office. Enjoy your ego, flatter it and demand that others do the same. You're an important personage, damn it, and you should be treated with respect.

For extreme cases of boredom and burnout, he suggested quitting, proclaiming that everyone had to come to the realization of when it was time to leave. But don't announce your departure, he would say, until you've nailed down a lobbying contract or a book deal and be sure to shape your legislative conduct to appeal to those who might retain you.

As a cure for paranoia, he would counsel, "suspect everyone." Never trust, never confide, keep alleged friends at arm length, always be on your guard and maintain no long term loyalties. Everyone is out to get either you or your job. "Even a paranoiac has his enemies," he wrote, quoting several famed paranoiacs on that point. Insecurity and fear are also to be admitted, Controller said. For your staff, hire unthreatening technocrats with paper credentials and zero ambition. You never know.

In the final analysis, he proclaimed, money is the root of all stability. Its four principal manifestations were:

1. the money you get
2. the money you could get
3. the money you give out from the public treasury

and

4. the money you raise.

Put money in thy purse, he would quote Iago, his favorite villain.

Finally, if you are called a liar or hypocrite, be both. You probably are anyway. Say one thing and do another. Demand no pay raise in public but twist arms to get one privately. If you're cornered, lie and lie again. There's no sanction for it in any event. On the latter point, he would use as evidence the documented conduct of several recent Presidents.

These, then, were the highlights of the Doctor's book.

Within a year, Washington was abuzz with rumors that the Doctor had parlayed his incredible success into a multi-billion dollar enterprise, buying up or taking a controlling interest in campaign consulting firms, lobbying organizations, polling groups, talk show radio stations, political fund raising outfits, direct mail companies and information technology think tanks.

It was also alleged that he had created a disciplined network of former and current government staffers and political hired guns who would dominate the public landscape: "team players with the right stuff," he was quoted as calling them. He then oversaw the placement of these individuals in sensitive positions at favored corporations, and on the staffs of the White House, Governors, Mayors and Legislators. Soon the airlanes of America became filled with private jets and helicopters whizzing friendly government staffers to Bowl games, golf outings, spa retreats and schmooze sessions.

When Common Good first appeared, The New York Times was the first to see through its hypocrisy, calling it "Common Greed," and a device to obscure the efforts of Common Cause. The Washington Post followed with an expression of "dismay and astonishment." But the editorials quickly died down, the initial furore was forgotten and the only question that remained was whether the IRS would designate Common Good a 501-c-3 charitable organization or a 501-c-5 business and commercial advocacy group. It settled soon after for a C-5 and from that moment on, Common Good became a billion dollar a year national selfish interest crusade.

Ludwig Controller understood long before anyone else that the American party system had died with the coming of electronic media and that so-called information highway. On private occasions, he would note that, because of the power of the advertising-television-consultant-pollster network, money had ceased to be the mother's milk of politics, as the old line bosses used to say, and had actually become a cancer of the political bloodstream, as he tactlessly put it.

And he, Ludwig, the Mad King of The Beltway, would take the place of the Bosses of Old, the ultimate in a long line of colorful Americans who had dominated the political scene at least since the advent of the Industrial Revolution.

"But with technology," he would proclaim. "We're all technocrats now."

Controller had indeed become the arch celebrity insider of his time.

And now, standing in the elaborate and stately reception lobby of the Grand Miradora, he was at the height of his power, affluence, influence, cunning, charm and scoundrel-like poise.

As I came down to the lobby to catch what was going on, I watched Controller greet the former and allegedly disgraced Speaker of the House.

"Ho ho, Ludwig," he declaimed. "God, it's good to see ya agin'."

Ludwig embraced the disgraced statesman, squeezed his hand and said that it was indeed good to see him again. "I'm working on that book deal for you, Mr. Speaker," he whispered. "I think you should title it 'Speaker Righter's Righteous Reign.' It'll get at least a $5 million advance."

"I don't know, Ludwig," the Speaker replied, looking chagrined. "The goddamn press keeps referring to me as Disgraced. I don't know if I can handle it."

"Now you listen to me, Mr. Speaker," Controller advised, piously pointing his finger at the Speaker in admonition. "Disgrace is in the eye of the beholder, not the doer. Nobody in this country gives a damn about disgraced. What they want is the dirt behind the disgrace. Just stick with me and you'll be vindicated."

"Doc, I'll never forget you," said Righter, squeezing the Doctor's hand in a physical bonding ceremony of bone crunching intensity.

"Hey, hey Doktor," said the former Secretary of State, extricating himself from the circle of his security guards. "It eez indeed a great pleasure to collect your check today. Ve must get togezzer privately and survey zee world situation." The Doctor nodded a vigorous assent as he reached out to grasp the authoritative fingers of the latest network sage.

"There are no secrets left in the world, Mr. Secretary. Sound familiar?" the Doctor proclaimed. "I haven't had the honor of seeing you since you appointed me as an observer at the Geneva Arms Talks years ago. And as we were standing outside the Great Hall, you turned to me and said that the technological age had exposed even the most confidential of national information. I remember everything. And I mostly remember that you were a statesman America and the world could be proud of. Nothing has made me happier on this weekend that to write the check which guaranteed your presence."

The great man beamed, already casting his eyes around the room for other VIP celebrities. But Controller wouldn't let him go that easily.

"Mr. Secretary," he injected, grabbing Kleppinger by the elbow, "I saw you the other evening on Midnight Report and I thought it was a terrific debut as a network commentator."

"It eez all bullshit," Kleppinger replied, whispering confidentially into Controller's hairy ear. "I get paid a goddam fortune to look like ze statesman and say 'on zee one hand...but on zee other hand' and everyone sits there as eff leestening to the word of God Almighty. But the way I see it, if zee asshole network is villing to pay millions to zee robotic anchors, why not me, huh?"

"Absolutely," Controller reassured. "By the way, I have the perfect organization for you to join," Controller continued, alluding to the newly formed Ass Kissinger Group. "You would be superb. And we very much need men of your stature and insight to give us credibility. We'll talk about it later."

"Loodvig," Kleppinger replied, "for a fee I do anyzeeng. Enough of theez public interest crap. Whatever you vant, I do. Right?"

Controller smiled his sly and knowing smile, patted Kleppinger on the arm he had practically twisted and bade him a momentary farewell, having spotted me on the periphery.

"Charlie," he grimaced, "can you believe the world of power and influence is filled with assholes like Kleppinger and Righter while you and I stand here in the background plying our humble trade? Why, that goddam Righter is so undependable that they used to say his vote depended on the last lobbyist that buttonholed him. One time, one of our boys called me in dismay saying Righter voted the wrong way. I asked him when he talked to him and he said right outside the House chamber in the hall. 'You made a mistake,' I said. 'The other guy got him as he walked in the door.'"

I had to laugh. On the one hand, he was right. On the other, he was far from humble. Ah yes, on the one hand...but on the other. Actually, I knew from prior chats with Controller that he hated both of them with a passion.

"Stick around on the periphery, Charlie," he advised. "I may need you. But right now I'm going to try and avoid Fletch Harrison, the ex-Chairman of Global Cleanliness, Inc. How the hell did he stay on the invitation list after he got fired? I'll kill that sonofabitch West."

But it was too late. Harrison headed right for him and began bragging about his settlement. "It's a golden parachute, Ludwig," he whispered. "Twenty million a year plus all benefits for the next three years and, of course, I'm still on several corporate boards. That's not even counting the options."

"That's all?" Controller asked, with a note of condescension in his voice. "That's not a parachute, it's a safety net. You should have demanded twenty five million a year for five years, the ingrates. And you a Rhodes scholar!"

"Well, why pay the fees for protracted litigation? I'm already a millionaire many times over. I can manage to live with it."

If you stay out of jail, I murmured.

Harrison moved on and it was a good thing too because, from across the room came Henderson Hutchinson, the new Global Cleanliness Chairman.

"Hendy! What a surprise!" oozed Ludwig. "Be careful though. Fletch Harrison is right ahead of you. I can't imagine why he's here. After his dismissal, I remember clearly taking him off the list. This is really embarassing for the both of us."

"Oh Ludwig, I'm not embarrassed," said Hutchinson.

"Not embarrassed? Well, I'm embarrassed. Things like this can really be embarrassing to important people. I mean, embarrassment is one of the real problems in life." Ludwig was puzzled at Hutchinson's lack of embarrassment.

"No, not embarrassed," Hutchinson repeated. "It's just business. We're still gentlemen. Fletch and I will get along fine after the first drink. Good to be here."

"Keep your eye on him, Charlie," Controller advised. "Global Cleanliness will be at the top of the Fortune 500 in no time and they'll be wanting to buy up the entire government."

Last but not least to enter the grand hallway that first afternoon was none other than the Chairman of the Senate Ethics Committee, Chris Livengood of Iowa.

"Chris old boy," Controller practically shouted. "I hope you're down here this weekend to confuse these new people as much as possible."

"Doc, I'm here to stand up for Congressional conduct. And the first thing I'm gonna tell them is to keep it in their pants. It's bad enough having to investigate official misconduct. Now I've got four sex cases on my hands and it's a real pain in the ass. Who the hell wants to play Judge on stuff like that? I've been thinking of establishing three subcommittees to handle all the work, one for the straights, one for the gays and the other for the White House," said Livengood, chuckling at his innovative initiative.

"I'll tell you what," the Doctor retorted, "set up a fourth for jerkoffs and assholes."

Both roared in unison, wrapped their arms around each other, pulled me along and headed for the bar. As long as Controller was buying it was fine with me. I can put up with anybody in return for a couple of free drinks.

For the next two days, the golf course resembled the battle zone of one of the world's many limited conflicts. Balls flew hither and thither, in creeks, behind trees, rolling onto the Interstate, bopping off little trolley cars which coursed their way around the resort. For extra amusement, Controller had imported from England some of the props from an old television show called "The Prisoner" which had been stored at Pinewood Studios near London. An ironic little devil, he thought the symbolism would be darkly humorous. But no one else remembered. "No memory left," he would mumble to me in passing. "No memory left." When he would offhandedly mention the show's sets to a newly elected Senator or Congressman, the reaction invariably would be "oh yeah? Gee, how much did that cost? All the way from England, huh? You sure do things first class Doc."

Interspersed with the athletic merriment, of course, were the motivational sessions and educational seminars. Controller was careful to arrange for the FBI to talk at the seminar on terrorism, the tobacco industry to host the seminar on smoking, the liquor industry on alcoholic beverage regulation and the dairy farmers' association on agriculture. The new members seemed transformed by the experience. Most had arrived wearing artificial smiles, a bit nervous, preoccupied with campaign debts, Washington expenses, relocation problems and political infighting at home. But as the weekend progressed, a kind of serenity fell over them, a renewed confidence, an inner peace. They seemed to stand taller, walk more erect, shake hands more vigorously, hit the ball more accurately, eat more heartily, drink more exuberantly and sleep more soundly. No more waking up at 3.20 A.M. writhing on the floor from political nightmares inspired by their recently endured opposition research. They seemed of sound mind and firm conviction, if not about the issues then about themselves. And they appeared to know exactly what would be necessary to guarantee their success inside the Beltway and their survival in the year round game of electioneering.

The closing dinner was a triumph, an outdoor barbecue of monumental proportions. The state of the nation and the world was discussed in travelogue elegance over racks of fire cooked salmon and barbecued chicken. Fortunately, I intercepted the one thing that Controller could have done to make the whole thing too obvious. Before the welcoming ceremony, he casually showed me the invocation he was going to use and I begged him to suppress it. He agreed with the greatest reluctance, I stuffed it in my pocket and only now do I feel safe in making it public. It went like this:

"Almighty Greed and Dollar
Honored Be Your Name.
Your Kingdom Come, Your Will Be Done
In Washington as It Is On Wall Street.
Give Us This Day Our Greenbacked Bread
And Pay Off Our Clients as Our Clients Pay Off Us.
Lead Us Not Into Indictments

But Deliver Us From Do Gooders
For Yours is the Money, the Power and the Jobs,
Forever."

What the man was thinking of is beyond me. It appeared to me that he had finally lost it all. But looking back on it today, I'm not so sure that it wouldn't have been the vulgar highlight of the weekend.

He did manage to do one last thing that finally shook my passive and indifferent reliance on the Beltway culture. At the close of the evening, he distributed to each guest a motivational tape, asked them to take it back to their rooms and to keep it with them at all times. And he suggested that each repeat the series of affirmations which followed the little lecture on self improvement.

It was a beautiful evening in Central Florida. The December temperature had dropped into the comfortable fifties. The windows of most bedrooms were open. Unable to sleep, I strolled through the courtyard, gazing at the stars and relishing the fresh air. As I did so, much to my astonishment, I heard the chant repeated from innumerable windows. It was the motivational litany Controller had given to his guests. And it echoed through the brisk evening air like this:

"AND NOW, REPEAT AFTER ME THE FOLLOWING INSPIRATIONAL SAYINGS:
"I LOVE MYSELF"
I Love myself, came the obedient repetition.

"MY EGO IS UNSURPASSED"

My ego is unsurpassed.

"THE MOST IMPORTANT EVENT IN MY LIFE IS A FUND RAISER"

The most important event in my life is a fund raiser.

"I HAVE FIRE IN THE BELLY'

I have fire in the belly.

"I CAN BE PRESIDENT OF THE UNITED STATES"

I can be President of the United States.

"AND LEADER OF THE FREE WORLD"

And leader of the free world.

"I MUST BEGIN NOW TO RAISE MONEY FOR THE NEXT ELECTION"

I must begin now to raise money for the next election.

"I MUST ALWAYS LISTEN TO MY POLLSTER"

I must always listen to my pollster.

"I LOVE MYSELF…BIG TIME"

I Love myself…Big Time

"I MUST BEGIN TO RAISE MONEY NOW TO PAY OFF CAMPAIGN DEBTS."

I must begin to raise money now to pay off campaign debts.

"MY EGO IS UNSURPASSED"

My ego is unsurpassed.

"MY NEWSLETTERS MUST BE SAFE AND INNOCUOUS"

My newsletters must be safe and innocuous.

"THE THING TO FEAR MOST IS THE THIRTY SECOND NEGATIVE TELEVISION AD."

The thing to fear most is the thirty second negative television ad.

"LOBBYISTS MAKE ME FEEL SECURE BY RAISING LOTS OF MONEY FOR ME."

Lobbyists make me feel secure by raising lots of money for me.

"I AM EDUCATED ON THE ISSUES AT GOLF OUTINGS AND JUNKETS."

I am educated on the issues at golf outings and junkets.

"I LOVE MYSELF…BIG TIME

I love myself…Big Time

"MY PARANOIA CAN BE CURED BY CASH."

My paranoia can be cured by cash.

"I MAKE NO MOVE WITHOUT MY CAMPAIGN CONSULTANT."

I make no move without my campaign consultant.

"I LOVE CONTRIBUTORS WHO MAX OUT."

I love contributors who max out.

"I CAN LEAP THROUGH ANY LOOPHOLE IN THE ETHICS LAWS."

I can leap through any loophole in the ethics laws.

"I LOVE THE SYSTEM AS I LOVE MYSELF."

I love the system as I love myself.

"AND MOST IMPORTANT OF ALL, I WILL FIGHT TERRORISM."

And most important of all, I will fight terrorism.

For a moment after it ended, I stood motionless, finally disturbed by the realization of how far things had gone. This was no longer a game, I said to myself. No longer merely the way things were done. Something profoundly wrong was going on here and I was suddenly growing up. I almost wished I hadn't witnessed it. Better to let life go on. But I had witnessed it and now I told myself I had to do something about it. Call it an instant conversion if you will. Call it phony and insincere. Go ahead and be cynical.

How to proceed? What to do? Job, money, even life maybe. But we don't think like that anymore, do we? Risk, courage, principle. Strength and honor sayeth the gladiator. Hollow concepts. But they took hold of me.

Stephenson, I suddenly thought. Yes, the Stephenson woman. That may be the way. Double agent Charlie Coons. Make contact. Be careful. Still one of the boys. But Pete. Pete O'Connor isn't. Chances are he won't believe me. Won't trust me. Can I trust him?

I rushed back to my room, breathing in the fresh air. I'll plot this out tomorrow when I get safely back inside the Beltway.

CHAPTER 6

ELECTED VILLAINS

It was on December 7th that I arrived back in Washington, the anniversary of Pearl Harbor.

Perplexed by my thoughts of the prior evening, and suitably hung over, I wandered through the crowds at Reagan Airport and almost missed the turn to baggage claim where, as I arrived, I was startled by the sight of none other than Josephine Stephenson, waiting, with another woman, for her baggage from a flight from Newark.

Now is the time, I said to myself. The moment is serendipitous. This chance meeting is meant to be. Go ahead, introduce yourself. Get it started.

She stood, passive, motionless and totally unrecognized while her companion fussed in a frustrating effort to identify the bags. Attractive woman without a doubt. My bag would be arriving at the same carol so there I stood, staring at her with this glassy gaze. If I didn't move soon, someone was bound to think I was very strange. My usual sure footed confidence escaped me as I faced this radical departure from my usually safe way of conducting my life. I shuffled around, paced awkwardly, started toward her and reversed, bumping into another pushy passenger who gave me a cold stare.

Try again, Charlie, I said to myself. Do it. It's perfect. Not a soul around who recognizes you.

And so, I looked up again, staring nonchalantly around the area, resting my eyes on the new Senator as if I had just noticed her. And around I went, appearing as casual as I could but stumbling mentally all the way.

"Excuse me, but aren't you Senator-elect Stephenson from Vermont?"

And so I did it.

"Yes," she said coolly, a little suspicious but obviously pleased to be recognized.

"My name is Charlie Coons. Political consultant. You might have heard of me." Obtuse thing to say.

"No, I don't think so," she said suspiciously.

"Ran several campaigns nationally." Was I communicating?

"Yes, I think I remember now. Ran Richard Jones' campaign for the Senate in New Hampshire a few years ago?"

"Yes, that's me. Dick Jones." I was relieved.

"You lost," she continued.

I laughed. And I thought I detected a slight grin even from her. "Yeah, tough race," I replied, loosening up. "Well, anyway, I just thought I'd say congratulations. As a professional, I appreciate smart campaigns and it sure looked like you ran one."

"Well, I don't know whether it was smart by your standards" she observed. "But it was right. And we won."

Right or righteous, I asked myself. I was about to do an abrupt but polite about face when my better self cautioned: Charlie, you'll have to put up with this sort of thing if you expect to accomplish anything. You know how reformers are.

"You're right," I said, graciously I thought. Keep the charm going.

"Look, I'd be happy to give you a ride. My car is here. And I don't have any pressing engagements."

At this point, the other woman appeared, luggage and all and we were introduced. Her name was Maureen Sullivan and I remembered it from my brief trip to Vermont.

"You were the campaign manager," I said.

"That's right," she acknowledged, obviously pleased that someone also knew who she was.

"Mr. Coons has volunteered to take us into town," Jo Stephenson commented. "How did you know about Maureen?"

"Keep up on things, I guess," I shrugged.

Maureen looked a bit apprehensive but left the call to the Senator-elect who seemed just a bit more comfortable with my presence.

"Okay?" I smiled.

"Okay," Maureen smiled back and after a short wait for my own luggage we were on our way.

On the congested ride into town, I learned that the Senator-elect and her campaign manager were in the city to check out office space and living arrangements.

"Do you know any more than I do about Turkmekistan?" she asked.

"Only that it appears as if the fundamentalist forces had beaten the progressive forces after the collapse of the old Communist government. Ancient tribal animosities and the desire to grab disputed territory were the root causes. Complicating the situation was the fact that the fundamentalists were welcoming terrorist groups into the country. The struggle is complicated not by an explosion of bombs but the explosion of media people on the scene. It's not only the armies of combatants but the battalions of reporters and cameramen that necessitated complex negotiations with the cable networks by both sides in an attempt to determine just how extensive the media coverage could be."

"You've got to be kidding," the Senator-elect observed with astonishment.

"Not at all," I replied. "How else will they influence world opinion?" I smiled slightly, wondering if they would get the irony in my retort. I don't think they appreciated it.

"Can we talk about something else?" she asked.

The conversation shifted to Vermont as Stephenson and Sullivan recounted some recent events.

The local press had variously reported on her conduct at the rally I had attended at the Radisson. "Secessionist Talk at Stephenson Rally," headlined the Burlington Free Press. The Associated Press wire had picked up the secessionist line and media outlets throughout the nation began to make the American people dimly aware of the rebellious tendencies of the newly elected independent Senator from Vermont.

"It's really ridiculous," she burst out. "This guy at the airport stopped me and said something like, 'hey I hear you wanna leave the union.' And then this waitress at the coffee stand says, 'don't let those radicals upset you honey. And whatever you do, try not to cry in public.'"

For the first time, in public or private, I began to detect an element of down to earthiness in this woman. In a fit of exasperation, she began to rail at the media. "Can't they ever get it right?" she asked rhetorically. "They run with the damndest things. And now I have to deny I'm a secessionist because some jerk hollers secession from the back of the room at a hotel rally."

"Let it die," counseled Maureen. "If you deny you're a secessionist, the next headline will say that you're waffling on your position."

What I did not know at that point was that Stephenson's son Raymond had had a run in at UCLA and had phoned home only the day before to give the vaguest hint of what had transpired. I learned later that he had become acquainted with Hollywood's sexiest teen alive, Buddy Roman and sexiest rock star in the universe, Mary Magdalene. They had lured the poor kid to a Mulholland Drive party where he was apparently seduced. And that had to be preoccupying her mind as we continued our drive.

Then suddenly she asked me to take her directly to the Capitol.

"But Jo, we don't have time," Maureen said. "And surely Mr. Coons here has things to do."

"I don't mind," I said.

"Mr. Coons doesn't mind, did you hear that?" Jo asked. "I haven't been in Washington for twenty years, ever since I interned during college. I just want to take a quick walk around the Rotunda and through the building. Just to get a feel for it again."

"You can't just do that," I said. "They've got security stations at all entrances to the plaza."

"Security stations? I don't remember that. I used to drive through there all the time," she replied.

"Can't now. Have to have an official pass. I'll park on Constitution and we can walk up," I suggested.

When we reached the Main Capitol steps, the line of tourists snaked around a cordon. Security police watched everybody. Metal detectors scrutinized bags and cameras.

"What is this, an airport?" asked Maureen sarcastically.

"Airports should be so secure," I replied.

She walked up to an elevator in the House wing which said "Public." She pushed the "Up" button and the elevator came.

"You can't get on here," said a surly woman operator.

"But it says public," Jo replied.

"I told you, you can't get on here," At that moment, a committee staffer I knew remotely walked up with a prominent badge on his lapel and slipped onto the elevator.

"This man is in a hurry, please stay off," said the elevator operator. The officious staffer stared ahead, unaccustomed to dealing with the public on his busy important rounds.

Finally, Jo walked back toward me under the withering gaze of the operator and out of range of the blank stare of the staffer.

"So much for open government and democracy," Maureen snapped.

I shrugged a 'that's the way it is' shrug and commented that "these days you never know what's going to happen."

"Let's get out of here," Jo said. She looked at me and asked, "would you get us to the Hart Building?"

"Sure," I said. "Follow me."

As we walked toward the Rotunda, it was apparent that a roll call vote was taking place on the floor since dozens of well dressed, blow dried and processed elected representatives of the people began to move toward the "Members Only" elevator.

"Hi yew," smiled one at Jo, figuring he must know her since she looked like she knew what she was doing.

Others nodded mechanically. One held out his hand. Another rubbed his palms together, anxiously waiting for the elevator to rescue him from the mob.

Several greeted each other with wooden nods and atrophied handshakes.

"Had a great fund raiser last night," commented one. "Fifty thou from the unions."

"Latest poll looks good," said another. "We're moving the undecided leans from leaning undecided to leaning to me. Lots of noise on the prescription drug bill did it."

"Hi yew," smiled another, nodding as he reached the elevator.

"Last newsletter brought in requests for five thousand calorie counters," announced a proud

79

member to two of his peers. "Consultant says if we keep up that pace, I'm a shoo in next time."

"Hi yew," echoed again through the waiting area.

Then one of them, much to my dismay, recognized me and asked why I was there.

"Showing our new Senator from Vermont here, Senator-elect Stephenson, how to get to the Hart Building," I said innocently. "Just sort of ran into her." Gutless apology, I thought. Not me. I'm not really with her. Please don't tell my boss.

At the sound of "Stephenson," all heads turned automatically to the rear. Agitation, distress and curiosity alternately showed in their collective countenance. Uncertain how to react to the presence of such an alien, Members turned and elbowed each other to get into the elevator.

A few unfortunate enough to miss the ride found themselves in the embarrassing and confusing position of having to say "hi yew" to the first independently elected member of the upper house in generations. As they did so, they looked around nervously, hoping they wouldn't be noticed by regulars who might rat on them to the boys.

Sensing their discomfort, I ushered the Senator-elect away and toward the Hart Building where she spent fifteen minutes being questioned, scrutinized, metal detected and ordered to "sign in" at the entrance. As Jo was about to be escorted to her temporary basement office, now that security was convinced she wasn't a bomb thrower, Maureen went off to meet with a local real estate agent. I took advantage of our moment of privacy to tell her, in abbreviated fashion, what I wanted to say. It was a bit awkward because, as the word spread, curious staffers would peer around the corner, staring at her as if she was from outer space. The buzz continued through the building, with word that "she's here" echoing down the halls. But nonetheless, I began.

"Senator, just a moment." I awkwardly grabbed her elbow and I think she thought it was rude. "We don't have much time right now. Briefly, I admire what you're trying to do. I'm one of the people you're trying to do it to. For the past twenty years I've bought into the system and I'm part of it. But you've got to believe that I believe it's got to change. And I think you have a shot at doing something about it. I want to help but I can't become visible right now. For all I know you're thinking you don't need or want my help. But just let it settle in for a while. If I think there are things you should know, I'll keep you informed. You've embarked on a dangerous business. The system doesn't fool around. And right now they don't take you very seriously but some of them, the smarter ones, do. And they'll stop at nothing to limit your influence, destroy your reputation, embarrass you or even worse. Now I'm not being melodramatic. I'm damn serious. I know you're going to interview people for your staff. And I know Rick Brewster is recommending people. Don't take them. They're all wired to the system. Villains all. Don't say where you got it but you should interview Pete O'Connor. He's on the Senate Budget Committee staff. Absolute integrity and smarts. Believe me. If you need me to help persuade him, I'll do it. We're friends."

Stephenson did nothing but looked startled. Yet, I could tell she was trying to absorb everything I said. Then I saw Brewster coming down the corridor. "Oh Christ, here comes Rick," I said. "He knows me and will think something's up. I'll get your things to Maureen at the real estate office. I'm in the DC phone book. Call me."

"Yes, I will," she said. "Can I call you Charlie?"

"Yes, can I call you Jo?"

"Yes." Amazing. She smiled.

I couldn't get out the door without being seen so I slipped behind a pillar in the hallway as Rick came up.

"Hi yew!" he called to Jo. The sound of the robot.

"Hello, Rick," Jo replied. "Or should I just say hi yew?":

She got it. She understood. So far so good.

And there was a hint of exasperation in her voice.

Then the big hug followed by the "it's been so long" niceties.

"I've got lots of good people lined up for you to see," Rick declared. Behind the pillar, I rolled my eyes.

"Oh thanks, Rick," Jo replied appreciatively. "By the way, somebody suggested I talk to a Pete O'Connor on the Budget Committee. Do you know him?"

"Oh Christ, forget him," Rick blurted out.

"Why, what the matter? I hear he's really good," Jo replied innocently.

"All the wrong qualifications, Jo. Been hanging around here for years. A troublemaker. Big time. Not at all a team player. In it for himself, not for you. Who suggested him?" Rick asked anxiously.

I cringed. Will she go along?

"Oh I don't know," she replied. "I think it was some reporter for The Washington Post."

"Oh yeah. Of course. That's where it would come from. The goddamn press. Look," Rick calmed down, "the guy's bright, no doubt about it. But can't work with people. Tough to get along with. Arrogant. Christ, he's been banished to the basement office of the Budget Committee. They only keep him around because he knows too much and they're afraid of what he'd do if they let him go. Used to be Chief of Staff to the former Speaker. But he was kinda crazy too. When he died, Pete became the forgotten man. Everybody just acted as if he didn't exist. Still, they felt they had to take care of him."

"Okay, Rick, don't get so anxious," Jo reassured him. "Let's get to the office and see some of these people. I really want to get started."

"Sure thing," said Rick, relieved.

Will she or won't she, I wondered. She will. She won't. She will. She won't. She has to!

As they walked away, I slipped out from behind the pillar in the hallway and headed for the real estate office.

****

Midnight in Georgetown and the phone rang. I had to climb over Dawn, who was staying for the night, to grab it before she foolishly picked it up.

"Charlie, put something on," she said in her droll manner. "You look ridiculous."

"Hello," I said, trying to sound like I wasn't drunken and debauched, then put my hand over the receiver. "Shut up," I warned in a shouted whisper."

"Is this Charlie Coons?" the voice asked.

"Yeah, who's this?" I asked the female voice in the commanding way I had adopted for use when late night phone calls from creepy people began getting commonplace.

"This is Jo," she said tentatively, "Josephine Stephenson."

"Oh hello!" I replied, gradually waking up. I grabbed my robe as if she were in the room.

And Dawn kept staring suspiciously.

"I hope it's not too late," she continued, "but I really wanted to let you know what happened today."

"Absolutely," I said. "I can't wait."

"It was hilarious," she continued. "These guys came in just like you said. One fat guy with a bald head told me he was on the Hill for twenty years and knew all the rules of the game."

"Harry Fisher, I'll bet," I said.

"Yes, you're uncanny. How did you know that?" she asked.

"Don't ask," I replied. "I just know."

"Then this next guy, a sleazy looking operator type in his forties tells me loyalty's the most important thing and he'll protect this lost lady from the system."

I chuckled. "Bobby Walsh," I concluded.

"Yep, you're right on top of it," she said, really loosening up now. "But you haven't heard the worst. The next one tells me you got to go along to get along and the final one reassures me that some of his best friends are the biggest PAC contributors. Can you believe that? Me with a PAC fiend?" She started to laugh.

"I could name the both of them but I won't," I said. "But let me just say something. You're being unusually frank and we've only met briefly. Why are you sharing this with me?"

"I don't know," she replied. "Maybe I'm making a mistake. But I have to talk to somebody in this city who doesn't start off a conversation by saying 'hi yew.' And besides, you were absolutely right about Pete O'Connor."

"Oh! He was in?" I asked, surprised and delighted at the same time.

"Yes, I saw him this afternoon. He walked in looking like a soiled English professor in khakis, blue blazer and a regimental tie. Almost a relic from the eighties."

"He is," I noted.

"Well, anyway, I want you to know I've offered your friend the job as my Chief of Staff," she said with satisfaction.

"No kidding," I replied in amazement. "You really did?"

"Of course. He's bright. He's cynical. And he laughed out loud when I told him I heard he was not a team player. And best of all, he's under no illusions about me. He said I came from a preposterous state that nobody cares about. He told me the place is drowning in money and the whole system is crazed. And he said that, for all he knew, I'd be just like them in less than a year."

"And what did you say?" I asked.

"I told him he may be right and then I laughed and offered him the job. And then he said something very funny. He wondered if I thought he wasn't over qualified and maybe I should hire a search firm to get the person with the best paper credentials. I loved every minute of it. And I want to thank you." She actually seemed appreciative.

"Oh, think nothing of it," I hastened to reply. "Did you mention me?" I was just a little apprehensive.

"Yes, I did," she said. "And he sort of winced and smiled and said he always thought Charlie had some redeeming qualities. But there's no doubt he was surprised and puzzled. I told him to keep it to himself. Oh, one final thing. He's kind of charming. After he accepted, he asked me if I remembered the last line of Casablanca and I pointedly told him I wasn't old enough. He didn't believe me, of course, but then he set the scene, where Bogart turns to Claude Rains after Bergman goes off with Paul Henried and says, 'Louie, I think this is the beginning of a beautiful friendship.' Goodnight Charlie, and thanks."

As I got back in bed, Dawn was looking very suspicious.

CHAPTER 7

BIG TOWN

There are times when it is glorious to be in the nation's capital. The morning after my talk with Jo Stephenson and night with Dawn Meadows was one of them. After the sojourn in Vermont and the conversion in Florida, it was good to be home and home it was because, despite its absurdities, there are moments when Washington glistens in the sun with the promise of what it was meant to be. And so it seemed on December 8th of that fateful year.

DuPont Circle. Adams Morgan. Jogging White House staffers. Past the fashionable hangouts. Down 16th Street, heading directly for the White House, stately and dignified in its lowland setting.

Radio news reported that the President was off on an early start to Medieval Weekend, annual gathering of the smartest, trendiest and most sophisticated of America's establishment. How lucky they were that one of their members became President of the United States. I could just see the crush and clawing of otherwise supposedly poised and successful individuals preening and posturing for the leader of the free world.

A few months earlier, I had gotten a schedule of events for this most sought after happening and decided, right then and there, that these people were off their rockers. Can you imagine supposedly mature adults attending sessions with idiotic subjects like "Oops! Booboos! Their Lessons and Consequences?" What flako moderator or group leader would have the chutzpah to collect big bucks for silliness like that? Plenty.

Flipped on the radio. Talk radio. National industry.

"Hullo, Lenny? Are yiz there?"

"Yes, I'm here," answered Lenny Lordan, the nation's most famous talk radio host, syndicated from Washington to three hundred stations throughout the country.

"Lenny, what's the President doing now? What's this Medieval Weekend stuff I hear about? Why isn't he stayin' in Washington and working to reduce our taxes?" Was this voice manufactured?

"I don't know but you're absolutely right," Lenny eagerly replied. "He's going down there with all those elitists, hobnobbing with the snobs."

"Well I don't like it," came the disembodied voice. "I think him and that wife of his ought to wise up. Sending their kids to that fancy school, what's its name?"

"Thorogood," Lenny answered. "Up there in Chevy Chase. Non-denominational too. No moral curriculum. Just like them. No principles. No values. Not even public schools. And against prayer too."

"What's happened to the old fashioned values Lenny?" It gradually became apparent that the whiny voice was a man. "Why all the talk about fags and people like that? I don't get it."

"Neither do I," said the sanctimonious Lenny. "But you know, there's a couple of them over in the White House itself. Did you know that? That's right. Fags in the White House. Big time. Is it any wonder?"

"Fags in the White House!" exclaimed the shocked voice. "I don't believe it. What's this country coming to?"

"Ask the President, don't ask me. Would never have happened when our man, Dick Nixon was President. There was a man who knew how to be President and Leader of the Free World. Big time." Lenny was on a roll. "Tell you what. All you out there in the great American heartland, write to the President today and tell him you want the fags out of there and an end to White House immorality. And e-mail me for your own private copy of my latest video tape on the shady escapades of this pretender at 1600 Pennsylvania Avenue. If you have a fax machine don't wait. Do it now. 1-800-GET-PRES. You won't forget that one! And you won't forget the title. Just ask for a video called SEX IN THE LINCOLN BEDROOM."

"Thanks Lenny," said the invisible caller. "I'm writing today. It sure is reassuring to know that people like you are still free to tell the truth to the American people."

No sooner had one call ended than another began.

"Lenny? Hi ya doin?"

"I recognize that voice," said Lenny sagely. "My old Marine buddy, Chuck Kinch."

Enough! I shouted at the radio. Turn the dial, get rid of this. Am I getting ready to betray the money Philistines only to fall into the hands of the self righteous Philistines?

I had two appointments that morning. The second would be with Dr. Controller at which time I would inform him of Stephenson's hiring of Pete O'Connor. Playing my double agent act, I would tell him I made contact with the newly elected Senator from Vermont and was now in a position to get inside information. He'd love it. And he'd almost have a cardiac arrest at the Pete O'Connor news. But he won't forget that I, Charlie Coons, was the man with the info.

The first meeting, however, was with a Beltway tycoon who had mastered the world of electronic media perhaps more successfully than any other entrepreneur in the nation. My interview with him was part of a study I was doing on communications precursors of the vaunted Information Superhighway. It was one of a number of reports I had to produce to justify my big salary at the think tank. And so my ride continued, past the Lincoln Memorial (does he know what's going on in his bedroom?), around the Washington Monument, down Constitution Avenue with its sometimes stately and sometimes dismal federal buildings.

His name was Muggeridge McMurtrie, if you can believe it, a financial wizard who originally made his money as a shopping center developer. His promotional skills knew no bounds, a born marketeer. Grand openings of commercial strips, usually sliced out of the side of a suburban roadway (zoning courtesy of the local board charmed and in some cases more directly influenced), always featured mob scenes of enthusiastic recession-proof shoppers. This phenomenon of success in good times or bad puzzled analysts who shook their heads in wonderment at the continuing success of McMurtrie's projects which progressed from strip to Mall with the changing mores of the times.

As for the long term, McMurtrie cared not at all since, long before economic and financial trouble would appear on the horizon, he would have taken his share out, leaving the project in the hands of the financiers and the shops stuck with long term leases.

In this manner, during the ebullient eighties and nineties, McMurtrie leveraged one center built on borrowed money into another as the banks and other lenders looked with awe upon his inexplicable success. Banks collapsed later but the cash flow turned him into a multi-millionaire via other people's money as he took out of each project his own hefty compensation as developer, creative director and inspiration, becoming, as his critics caustically commented, another "legend in his own mind." From there it was only a short leap to complete acceptance by the Beltway crowd as he became a contributing patron to arts organizations, a huge funder of political campaigns and ultimately, the owner-operator of a far flung national network of cable television stations serving the American public with everything from silent movies to home video shopping. In the process, he also became well known as a personality, insisting on presenting his own editorial views each night after the conclusion of the evening news and comfortably before the cocktail hour at which time he would begin the drinking which would carry him through the entire evening. Although he never acknowledged it, his rather odd first name was rumored to have been given him by his mother, a great fan of the English writer Malcolm Muggeridge. As it happens in the media profession, he soon became known affectionately as "The Mug" and, after his bonding with the pros became complete around the newsroom, he was fondly dubbed "The Mugger." When the Mugger gave his first commencement speech at an Ivy League University, everyone knew he had finally arrived.

And I had finally arrived at his elegantly decorated but modestly sized office in a downtown office complex conveniently annexed to a stately old hotel not too far from The White House.

Mustachioed, impeccably dressed (except for those gauche wide orange suspenders), smoking a morning cigar, sporting tinted glasses, suitably tanned from another weekend in Florida but clearly showing the midsection signs of excess inevitable at middle age for affluent eaters and drinkers, McMurtrie greeted me impassively.

"Coffee Coons?" he asked in a dull monotone.

"Thanks, black," I replied. "Will you have some too? I'll ask your Secretary."

"No, drinking orange juice these days," he said, pointing to the glass on his desk. The orange juice looked awfully pale to me.

"See the latest edition of 'Hedonism Display,' Coons?" he asked. I hated the magazine. The ads were more vulgar than the articles and the articles were vulgar enough.

"No, haven't seen it yet," I replied.

"I'm in there, Coons. Full page color glamour picture portrait. Man on the white horse. Out at my ranch in the West. All of us are in there. Big time. The new powers. Golf outing at Humbert Randolph's in Telluride. Deal makers. The real players. Billions tossed around on cellular phones. It's the new world, Coons. This Beltway stuff is bullshit. We control the wave lengths. Just need guys like you to keep this crowd off our backs."

"Now before we start reinventing the wheel here," he continued, "let me pick up where we ended the last time. I was reviewing the tape of our conversation and want to make sure you understand exactly what's going on. I've gone beyond the local station stuff. I'm way above that. International reach. More than you'll ever comprehend. Selling jewelry now on cable. Stable's got the top talk show hosts. Influence millions. The local station's just a toy. My way of having fun with the political establishment. WSLZ, Channel 55 has only one reason for success and it's the decision I made a few years ago to go to the 9 o'clock news."

"I was wondering about that," I said.

"It was clear to me that the 10 o'clock news was outpacing the 11 o'clock news in this market for two reasons. First, the networks are boring. Goddamn sitcoms. And other cable is bullshit. Goddamn movie replays. Second, nobody I want to reach is watching at 11 P.M. anyway. They're either drunk or exhausted. So I figured I'd give 'em a last shot of scandal and mayhem before they passed out and 9's the time to do it. Besides, this way I really get the breaking news. Breaking news fashioned into developing stories, Coons. That's the game."

"Yes, of course," I noted. "I did notice, in monitoring your news that there's an excess of murder, fires and scandal. You surely have to know that, with those call letters, WSLZ, everybody inside the Beltway refers to your station as SLEAZY 55." I watched carefully, wondering how he would react.

"I could care less," he retorted. "It's breaking news."

Stupid statement. What he really meant is that he couldn't care less. If he could care less, then he cared more.

"What goes around comes around," he continued. How the hell did that cliche make any sense? "Just like the big networks I started tracking every minute of the news. As soon as we put on a foreign dignitary visiting The White House, people changed channels. As soon as there was a murder, they were back. The President signs a bill, the viewing dies. The President's accused of sex crimes, the ratings soar."

"But don't you think you have a responsibility to cover the positive side of the news?" I asked.

"Coons, we don't go to the airport to cover landings. We go to cover crashes. It's what I call the technique. I'm the granddaddy of the mobile television unit. And I tell my people there's one rule of conduct: shove the microphone into their fucking faces and shout! That's it. That's the whole nine yards."

"Let me get that down," I interjected. The whole nine yards indeed. I didn't even know what it meant.

"And what I'm looking for right now is a big fat scandal and I'm willing to pay big time bucks to whoever gives me the scoop. My old college classmate, Pete O'Connor just went to work for that new Senator from Vermont and promised me he'd let me know as soon as something breaks. And now I've got to cut this short. Vice President called and wants me to come over to talk about a fund raiser. I play both sides, give to everybody, regardless of party. Would you like to join me? See some of your campaign buddies. If you do, I'll need to phone over and give your social security number."

My social security number! Why the hell my social security number? None of their goddamn business. What the hell do you have to do to get in to see the Vice President of the United States? Christ, I ran his first campaign! But I calmed down and began speaking slowly.

"That just may do it," I concluded. So he went to school with Pete. And he already knows. Amazing! Small world indeed.

What goes around comes around.

"Have a good one," the Mugger said as we parted.

"A good what?" Forget it Charlie.

****

"SHE DID WHAT?????" Controller bellowed when I informed him of Stephenson hiring Pete O'Connor. Went ballistic, as they say.

He screamed over the phone to Ronnie West. "Do you mean to say that, despite all your plans and the Brewster connection, you just sat by and let that woman hire the biggest pain in the ass on Capitol Hill?"

"I didn't even know about it," West replied with agitation as I quietly got on an extension to listen in. "We drew up the list. We gave it to Brewster. He gave it to her. He says she interviewed them all and then called O'Connor on the recommendation of some guy on The Washington Post. Brewster says she promised to talk to him before making the decision but didn't. She was so taken by O'Connor that she just then and there hired him."

I was breathing easier. The cover was being maintained.

"Oh she did, did she," interjected Controller sarcastically. "Just like that, eh? Well, she damn well better unhire him and you and Brewster better make sure she does unhire him or it's your ass and his! O'Connor, in case you don't fully realize it, is an arrogant son of a bitch who has no respect for the system. He not only doesn't have any respect, he hates it. And he knows, HE KNOWS, how to fuck it up. This is bad Ronald. Really bad. Big time! One of your very worst."

"But what can I do," asked Ronnie helplessly.

"I don't care. But do something. You tell Brewster to tell her he's a Commie or a queer. Tell her he's on drugs or a child molester. Make something up. Do anything but get this undone, do you understand?" ·

"Alright. I'll talk to Brewster. I'll talk to Frankie. I'll do what I can," he said with resignation. "Chances are, she won't budge. But I'll do what I can."

Still on the extension I wanted to comfort Ronnie but he wasn't to be appeased. "Thanks a lot, Charlie," he said. "You had to go to Controller, didn't you? Why didn't you alert me first? And how the hell did you know?"

"HANG UP THE PHONE" Controller ballistically shouted at me. "Let that stupid bastard stew for a while. And Charlie, will you keep an eye on this for me? You're the only one I can trust."

"The whole nine yards, Doctor," I replied. "The whole nine yards."

CHAPTER 8

INAUGURATION

Rick tried. And Frankie Phillips tried. But neither, to the dismay of Ronald West, could shake Jo's determination to hire Pete O'Connor. In desperation, Ron had even asked me to join Frankie and Rick as they took her to dinner at trendy and fashionable Bice that night. Thank God she played the game, acknowledging me as someone she happened to meet casually. Of course, I did the same.

"I like him," she laughed, when they brought up Pete. "He's kinda cute."

"Jo," Rick replied with exasperation, "this is serious business. It really isn't funny. The guy's crazy. He'll get himself in trouble, you in trouble and ultimately a lot more of us in trouble."

"Yeah, and I hear he's no good too," chimed in Frankie. "Me, I got an old dependable Hill hand who will at least make sure I don't miss quorum calls."

"Oh Frank, stop it," Jo shot back. "I'm not you and I wasn't elected the way you were and Vermont is not Pennsylvania. Can't you guys understand that I'm not here to make quorum calls? And Rick, I don't understand this trouble business. What do you mean, he'll get us in trouble?"

"He's just not one of ours," Rick blurted out, realizing too late that he had made a mistake.

"What do you mean, one of ours? One of whose? He's certainly one of mine." Jo was getting irritable even before we ordered.

"Cocktails!" I called to the waiter, keeping our priorities straight.

Over drinks Rick calmed down, careful not to appear concerned about his comment. "Jo," he said deliberately, "you will soon learn that the system simply isn't going to change just because you got elected to the United States Senate. And only to complete the last two years of a term at that. The other day you complained about the heavy security of the Capitol and the lack of freedom. If I may grab a phrase from my English student past, that security is a metaphor for what's been happening in this country. The system is now locked in by money, power and influence. Maybe it was always that way. What did Shaw once say? Every profession is a conspiracy against the laity. Well, this one is the biggest of all. We pay lip service to democracy but in reality, we're a highly sophisticated, carefully refined and subtly tuned instrument of special interest survival in a mechanized subculture with the trappings but not the realities of an open government. All I'm saying is that you can do what you want and hire whomever you want, but if you think things are going to change, you will end up as a most disillusioned woman."

Jo looked over at me for a reaction but I sat impassively because I agreed with the assessment but didn't want to tell her.

"That's not bad, Rick, not bad at all," she replied, having failed to elicit anything from me. "In fact, I think you put your finger right on the problem and it's precisely why I ran for the Senate, to try to change it."

"Rick's right, Jo," interjected Frankie. "You gotta go along to get along, that's what they told me. In ten years, I'll still be around here and vested when you're sitting up in Vermont teaching political science. Hell, I can even vote for my own pay raise and don't have to worry about it being in a negative ad. In my district, who cares?"

"Well, in any event, I'm sticking to my decision. There's just no way I'm not hiring Pete O'Connor," Jo said with determination.

"Another round!" I called to the waiter.

"Fine, then go ahead," Rick responded. "What's the difference? Why should I tell you otherwise? Do you realize there are more than 30,000 so called aides working on Capitol Hill right now? Thirty thousand operators with their own agendas? What possible difference will your one maverick make among thirty thousand any more than you will make a real difference among 535?"

"And 90,000 in the lobbying game," Jo shot back. "What difference does that make?"

"Now wait a minute," Frankie butted in. "They're good people, loyal and realistic, most of them. They make this government go around and don't doubt it for a minute. And most of them will be here long after we're gone. You know what they say, these elected guys are here today, gone tomorrow but we go on forever."

"The permanent establishment," I interjected.

The conversation moved on to other things, old times, college days and families, things that were really none of my business. It was clear that, twenty years later, Jo could still be charmed by Frankie's rough edged but basically decent approach to life. But Rick, more polished and stuffy, seasoned and experienced, seemed distant in his formality and almost robotic in his insistence on playing by the rules of the game. Repeated dinner conversation references to fund raisers heightened Jo's curiosity. Of course, she had never been to bed with Rick, something I would have bet she could not swear to about Frankie. Her memory of their brief college romance still brought a smile to her face and there were moments when I suspected she would do it again, here in Washington, which had a way of providing its own veil of anonymity to wayward politicians.

But enough of that. There were sufficient problems without adding that one. And, as we dropped her off at her hotel that night, she watched as the car drove away, I felt for the first time that she was beginning to be just a little perplexed by the situation she was getting into. And the closer I got, the more uncomfortable I became.

Controller of course was furious when I reported Rick Brewster's notable lack of success in getting rid of Pete O'Connor. But what to do? Clearly, his initial and impetuous suggestion of assassination was, at least for the time being, out of the question. He did manage to cut West's Christmas bonus in half but that was the spiteful reaction of a petty boss, not the stroke of a political genius. He did threaten never to raise a dollar for Rick Brewster if he ever ran for Governor of California but he knew he had him under control when the chips were down so why upset the applecart?

It came as no surprise, therefore, that within a few days, the entire political world became aware of the street talk that the woman from Vermont had hired that crazy bastard Pete O'Connor. And within a week, O'Connor was sitting at his desk in the low seniority Senate office of newly elected Josephine Stephenson.

By then, the Senator-elect was back in Vermont, making plans for her swearing in which would occur in just a few weeks at the beginning of January. Everybody wanted to come, of course: the Governor, the other Senator, Bernie himself, her gaggle of loyalists and supporters, environmentalists, micro brewers and ice cream makers, small town reporters and mountain people, transplanted blacks from Burlington and academics from the University. And, above all, George, Raymond and Henry, together with her adoring, proud mother, envious sister and two impatient brothers from other parts of the country.

As she reminisced with me later, it was a bittersweet time, unforgettable in its historic context, with each day bringing new psychic rewards of realizing how deeply appreciative, hopeful and full of goodwill so many human beings can be at that special time of unexpected victory. And then the emptiness of victory, the feeling of 'is that all there is?' And the silliness of the press, constantly hounding about secession and that night at the Radisson rally, people pushing her where she did not want to go, a cerebral radical with a moderate temperament, one step forward, two steps back, typical American middle of the roader, yet, undeniably, a maverick elected outside the system of whom much was expected.

And so she went back and forth, between anxiety and peace, tension and satisfaction, extremes and moderation. And then there was Raymond, the older son.

We knew before she did. Controller and West actually were in possession of a video from the Hollywood party with the kid apparently sniffing cocaine with sexiest teen alive Buddy Roman and actually having sex with the notorious goddess of hedonism, Mary Magdalene. (Ah, the marriage of Beverly Hills and the Beltway. How enticing to both. How heady.) And we also knew the kid knew about the video because Mr. Roman, king of the cinema opportunists, slipped the word to his agent who slipped the word to Controller's Los Angeles lawyer that Roman had informed Raymond of the missing tape. How Controller actually got his hands on it remained to be discovered but he got it indeed and poor potentially blackmailed Raymond was now a factor for Jo to reckon with in her pursuit of righteousness. I quietly let her know over the phone about the tape. She already knew what happened vaguely from Raymond but she had no idea that it now was in the possession of a mortal political enemy. Frozen, she replied in a monotone: "if it becomes a public issue we'll just have to deal with it. At the moment, I'm more concerned about Ray than about me."

I spoke to her on the phone on several occasions during the holidays. For some reason, she couldn't stop talking. Why this trust? Why me? What to do next? Embarrassing having her tell me about Raymond and her perception of George's increasing discomfort with his wife's celebrity and their constant separation. But apparently, peace reigned through Christmas as all went through the motions of the loving family and to some extent it was a loving family. George apparently loved Jo and Jo sort of loved George, everybody loved Henry, Henry lived in his own world, all were solicitous of Raymond and Raymond really cared about them. And then the lighting of the tree, the giving of presents, the family dinner on Christmas with all the relatives, fueled by the appropriate fire and rendered picturesque by the Vermont snow through the window. Evidently, Maureen had a gigantic New Year's Eve Party and on the very next day, burdened with hangovers and exhaustion, Jo and George piled into the proverbial station wagon with Ray and Henry and began the daylong trek to Washington, D.C.

I had been invited to the swearing in, much to Controller's delight that one of his boys was now on the inside of her operation. Afterwards, a regular session of the Senate was convened, with members, staffers and pages buzzing back and forth through the doors of the lordly Chamber. I was honored – I really mean it -to have been included and was delighted to meet George, Raymond, Henry and the others. Henry was particularly amusing.

105

"Mom, what's with these guys?" he asked undiplomatically after hanging around the Senate chamber and the Senate Building for the first few hours. "They all act like droids in a space movie."

"Quiet, Henry," cautioned Jo, fearing that Henry's loud mouth would spill over into the chamber.

"All I'm saying is that they're all kinda creepy," whispered Henry, determined not to give up on the point. "They look the same, they act the same, they smile the same, they even dress the same. And they all keep saying 'hi yew' to me and they don't even know me. It's weird. And Mom, can I ask just one more thing?"

"That's because they've been here too long," smiled Jo, adjusting to her new surroundings and trying to appear one of the boys in face of Henry's insistent grilling. "What's the one more thing," she asked patiently.

"What's a fund raiser? All I hear these guys talking about is their latest fund raiser. Are they collecting money for the Boy Scouts or something?" Henry looked intently at his mother.

"No, son. Fund raisers are parties that elected officials hold to raise money to pay for their campaigns."

"But you're an elected official and you never had a fund raiser," he persisted.

"Well, I did raise some money but not like most do. And because I was an independent, running against the excessive use of money in politics, I just didn't hold any fund raisers." Jo was desperately thinking of some way to change the subject, particularly since several of Henry's "droids" kept coming up to shake her hand and say "hi yew."

"But the campaigns are over, Mom," Henry remarked.

"Yes, dear, the campaigns are over. But a lot of these people have campaign debts and some are starting now to raise money for the next campaign. That's why 90% of this representative body – those that don't die or retire, keep getting elected and re-elected every six years. It makes the Russians look like the real democrats."

"The next campaign? But they just ended this one. Aren't they supposed to be governing now and campaigning later?" He wouldn't let it go and I couldn't help chuckling out loud.

"One would think so," Jo replied, glancing at me sideways to indicate her exasperation with her younger son's persistence. "I agree with you. As I said, that's why I ran the way I did. But not everybody does it my way."

"Give it a rest, will ya?" Raymond interjected. He had been standing nearby watching the proceedings while following Henry's dialogue.

"Hi yew," came the greeting from another member. "So you're the little lady from Vermont, huh? Welcome aboard. It won't take you no time to learn the ropes around here."

Frankie Phillips appeared from the lower body, inviting Jo to his inaugural party and celebrating the fact that he was the only freshman Congressman elected to the powerful Ways and Means Committee. "What did you get, Jo?" he asked.

"I don't know yet. I asked for the Ethics Committee but since the two party caucuses make the decisions, I'll probably be dead last on Merchant Marine and Fisheries."

"That's an important committee," Frankie reassured her. "Don't knock it. I want it for my second assignment. Lots of PAC money from Merchant Marine and Fisheries interests."

"Somehow, I knew you'd have your eye on the ball, Frank," Jo responded sarcastically.

"I'll put in a word for you with my new Senatorial buddies," Frankie volunteered. "If you go on it that's at least one Senator who won't be slicing up the pie with me." Frankie laughed and so did Jo.

"Mom," Henry came back again. "That guy just went down to the microphone and started screaming about family values. He only talked for thirty seconds. I timed him. And he didn't say nothin. And nobody was paying any attention anyway."

"Nothing's going to happen, Henry," Jo replied. "Nothing. The gesture is meaningless. I suspect that that particular man just took a poll in his district that showed that 77% of the people favor family values. That thirty second speech will be mailed all over his state and he'll put out a press release and his local paper will have a big headline saying that he got up on the floor of the Senate and demanded a return to family values. It will play very well with his constituents. Now let's get back to the office. We have to go to the party. A lot of people came down from Vermont to celebrate."

As we left the Senate Chamber, Jo came face to face with a handsome blonde woman dressed in pink, drowning in perfume, covered with jewelry and smiling waxenly at one and all. Oh my God, I thought, she knows me. Better duck before she begins to bore the hell out of me!

"Good afternoon," she intoned warmly. "I'm Juliette Wilson, newly elected Representative from Connecticut and you must be Josephine Stephenson, newly elected Senator from Vermont. I just came over to see this lovely Senate chamber."

"Why yes," Jo replied, somewhat taken aback by the formality of the encounter. "We should really get to know each other. There are few enough of us as it is and only you and I are newly elected women." She felt a little foolish but didn't know what else to say.

"Yes, we must," Congresswoman Wilson stated. "My office is in the Longworth Building. Please stop by and see me. My husband says he's always happy to meet new people and so am I. I'm here only to serve my constituents. Isn't that what the democratic process is all about, Mrs. Stephenson?"

"Please call me Jo," said Jo. "And may I call you Julie?" She avoided the more philosophical question.

"Juliette, please," answered Juliette. "My husband says that all women should use their formal names. But I'll call you Jo. Just don't tell Edmund. That's my husband." She smiled sweetly. "It will be our little secret."

"Well," said Jo uneasily, "it's nice to meet you. And I do hope we can get together soon. Bye now."

"Goodbye, Jo," Juliette smiled again. "See you soon."

Raymond and Henry had stayed in the background, observing the scene from a little distance.

"Now I've seen it all, Mom," pronounced Henry. "This place is really weird."

"I'm beginning to agree with him, Mom," added Raymond.

"So am I," said Jo, shaking her head in wonderment. She turned to me and asked: "what was that all about?

"Beats me," I said.

At the office, Pete was holding forth as the informal master of ceremonies, the one who knew everything, the old pro, the suave and debonair veteran, squiring old ladies and bearded gentlemen to rest rooms while arranging network television interviews for the first independently elected member of the Senate in memory.

Pete was going out the door giving directions to another contingent from Vermont as we were returning to the office. Pete and I had already talked on several occasions. He knew that I had recommended him. He was surprised and grateful. He also knew – but really didn't believe – that I was secretly going to help the cause. But we agreed to be a bit formal in public so as not to tip anybody off to our possible collusion.

"Everything ok, Pete?" Jo asked.

"Fine. I'm suggesting to everyone that they start now to go over to the hotel for the reception. And

I've got two network interviews scheduled for this afternoon and a photo session with the Burlington Free Press."

"Good. I'm especially interested in the Free Press and anyone else down here from the Vermont media. The network stuff is fine but I want to concentrate on the hometown people."

"Oh, I almost forgot. You also got a phone call about a half hour ago. Senator Chris Livengood of Iowa asked if you'd call him this afternoon. His number's on your desk." Pete started to walk away.

"Livengood? Wait, Pete. Livengood? Isn't he Chairman of the Ethics Committee?" Jo asked.

"Indeed he is," said Pete, stopping for a moment in the hall. "An old buddy of mine from the days when he was in the House and I was in the Speaker's Office. Interesting, huh?"

"I wonder what he wants," Jo asked me as she walked into the office, smiling and shaking hands with all the people from Vermont. I just shrugged.

Jo was especially pleased to see her other Senator from Vermont, Jim Webster, a Republican. She knew he had been shaken by her election since it not only indicated a deeper rebellious strain in the state than he had suspected but also set Bernie or another coalition member up as a leading contender for his seat, a prospect already being discussed in the local press.

Webster stayed only briefly, explaining that swearing in day was a particularly busy time for holding fund raisers. "I'm going to five in a row tonight," he said without emotion, "and I'm taking the Governor to every single one."

Jo stared at him in wonderment, smiled and said goodbye. "What the hell does that have to do with the price of maple syrup in Vermont?" she murmured under her breath.

Sliding by the punchbowl and the cookies, the volunteers and the relatives, she slipped into her office and called Senator Livengood. "Yes, I'll be right over," she said. "And thanks for seeing me."

CHAPTER 9

THE ETHICS COMMITTEE

The Russell Senate Office Building is one of those structures which, when excavated in a thousand years, will cause the people of that era to wonder what in the hell was in their ancestors' minds when they built such an awkward, gross and imperious mausoleum to shelter their elected officials. The ultimate symbol of 20th Century empire, its environs were reserved for the really senior members of the world's most exclusive club when they weren't hiding out in their private little cubbyholes in the sheltered environs of The Capitol itself.

Of these, Chris Livengood was fast becoming an institution himself. After forty years in the Congress, he stood third in overall seniority. Chairman of the Ethics Committee, he also was a ranking member of Appropriations and Rules. A product of the old system, he had seen his club evolve from an oligarchy controlled by a few powerful bosses into a colorless collection of pin striped egos, all dominated by one overriding common denominator, fund raising.

Unlike many who had retired or faded away, he adapted to the change, played by the new rules and actually managed to enhance his power and influence as the years went by.

His office was palatial, adorned by fine works of art from the National Gallery and draped with the American flag. Plaques, pictures of award ceremonies, informal photos from innumerable golf outings and endless memorabilia from Iowa covered the walls of the reception area. His door was always open as were those of most Congressional offices. But it wasn't easy to get by the staff.

This is what transpired, as Jo recollected it for us later. When she walked in the door, six aides instantly stared at her apprehensively. This was her, that woman who was threatening to upset the applecart. Two women staffers quickly turned to their computers, two young men picked up their phones, the receptionist froze and the top banana himself, the Administrative Assistant, peered around another visitor who hadn't noticed her entrance.

"That's twenty thousand in there," said the other visitor, placing an envelope in the hands of the A.A. "I'll have more tomorrow. Tell Chris I hope he makes it to the fund raiser tonight at the Madison. Controller will be there with some of the New GOP crowd. Should be worth at least twenty more."

Then the other visitor realized someone else was behind him. He turned slightly, gave Jo a sidelong glance, moved ponderously toward the open door, turned and said, "see ya later," disappearing into the corridor.

"Can I help you," the A.A. asked, with what Jo later mockingly refereed to as "a superiority befitting the Russell Building."

"Yes, I'm Senator Stephenson from Vermont. Senator Livengood called a little while ago and asked me to come over."

"Yes, he told me to expect you. I'm his A.A. Thomas Gracie," said Gracie coldly. "If you'll wait a moment, I'll tell him you're here." Not Tom, Thomas.

"Thanks Tom," Jo said offhandedly.

"It's Thomas, Mrs. Stephenson," Gracie corrected.

"Right, Thomas," Jo repeated.

Before getting up to go to the Senator's office, Gracie slipped the envelope into the center drawer of his desk. Jo got just a glance. It was obvious that the envelope was one of several collected that day. Pretty good catch for opening day, she thought.

Within moments, the vanguard leader of the new reform was seated before the old guard standard bearer of the system. He was an imposing gentleman, not at all a caricature of the comic books, not a trace of Senator Claghorn. Fairly trim and extremely well dressed, with Congressional cufflinks on his custom shirt, Rolex watch and regimental tie, Livengood, although in his seventies, could have been in his mid-fifties. With horned rim glasses and dyed black hair slicked back, he was clearly a throwback to, Jo guessed, at least the fifties, if not earlier. His eyes were pleasant and direct. He sat with both arms on his desk, all five fingers of one hand touching all five of the other, and stared at her.

"So you're the young lady who's causing all the fuss," he said warmly.

"I was sure you were going to say 'hi yew' like your colleagues, Mr. Livengood. But yes, if you have to put it that way, I'm the not so young woman who's causing all the fuss."

Livengood chuckled at the 'hi yew' reference, sat back in his swivel chair and proceeded to feel more comfortable.

"You know, I've seen them come and go around here for the last forty years and I must say that it's usually not very interesting. But you're interesting. And so's my friend Pete O'Connor whom you had the good sense to hire."

"Thanks," Jo said. "You're the first person around here with any power who's said that to me. I think I made the right decision and, in any event, it's done."

"Good for you. I like that," Livengood smiled. "What do you want?"

"What do you mean, what do I want? You called me if my memory serves me correctly."

"No, I don't mean what do you want here, I mean what do you want? What's your agenda? Majority Leader of The Senate? First woman President?"

"Honestly, I don't know what I want. I don't have what you call a personal ambition agenda. Does everybody in this place have to have an agenda? Does everybody have to be preoccupied with controlling everybody else's agenda? Must everyone be suspected of having a 'hidden' agenda? My running and winning look more accidental to me every day. And now that

I'm here, I'm not sure how I can either meet the expectations of my supporters or get anything substantive done. Frankly, I'll probably be a two year member and a footnote in the history books."

"I'm not so sure about that. I'm an old pro, Mrs. Stephenson, and I think I can detect ambition when I see it," Livengood interjected.

"Maybe," Jo responded. "But I don't think I possess your kind of ambition, Mr. Chairman, if I may call you by your more familiar title. Speaking of ambition, you seem to have more than your share. What is going on out there with envelopes full of checks piling up in your A.A.'s desk drawer? Isn't that a bit too ambitious and possibly illegal?"

"Completely within the rules, young woman," Livengood shot back, getting a bit testy. "Besides, I can raise money other members can't. And then I give it to them. Increases my power. Now I can't talk money on the premises but my A.A. can collect it right out front and it's all legal. How do you like that bullshit?"

"I don't," replied Jo, somewhat taken aback by the revelation and the crudity.

"Let me get right to the point, Mrs. Stephenson. If you go ahead as you are, as a maverick lone voice in the back of the Senate, you will achieve nothing and, indeed, will in all probability, be gone from here in two years. Even the worst of us can wait out that short length of time. You will be drowned, smothered, isolated and humiliated at every turn. A thousand little slights will come your way and your life here will be one long and lonely period of misery. You see, nobody gives a good goddamn about you or your causes. All that you represent to them is a momentary inconvenience."

"I think I'm aware of that," Jo interjected.

"Let me finish and don't be so impetuous," Livengood commented, loosening up as the conversation continued. "The system stinks. It's out of control. Some of us know that but we keep it to ourselves. Others who can't change it leave, disillusioned and weary. We who hang around played within the system so long that we wouldn't know how to do otherwise if we wished. That's why I keep collecting those checks. It's raw political conditioning. They think I'm one of theirs. And I guess I am. At least, I put on a pretty good act. But something has to be done and I've decided to try to do it through you. I wasn't so sure at first but when you hired Pete, that convinced me. That was the first time I really thought you were serious. And I must say that your conduct here in this office so far has reinforced my opinion."

Jo just sat there wide eyed.

"I'm Chairman of the Ethics Committee. In that position my responsibility to the powers that be is to do nothing to upset the applecart. Yes, we investigate personal misconduct and I must say this sexual stuff is getting out of hand for an old Puritan like me. But the heavy stuff, the money, the lobbyists, the conflicts of interest, forget it. Now, what I am going to tell you is strictly between you and me, do I have your agreement on that?"

"Well," Jo hesitated, "I'd like to know what it is before I agree."

"Now you can't do that, goddammit," Livengood shot back. "If we're going to work this thing out, then I have to be able to trust you and you have got to trust me."

She hesitated again. Is this the way they buy and makes deals, she wondered? Already a party to the game? Indoctrination into the old boy network?

But then she blurted out, "okay, it's a deal."

"Mrs. Stephenson, my doctors have told me that I don't have long to live…"

"Oh, I'm terribly sorry," she said suddenly.

"Fine, fine, I appreciate that, but I'm not looking for sympathy. The fact is it's the Big C and it looks like anywhere from six to eighteen months. No one knows that. No one. Not even my wife. I'm telling you because you must know if we are to work this out. You have got to understand why I'm doing what I'm doing. Frankly, I want to be remembered as something other than one of the longest serving hacks in the United States Congress. I want my footnote in history, Mrs. Stephenson, and I want it to say that I did what had to be done at a crucial moment in our nation's political system. That may sound corny or insincere to you but that's how I feel and I don't intend to elaborate. Just take it for what it's worth."

"I believe you," Jo said quietly.

"I am prepared, Mrs. Stephenson, to place you on the Ethics Committee. We have one vacancy. I will say it's either you or the minority party so I decided to screw the minority party on this one. Everyone will understand that even though they won't be happy. In a few months, it is my intention to create a subcommittee on the role of fund raising, lobbying and campaign consulting which will have broad investigative and subpoena powers. At that time, I intend to name you its Chairman. All hell will break loose of course but I have virtual dictatorial authority in this matter and I'll just stick it out. At that time, you can assign Pete to the subcommittee staff. I'll give you all the help I can but my ability will wane in the coming months and you must understand that hostile and powerful forces, even my own loyal staff, will do everything possible in their sheer audacity and guile, to stop you. Your life may even be in danger if this goes too far. Do you understand what I'm saying?"

Her head spinning, Jo could do nothing but nod. My God, he's opening the door to consequences that could shake the Capitol to its foundations. "Yes," she finally said, "but you don't even know me. I can understand your motives but why me?"

"I know you, Mrs. Stephenson, just as the people of Vermont knew you and just as you knew Pete O'Connor and he knows you. He told me the story of your interview and that did it. You'd better get that resume he promised. He also told me who recommended him and I find that very interesting. Mr. Coons was last seen by me at Ludwig Controller's Golf Outing and he didn't look like a rehabilitated member of the Brotherhood. But one never knows."

Jo smiled. "I trust Charlie," she said. "At least I think I do. And I'll get Pete's resume," she said, "but only to see if he's qualified to work on the subcommittee."

Both laughed, then Livengood continued. "You know, it's really bad. Not only is the money out of control but it's turning into a racket. The outrageousness of madmen like Ludwig Controller actually creating organizations like the New GOP. I hate that bastard with a passion. I went down and backslapped at that golf outing of his last month and couldn't get over the sheer audacity of it all. That's your other job as I see it. The only reason this stuff continues is because of the massive indifference of the American people. Not only do you have to challenge the system, Mrs. Stephenson. You're going to have to attract and keep the support and loyalty of the media. Don't get done in by the Iron Triangle."

"What's that?" Jo asked with a puzzled look on her face.

"The Iron Triangle, Mrs. Stephenson, the Iron Triangle. The entrenched politicians, the media and the special interests. Pete and Charlie must take the media out of the equation. Or you'll find yourself on SLEAZY 55 in a way you never expected." He looked sternly at her.

"SLEAZY 55? What's that? Oh, I suppose I understand," Jo said solemnly. "What happens next?"

"Well, do you accept?" he asked.

"Do I have a choice?" she asked in return.

"No, you don't," he said flatly. "Go back to your reception with all those nice people from Vermont. If anyone asks where you were, tell them that I simply wanted to interview you about committee assignments. Don't even tell Pete yet. And especially not Mr. Coons. I don't trust him like you do. At least not yet. In about ten days, we will meet again with Pete present. Get your feet on the ground, get used to the place, and we'll get started soon. Okay?" He smiled.

"Okay," she said. "Okay. I can't believe this. But I heard it and it's, well, okay. Thank you. Yes, we'll talk again."

As she left, Livengood shouted "Thomas, get in here! And show the Senator out. We've got work to do."

CHAPTER 10

THREE POWERFUL VILLAINS

I was furious at Jo's report of Livenghood's impression of me but predictably, he was right. Widespread public approval of Jo Stephenson's selection for the Senate Ethics Committee and the chairmanship of the newly created subcommittee was balanced by an astonishing amount of backroom Beltway dismay.

Senator Larry (not Lawrence) Johnson of Kansas was quoted in the New York Times as expressing "tremendous approval of this courageous act on the part of my good friend Senator Livengood." Senator Johnson was quoted privately in the Senate Cloakroom as having shouted, "is the old fucker off his rocker?"

The Senator's, shall we say, mixed sentiments were shared by most of his colleagues. Some of Livengood's more discerning and sophisticated associates saw a deeper and more venal stratagem on the part of the wily old master. Bill (not William) Kenworthy of Missouri, over cocktails the evening after the appointment, allowed as how the Ethics Committee traditionally had been peopled with Southern Senators from safe states. The reasoning behind the selection of such safe club members had been that they could protect their colleagues in Ethics investigations and cover up their dubious conduct with little fear of reprisal from voters at home who were not only immune to criticism from The New York Times, The Washington Post and the networks but actually rebelled against the establishment press knocking their favorite sons.

Ergo, continued the learned gentleman from the "show me" state, Livengood was actually setting up Stephenson for a fall. "Wait'll she starts makin' a fuss and we retaliate by cutting off projects for Vermont. She won't get shit done for her constituents and she'll be in hot water in no time with just two years to serve. And she won't get nothin' on us because nobody will talk to her. To somebody else, maybe, but not to her. Smart cookie, old Chris."

And so it went.

For once, however, the wily Controller kept his cool. After counseling with Ronald West, Dickie White, Paul Pinafore, Tommy Rock and myself at the Congressional Country Club on the evening of the momentous news, the Doctor kept his detestation under control and announced that he would set off for a vacation of several weeks in the Caribbean. As it happened, he had just been reading a book about Joe Kennedy in which the author said that, at one moment of setback in his ambitious career, Kennedy adopted the course recommended by James Joyce for people out of power: exile, silence and cunning. He loved it.

"Gentlemen," he said, "I'm going into exile. But only for a little while. And I'm going to shut up. But I'll be thinking about this big time. You can bet on that. Yes sir, I'll be thinking about that little bitch and that smart ass assistant of hers. Smart son of a bitch, old Joe Kennedy. And what's that other guy's name? Joyce. Yeah, Joyce. Smart too. Can't beat the Irish for conniving. As for Livengood, he's a dead man."

All of us reacted with dismay. West particularly squirmed in his easy chair recalling that Controller had suggested, if ever so casually, the assassination of Jo Stephenson.

After a moment of ominous silence, he got to the point. "Look, when I say he's a dead man, you really don't know what I'm talking about, do you? Now don't worry Ronald. I'm not gonna have him killed. The old man's dying of cancer. He'll be in the ground in a couple of months."

"What?" we shouted in unison. Jo hadn't told me yet so I was just as shocked as the others.

"Got it from his Doctor. One of my boys. It's fatal. And this little act is his swansong. The guy's an old time Catholic and probably wants to straighten everything out before he meets his maker."

Tommy Rock timidly tiptoed into the conversation. "Well, Doctor, if I may venture an opinion…"

"Yeah, what opinion? What've you got to say?" asked Controller scornfully of this, the least of his followers.

Jiggling the knot of his tie, Rock came out with it. "Well, sir, that may be an explanation but it's not a solution." There was a noticeable lack of concern being expressed about the plight of Senator Livengood.

"What do you mean, solution?" Controller impatiently demanded.

"I mean, there she is whether Livengood has cancer or not. Whether he did it to meet his maker or not. The question is: what do we do about it? I mean, Common Good, the new GOP, the whole house of cards is threatened by this. Her chairmanship of that subcommittee is a distinct challenge to our business...*your* business." Tommy was getting eloquent.

"Cunning, my boy," the Doctor observed, feigning confidence. "That's what I'm going away for. A little time to plot and plan."

For the first time in our association with Controller, all of us knew that he didn't have an answer. It made them nervous and gave me encouragement, something I badly needed to shore me up as I began, ever so slowly, to vacillate between reformer Jo and manipulator Ludwig. At that moment, I could tell that the others began to look around in their individual mentalities for alternative means of survival. It doesn't take long for insecure people to start checking out the life rafts instead of the deck chairs.

Then he added the one dirty line: "and there's always the video, gentlemen. Always the video."

****

Personally, I wasn't sure myself whether to check out the life raft or the deck chair. But the angels of my better nature, Lincoln's timeless spirits, kept bringing me back to Jo and the white hats. And so I found myself once again in her presence, reassuring myself that, even with the threat of scandal at our disposal, Jo need not have been so concerned. As is usual in such affairs, the enemy didn't know much more about what to do than the adversary.

Jo sat at her desk, in her modest Senate office, peering at Pete O'Connor who sat staring equally at her as I slipped in the door, pad and pencil in hand, like some sort of stenographer waiting for dictation.

"Pete," she started.

"Yes, Senator," he dryly retorted.

"Do you remember the last scene of The Candidate where Redford wins the Senate race and his consultant says…"

I cut her off and then we all said, simultaneously, "okay smart guy, now what do you do next?" We broke up. And then silence after the laughter died down.

"This is serious business, guys," she said.

"I know, Senator," said Pete.

"People expect a lot," she said.

"Yes indeed, Senator," said Pete.

"The Times, the Post, the networks, cable. They're crawling around here looking for something," I chimed in. "And they must be fed or you will end up as the do-nothing disappointment of the year. They will write of high expectations dashed on the rocks of expediency and compromise or, worse, on the quicksand of incompetence."

"Oh stop it, stop it. What are you doing to help? You're no help at all," she shot back at me, showing the first signs of irritation at me since I met her. "The Iron Triangle," she murmured. "The Iron Triangle."

The Iron Triangle? I thought. Ah yes, the Iron Triangle. No, the Unholy Trinity. And Pete and I will have to deal with it. But first, reality.

"Well," Pete said, "the fact is that we've been through scandal after scandal. It's pretty hard to keep the momentum going. You may be old hat by now, especially if one more corporation declares bankruptcy after phony audits. Who cares about us when the private sector is being hung for a change?"

"It's all the same interlocking business, whether its Washington or Wall Street," she insisted. "This place is a racket. The corporate guys feed the money to protect themselves. You can sense it in the halls. You can smell it in the cloakroom. It reeks of big money and is strangled by lobbyists."

"Good speech," he replied calmly. "But probably nothing illegal. That's the problem. Everybody knows how to stay within the laws that were written precisely to protect the game. Appearances and improprieties don't make indictments and illegalities. And anything short of indictment doesn't satisfy."

"Then let's go for real change. Let's just push substantive legislation that will change the system," Jo suggested.

"Real change. Hmmm. Isn't that the slogan of your favorite President?" Pete smiled.

"Don't be so cynical," she retorted. "Besides, he can't run again."

"And her an Independent," I commented sarcastically.

"The problem with real change is that nobody really wants it. Anyway, I have been thinking about this and I have a suggestion." Pete looked down at his notes.

"It's about time," Jo said, but smiling as she said it.

"I suggest we introduce two pieces of legislation. The first would ban federal officials, both elected and appointed, from ever lobbying for commercial interests after they leave office...no time limits...no qualifiers...no maybes. That obviously would include – and start with – foreign interests. If you're serving the United States of America, you can't take your know how with you and give it to commercial enterprises and other countries." Pete looked pleased with himself.

Jo became thoughtful, musing about the roadblocks.

"How about your constitutional right to do as you please?" she asked.

"I thought about that. It's risky. But it's worth the chance. We'll worry about that later. Good PR," said Pete.

"Forget the PR," Jo shot back. "Won't some of these guys hide behind the constitutionality business as an excuse not to support the bill?"

"Probably," Pete retorted. "That's their problem. Aside from your sanctimonious comments about PR, we need some momentum. Take one example. Some of these guys sit over there in the Trade Rep's office, negotiate all our deals with foreign countries then leave office and get big fees for representing the very countries they just negotiated with. The second would not only ban soft money but finance all federal campaigns with public funds and require television stations to grant free access to candidates at all levels while banning the use of political ads that don't feature the candidates speaking directly and forthrightly to the people. That way, you get rid of the negative poison that's corrupting the system and you turn the whole media world into one big C-Span."

"Speech over?" Jo asked. "You're right, Pete. It may not work. Maybe it won't happen. But we have to start somewhere. Besides, that's what I campaigned on. Get the bills drawn up. I want to look at them very carefully. With a couple of good constitutional lawyers too. If we're satisfied, let's hold a press conference and circulate them for co-sponsors. It'll be interesting to see what happens. Maybe something."

Jo looked out the window. Pensive. Thoughts far away.

"That view is not in the direction of Vermont," Pete commented. "Or Los Angeles. That view is only Beltway."

"I know," she responded without turning around. "I'm just thinking about them. I'm thinking about the state too. It's hurting economically. I have to get things done, just ordinary bring home the bacon stuff that we need. This legislation will fly in the Times but not necessarily in the Burlington Free Press. Get Maureen to call Jim Webster's office and check on the progress of those highway maintenance funds and the housing money for Burlington. Do you realize how many people in my state can't afford a home? What do they say about reformers?"

"Don't get so far in front of your troops that you get shot in the ass," I warned.

As Jo nodded agreement, Maureen Sullivan appeared in the doorway, carrying what looked like a Senatorial press release. And a press release it was, from the office of Senator Chris (not Christopher) Livengood.

"Livengood just announced the other three members of the subcommittee," Maureen announced. "And you won't believe it."

"Without consulting me?" Jo asked in amazement.

"You're surprised?" asked cynical Pete.

"But I'm the Chairman or Chairperson or whatever," she retorted.

"Yeah, but he's the big cheese. New subcommittee, new and inexperienced Chair, the big guy has all the power. I can just imagine what's coming," I observed.

Maureen handed the statement to Pete. "Read it," she said.

As Jo stared intently, Pete began:

"Senator Chris Livengood today announced three additional appointments to the newly formed Subcommittee on Fund Raising, Lobbying and Campaign Consulting of the Senate Ethics Committee, to support the work of newly designated Chairman, Josephine Stephenson. The members are: Senator Alvin Bushey of Alabama, Senator Bobby Bagot of

Mississippi and Senator Floyd Green of Texas. In making the appointments, Senator Livengood cited the long experience, extensive knowledge and political wisdom of the three appointees. 'Senator Stephenson is going to need all the help she can get as she undertakes this historic mission,' Senator Livengood commented. 'I know of no finer pillars of support that the team of Bushey, Bagot and Green.' The appointments take effect immediately."

"End of release," Pete said coldly.

Jo was dumbfounded. How could he do this to her? No consultation? Just like that? Not even a phone call?

"It's worse than that," Pete said. "You don't know these guys but I do. They're known around here as the Wimp, the Wonk and the Windbag. Let me tell you a couple of..."

Before he could finish, Jo lunged for the phone.

"Hello, yes, this is Senator Stephenson. Is Senator Livengood there? No? He's where? In Iowa? When will he be back? Tell him I called. I need to talk to him immediately. It's urgent."

"Oh, don't use that word," I said. "Everything's urgent around this place and that means nothing is urgent."

"If you would stop being Mr. Observer of the Passing Scene and start getting involved in this thing, we'd be a lot better off," Jo retorted.

That, of course, had always been my problem, a hesitation to get fully involved. The normal human fear of being cut off. No more political consulting. No more big bucks. Shunned by my friends. And besides,

Controller's done me a lot of personal favors. He invites me to his Super Box and includes me on jaunts. My world would be over. My life could even be in danger. The post golf outing resolve was softening.

Maureen broke in. "Can I ask a practical question? What do I tell the Times, the Post, the Free Press and the networks? You know they're gonna think something's fishy."

"Well," Pete volunteered, "we can't say we knew. But we can't say we didn't know. Oh shit, what a goddam mess. Limited options."

"Options! Options! You're beginning to sound like Mr. Sound Bite. Maureen, when in doubt say nothing," Jo instinctively replied. "Nothing until I talk to Livengood. But he'd better call fast. Just tell them – if they call – that I'm tied up and will get back, okay?"

"If you say so," said Maureen, looking exasperated. "But I think you've been set up."

"I don't need that," Jo said testily. "We'll…we'll work this out."

The buzzer sounded. Maureen picked up the phone. "It's Livengood," she said, handing the receiver to Jo.

"Josephine, hello, I hear you're trying to reach me," intoned the relaxed voice in Iowa.

"Yes, yes, of course I'm trying to reach you. I just got this press release about the subcommittee."

"Oh that," Livengood replied calmly. "You sound concerned. I wouldn't worry about it. They're good old boys. I'll control them. Just did it to reassure the troops."

"But couldn't you have consulted me?" Jo was trying to remain calm.

"Oh I guess so," Livengood replied. "But I would've done it anyway. You're new. You'll get used to these things. By the way, I just talked to Alvin Bushey. He's going to call you to set up a meeting with the other members as soon as possible. Maybe this afternoon. Why don't you just go ahead and meet with them."

"But what do I tell the press? They're going to want to know how all this happened and did I know and did I approve."

"Now you just tell them it was my idea and you went along on the assurance personally from me that these here fellas have agreed to give you all the backing you need. Tell them you're meeting to plan the agenda as quickly as possible. It'll all work out. You'll see, young lady. It's how we do things in Washington."

"But what about all those things you told me in your office when I agreed to accept this thing?" Jo asked in exasperation.

"I'm committed to them. I told you that. And I mean it. We just have to out-maneuver the system by playing by its rules, that's all. Trust me. Everything's gonna be alright."

Jo didn't believe it but she had little choice. And she did hold onto the vanishing hope that Livengood meant what he said. Maureen slipped a note under her nose that Senator Bushey had already called. Good news. Maybe this will work out after all.

"Hang on.   Don't do anything radical," whispered Pete.

She hesitated for a moment, then said: "alright Senator. I'll give it a try. That's Senator Bushey on the other line. I'll get together with them this afternoon."

"Good girl. Have a good one," said Livengood as he abruptly hung up the phone.

"Jo, I have an idea," I interjected.

"It's about time," Pete shot back.

I ignored that remark and continued: "let me sit in. If I do, those three guys, all of whom I know and all of whom think they're wired to Controller through me and the others, will be absolutely reassured that they've got you surrounded. Believe me, I can help on this one. It'll get everybody off guard while we plan what to do."

On my part, this was not an instant and total conversion. And it wasn't a long term commitment. It was really the old balancing act. I could help her out and still have Controller thinking I was his plant.

"Pete?" Jo asked.

Pete looked at me. He hesitated. In any event, he knew it couldn't be him and it probably had to be somebody, even someone he wasn't sure he trusted.

"Yeah," he said, to my relief. "It can't do any harm."

And so we decided to meet with the Wimp, the Wonk and the Windbag.

CHAPTER 11

THE BIG GRAB

"Good girl indeed!" she mumbled as she picked up the phone.

Jo didn't need that little bit of condescension. But call Senator Bushey she did and made her next mistake. She agreed to go to his office in the Russell Building rather than convene the meeting in her own office.

"What difference does it make?" she demanded when Pete complained about the arrangement.

"Symbolic geography," Pete replied. "Power has a lot to do with who calls whom to where at what time."

"Oh nonsense, that's not the way I do things," Jo shot back. "Anyway, we'll just slip on the private elevator. Nobody will notice."

"Don't bet on it," Pete warned. "But before you go, Charlie and I must brief you about the Wimp, the Wonk and the Windbag."

Jo smiled. Wanly. But she did smile. "Okay," she said, "tell me."

"Bushey's the Wimp," I began. "Been in the Senate for forty years. A lot of seniority. Survived by bringing home the pork for Alabama. Funny little man. No chin. Pursed lips. Wears a gold watch on a chain. Shifty bulging eyes. Never takes a stand, except for Alabama and states rights. Hasn't had an opponent in a decade but he's scared of the emerging Republican Right. Collecting PAC money like a madman. Now says some of his best friends are black. No help there at all. Should have retired, or been retired, years ago. Nothing will get him out but the grim reaper."

"That's real encouraging, Charlie," Jo commented. "And the Wonk?"

"That's Bagot," I continued. "Unsteady. Shaky. A little feeble. Tends to go off. Wanders. Frequently isn't there for important votes. But he's shaken every hand in Mississippi for the past thirty years, black, white, young, old, rich, poor. Just what they want. Gray, cautious, meticulous. Wears white suits. The movies would type cast him easily. No guts. But canny. His physical shakiness gets him sympathy. Big fundamentalist darling. Loves lobbyists, especially corporate, and never missed a free meal or a corporate cocktail reception."

Pete continued with "some people swear he leaves church meetings, Boy Scout dinners and American Legion picnics, gets in his car and drives to gay bars in New Orleans. I can't believe it myself. But that's the gossip. At any rate, I wouldn't count on him. The religious right would never believe anything about him anyway. Daughter married a Mormon elder."

"Thanks a lot. That's all I need," Jo responded. "Okay, how about the Windbag?"

"Power, strictly power," Pete commented. "Tall, stately, lanky, formidable, piercing eyes, patrician demeanor, double breasted blue suits, Cowboy boots. Skin leathered by the Texas sun. Chairman of Appropriations. Major player. Ego to rival Johnson or Connally. Slippery. Dominant. Cunning. And corrupt. Extremely close to Controller and the Common Gr...Good Crowd."

"I met him at the Inauguration," Jo recalled. "Very courtly, extremely masculine. But the eyes had that phony piercing quality. You know, the message is 'I'm paying attention only to you,' but the reality is 'I can see through you, will know your vulnerabilities so you better think twice about double crossing me.'"

"Very perceptive," Pete interjected. "But you must know that he dominates the other two. The meeting may have been called by Bushey but the agenda will be set by Floyd B. Green. Actually, like most people around here, chummy as they may be, they really hate each other with a passion."

And indeed they did.

The private elevator worked. Quiet in the halls. No press people hanging around. Jo and I slipped into the Russell Building only to be blocked again at the security station. Will they ever get to know her? Accept her? Then the deferential half bows. Go right on up.

"Oh dear, dear, come right in here, Senator," slurped Alvin Bushey the Wimp. "It's so fine of you to come all the way over here. You know, we could have come over there but, well you know, the three of us are here. Ha. Ha. Anyway, please come into my conference room. And Charlie! This is indeed a surprise and a pleasure. Do come in!"

We smiled, shook hands and followed Bushey through the partitioned cubbyholes of an overstaffed Senatorial office and into the small conference room furnished with easy chairs and lined with wall to wall pictures of Bushey and Truman, Bushey and Eisenhower, Bushey and Kennedy, Bushey and George Wallace, Bushey and Martin Luther King, Bushey and Johnson, Bushey and Nixon, Bushey and Ford, Bushey and ("one of our very own") Jimmy Carter, Bushey and Reagan and, two peas in a pod, Bushey and Bush. The man was living in the past. In fact, he was the past.

Bagot the Wonk and Green the Windbag were already waiting, Bagot shakily extending his hand to "Madame Chairman" and Green bowing in courtly manner to this "fine little lady from, where was that, oh yes, Vermont. And Charlie. How reassuring to see you. A real pro, Madame Chairman. Real pro. Big time. You listen to Charlie and everything will be just fine."

I could tell that Jo felt uneasy. In fact, that she felt terribly uneasy. Here was the inner sanctum, the very core of democracy at work. In this darkened, unprepossessing, power lined and smokily masculine little room, the conniving and the nondescript pulled the levers of power and exercised the prerogatives of Senatorial tradition. Carefully crossing her legs as she took one of the leather seats of success, she barely waited for them to sit down before having the first word.

"Gentlemen, I'm glad to meet each of you personally and hope that we can get down to business as quickly as possible," she announced in her best authoritative tone.

Bagot reached for a cigar. "I, I, I, I would offer you one but I'm sure you don't smoke, Senator," he said with a feeble smile.

"That's right," Jo replied. "Is smoking allowed in here?"

"Oh not everywhere," Bushey answered as Bagot lit up, blowing the smoke in the general direction of their visitor. "Charlie, cigar?"

"Not right now thank you, Senator," I replied deferentially. All through this meeting I was hoping that Bagot wouldn't remember the time I ran one of his opponent's campaigns and almost beat him.

"But here, in our private quarters, anything goes," Bagot chuckled.

"I was hoping," Jo persisted, "that we could agree on a time for our first public meeting."

This sort of instant demand made me really uncomfortable. Doesn't she realize that this thing had to shift, bob and weave before anything got agreed to?

"Now, now, young lady," Green predictably interjected, "there's plenty of time for that. We thought it would be preferable to spend some time getting to know each other better. Make things comfortable so we can establish a meaningful working relationship."

"Perhaps a little brandy, Senator, in lieu of the cigar?" Bushey chuckled.

"Uh, no, no thanks," Jo replied, a little off balance. "I don't drink…"

"Don't drink! Oh my, you'll never last in the Senate," Bushey said with another chuckle. Chuckling was a frequent habit of the powerful. "We'll have to get her a membership in Alcoholics Unanimous," he added, turning to the others.

"I mean, I don't drink at three o'clock in the afternoon," Jo continued. "Perhaps later, when we get together occasionally for a cocktail after work."

"Fine, fine!" Green interjected. "That's the spirit. Charlie, brandy?" Boy would I have loved one but again I said no thanks and after an awkward pause, he declared, somewhat condescendingly, "so you're the little lady who started the latest reform movement."

Little lady my eyeball, I thought. Is that a paraphrase of what Lincoln said to Harriet Beecher Stowe? The thought ran through my mind. Ironic. She looked directly at Green, determined not to be intimidated. But that piercing look of his clearly sent shivers down her spine. Smarmy wasn't the exact word but it came close.

"Well, I'm not sure I started anything," Jo retorted confidently. "And I don't know whether it's a reform movement in the sense of a movement. But I know something is going on out there and I think we have to respond to it."

"Absolutely, no question about it," interjected Bobby Bagot. "I just wish I felt strong enough to carry it off. But I've been around here a long time and I know one has to go along to get along." A trite phrase for a trite little man, I thought.

"Now Ms. Stephenson," Green stiffened, "we know about those bills that Mr. O'Connor is having drawn up for your sponsorship. Laudatory aims, Ms. Stephenson, laudatory aims."

"Perfectly laudatory," chimed in Alvin Bushey.

"Laudatory and timely. But we've got to go slow on some of these things," added Bobby Bagot. "Even the Beltway, like Rome, wasn't built in a day. This great country of ours mustn't be permitted to go awry." He glanced unsteadily at Floyd Green for approval. It was not forthcoming and he became very unsteady, dropping cigar ashes on Bushey's oriental rug. Bushey meanwhile poured another brandy and I was getting quite uncomfortable.

"I would like to have all three of you as co-sponsors," Jo interjected.

Bushey and Bagot fumbled but Green kept his cool.

"Well, now, that's mighty considerate of you, Ms. Stephenson. Oh, may I call you Josephine?" he inquired.

"Jo is fine," she responded. "What do you think?"

"Of course we'll take a look at them," Green responded easily. "Frankly, I don't put my name on anything I don't examine carefully. Neither do Senators Bushey or Bagot. Do you boys?"

"Of course not," they responded in unison.

"So let us take a look. We'll examine them carefully and let you know in just a little bit. Now how's that?"

"Fine. I have to look myself," she said, as the momentum inexorably slipped from her side to their side.

"And let us get our busy calendars, check our other committee schedules and constituent responsibilities and we'll see if we can't set up an organizing meeting in the very, very near future," Green assured her. "Oh, by the way, we'll have to think about staff. Now I know you've got good old, bright, dependable Pete O'Connor on your staff. I'd advise you to keep him there for a while. As a new Senator, you're gonna need all the personal office help you can get. In the meantime, I'd like to send over a bright young man named Tommy Rock to be interviewed for Chief of Staff for the Committee. No commitments necessary, of course, but I think you'll find him to be your kind of staffer. Charlie knows him well. Fine young man, isn't he Charlie?"

"No question," I replied. "And experienced, Senator." God, I could have killed myself.

"Alright," Jo said clearly, wishing for nothing but to be out of there, out of the smoke and brandy smelling environment. "Of course, I'll have some thoughts about that too."

"Course you will," Bushey assured her.

"Course," added Bagot.

"Certainly," concluded Green. "Now we were hoping you might be able to join us for dinner tomorrow night so we can relax, get to know each other better and do a little more long range plannin'. We'll take you to one of the best spots in town, that new Eye-talian place called, what is it? Leonardo? May we have the honor of your presence?"

"I'm sorry Floyd. I think you mean Galileo," Bagot delicately interrupted. Annoyed at the correction, Green glared at Bagot and said coldly, "of course, Galileo. I'll make the reservation."

"I'll have to check my calendar but I think I'm free. And I am anxious to get moving," Jo responded.

"Good," said Bushey. "Nothing like a little good food and drink to oil things."

"Very good indeed," said Bagot.

"Excellent," said Green. "And Charlie, we're dependin' on you, my boy, to help this young lady get acclimated to the system." He winked, I smiled, winked back and headed for the door.

The Wimp, the Wonk and the Windbag had circled their prey. She wasn't caught but considerable progress had been made in their opinion. It was obvious from the glances around the room.

Bushey and Bagot remained to finish the cigars and brandy. Green ushered us out of the conference room. As the door opened, Bushey's Secretary was announcing a call from "The Doctor, long distance, from Saint Croix." Bushey rushed in to take the inside phone as Green hastened to say "be sure to give him my very best regards."

"And mine," I insisted, not wanting any suspicions to arise.

At that point, Green asked if he could speak to me privately for a moment. Jo looked suspicious but couldn't say no.

In the foyer of his office, he grabbed my lapel as if he were about to choke me, almost lifted me off my feet and said quietly, "Charlie, what's this woman worried about? You'd better straighten her out."

Startled for a moment, I collected myself and said, "Senator, she really means it. She's a crusader. She thinks the whole system is corrupt and that all of you are controlled by the lobbyists and consultants."

"Oh Charlie, for Christ's sake, can't you bring her down to earth, my boy?" Green inquired.

"What do you want me to do?" I asked.

"Charlie, Charlie, don't you remember Jesse Unruh's advice about lobbyists when he was Speaker of the House in California?" he demanded.

"No, I don't sir. Too young maybe," I answered somewhat apologetically.

"Well, remember it now and tell it to her. To paraphrase old Jesse, if you can't take their money, eat their food, drink their booze, fuck their women and vote against them then you don't belong in the United States Congress. Bottom line: don't take all this too seriously. And if you can't wake her up to reality, I will."

"But Senator, the complicating factor is that they know you might not be for them but they're really afraid of what you might do to them." I paused. "If they don't come up with the money, you know?"

He gave me one final knowing stare and ushered me to the door.

Green joined us on the private elevator which, by that time, was almost filled with staff. Close quarters. Green stood behind Jo for the ride down. Suddenly, she started. Clearly something had happened. She quickly turned around with a puzzled look on her face. Green was expressionless, staring straight ahead. When the door opened, she kept going straight for the exit, shaken and dismayed.

"I don't believe it," she said almost out loud, "that dirty son of a bitch grabbed me! He did. I'll swear it!"

I reacted with amazement. One more push over the line. Damn it, I thought, can't these guys control themselves? This woman's a loose cannon on the political deck. She might tell the Washington Post. But Green had that 'so what, get real' demeanor. He'd deny it and nobody could or would corroborate it, least of all me. And I didn't observe it anyway. Don't get me into this.

CHAPTER 12

GRIDLOCK

Jo was so shaken that she couldn't return to the office. She asked me to please leave her alone and, despite my protestations, she bundled her coat up against the winter cold and walked away. I watched nervously as she passed the Supreme Court Building and the Library of Congress, southward on East Capitol Street. What there was of the sun on this gray bleak day began its descent toward dusk. From many years of wandering around Washington, I knew that the streets there begin to change, from semi-fashionable town house to ordinary neighborhood. And then to the bottom. Beggars on the street among the trash cans; I could envision sullen, angry faces staring at this blonde apparition from another world. Abandoned cars; broken glass; trash; dim yellow street lights; seedy corner stores.

Into the third world.

And only after insistent questioning later that night oh the phone did she confess to me what happened.

Three young black teenagers over by a No Parking sign. They glanced, she said, and quickly turned away. They split. She hurried along. Where did they go? Disappeared. Only to reappear from the back and two sides, poised for the ambush and assault.

A brutal blow to the back.

147

She started to run. Then a body punch to the stomach. She stumbled. They kicked. Viciously. She covered her face and screamed. She knew there was no hope in fighting back. As she fell, the pocketbook was ripped off her shoulder, its contents dumped on the sidewalk, the wallet ripped open. Forty three dollars and twenty nine cents. Count it.

As quickly as it began, it ended. "Thank God they didn't rape me, murder me," she told me as she attempted to keep her composure.

"What did you do Jo, what did you do," I pleaded, envisioning her spread out on the sidewalk.

A black woman, young, attractive, stylishly dressed, had stopped her car and apparently had scared away the young men.

"She saved me from something much worse," Jo continued.

"And she knew my name. Works in the Senate. Wanted to take me to the hospital but I said no, no, not the hospital. It will be all over town." And for the first time, she began to cry. "She drove me home. I asked her in. She declined. And, can you believe it Charlie, I didn't even get her name. I didn't even get that woman's name. How stupid of me. What must she think? We're all alike, right? Or they're all alike. Black and White. Never been worse. Never been farther apart. I'll find her. I'll thank her again. Be thoughtful and considerate. And those mean faces full of hate. Where did I read recently about the murders, the mindless killings, of each other, of strangers? The violent children, their ranks growing, their viciousness spreading. And here we are talking about lobbyists

148

and highway funds, election reform and fund raisers. Are we crazed? Building walls of polls and focus groups to keep out the horror, hold it at bay, do nothing. And I didn't even get her name. Idiot!"

And I didn't know what to say. I was terribly worried about her. It wasn't the first time she wandered off on her own. This is not Burlington, I warned her once before. There was nothing I wanted to do more than console her. I asked if I could come over and she said no, she didn't want to see anybody.

The psychic shock remained as the physical bruises healed. The next day, a few questions and comments from Pete, Maureen and the staff. "Why do you bend over like that? Is your back hurting you? You look pained." But the secret was kept, shared only with me as I rushed to her apartment that night despite her protestations to the contrary. The other woman was never seen. When I accompanied her to Galileo the following night, she shuddered as three black teenagers walked anonymously by. Cocktails, rack of lamb, wine, warmth, politeness, money, straining necks looking for political celebrities, obsequious head waiters. Bustling waitresses and busboys and behind them dishwashers and other specimens of the service sector. The wage slaves at work in the growth economy. And the world outside, she kept haunting herself, was continuing to come unstuck. A few days later, Maureen caught Jo looking through the staff photos of Senate aides. "What are you doing that for?"

"Oh, nothing. Just trying to find someone more capable than you."

Laughs. And then it was buried.

Jo had her press conference. The bills were introduced. Her subcommittee members amazingly enough agreed to co-sponsor. As did 45 other Senators. Just one short of a majority.

But Pete and I knew the names of the co-sponsors weren't worth the paper they were written on. Many agreed simply to associate their names with reform. Besides, most did it because they were told to.

****

Controller had returned from Saint Croix with his latest brilliant stratagem in mind. After talking to Bushy on the day Jo visited his office, the Doctor thought and thought and then realized the incredible potential offered by Stephenson's initiative.

In his office, half way between the White House and the Capitol, he convened the leaders of the New GOP. Incredibly enough, I was still considered one of the in crowd.

"Call your Senators," he declared. "And House members too. Get just enough to sign on those bills to make them look like a real threat to the system. Then we go around to every affected interest we can find and warn them that this time there's a real threat. New reformer from Vermont. Lots of support. Public indignation. It's gonna take every dollar we can spend to stem the tide, bottle these bills up. Christ, we'll rake in the fees like never before. Every Senator and Congressman who co-sponsors the bills has a fund raiser. The interests all contribute to the coffers while coughing up the lobbying fees for our boys."

"But Doctor, isn't that getting dangerously close to passage if all those guys sign on?" asked Tommy Rock who, incidentally, had been soundly vetoed by Pete O'Connor and myself as Ethics Committee Chief of Staff (O'Connor crying "no fucking way!" when the name was surfaced by Jo Stephenson).

"Of course not, you idiot. I don't know why we keep you around here, Rock. You can't even con that dumb broad into putting you on the Committee staff. Even with the support of Bushey, Bagot and Green. It's not a question of how many guys put their names on the bills! That doesn't mean a damn thing. Christ, all hundred Senators could put their names on one of these things and they don't move. It's the system, young man, the system. Nobody really means it, except maybe the woman from Vermont. And sometimes I wonder about her. Nothing moves, you hear me? Nothing moves but the cash and the checks. If she forces a subcommittee vote, our boys amend the bill. If it goes to the full committee, amended, it gets amended again and sent back to the subcommittee. If it comes out again, and even passes the committee in a watered down version, it gets bottled up in Rules. If it gets out of Rules, even more watered down, it loses on the floor. Even if it passes on the floor, it goes to the House and we play the same game over again. Maybe that's even better because we need a lot more lobbyists in the House. So let's suppose it passes the House. Then we get the ultimate weapon, the Conference

Committee. And if that doesn't work, we con the President into a veto and if he won't veto, the Election Commission review and court challenges take ten years and finally it gets overturned. Shit, Rock, don't you know yet how the game is played? Meantime, we cash in. Big time! What a world! Get their names on the bills. Now! I always wanted to be a reformer!" He laughed. A tedious master at telling us what we already knew.

Jo went home – had to go home – for the weekend. I could just imagine it, dwelt on it: a hug from George and Henry's arms around her neck. With Jo for days on end in Washington, sometimes not even reachable by phone, the living arrangement had to be impossible. Had to change. Here's George making pots of money on Jo's notoriety. And Henry wandering around Burlington with his friends doing – as she always said – God knows what. There but for the grace of station, race and location goes Henry walking down that street off East Capitol. Thank God her mother had moved in to look after him and clean and cook.

No time for peace. A weekend at home was not played out to the tune of Moonlight in Vermont. On the schedule we had drawn up were two constituent gatherings, a meeting with the editorial board of the Burlington Free Press ("where's the highway money, Senator?"), and an endless dinner with close friends and supporters. By Sunday morning, sitting in the back pew of the church, with a dutiful George and indifferent Henry, she bowed her head and prayed.

Yes, actually prayed, probably for her fragmented world to come together.

Meanwhile, I was fantasizing as I had many times before. Maybe they'll have a fight, a really big one and break up, I mused. Maybe she'll come back to Washington and want me. And maybe I'll say yes. Of course I'll say yes.

The Monday papers greeted Jo with a front page analysis of her reform package of the prior week.

"The President thinks it's a laudatory effort but has serious concerns about its practical application," a nameless White House aide was quoted.

Senator Floyd B. Green floridly praised his "distinguished colleague" for her vision and courage while predicting a hard fight for passage.

Anonymous lobbyists and campaign consultants falsely described the bills as real threats to their livelihoods but did so only to buttress Controller's strategy of scaring the hell out of affected interests.

And so the gridlock began. Pete, of course, knew it all along. So did I. The Wimp, the Wonk and the Windbag agreed to public hearings. Jo did a great job of arousing public support. Editorials praised her. Reform groups mobilized their own lobbying efforts, contributing even greater dollars to the Gross Beltway Product (GBP). Two sides could play the Beltway game. Common Cause vs. Common Gr...ood. Ralph Nader vs. Ludwig Controller. Reformers enlisting their environmental allies who were not so sure where they stood on the bills since they too wanted their kind of money to influence legislation.

Vermont seemed less impressed. After her editorial board meeting with the Free Press, the paper editorialized its admiration for their newly acquired national voice. But where were the highway dollars? The housing funds? And for the rebels who agreed with her efforts, where were the results? Quietly, Hap Mandell began to poll and focus group the Green Mountain State. What he was finding out was very revealing. Jo's positive rating was a mediocre 44%. But between her inauguration and the late Summer, as the hearings dragged on and as she became more and more preoccupied with Washington, her negatives rose from 13% to 24%. For the first time, in late August, it was beginning to seem possible to undercut and ultimately deflate and defeat the woman from Vermont.

The call from her Senior Senator from Vermont, the Honorable Mr. James Webster, could have been foretold.

"Senator," he said crisply, "I think you ought to know that the highway and housing funds are getting bogged down in the bureaucracy. Didn't you agree to do the work on this?"

"Yes," she replied, completely dismayed. "What happened?"

"Sloppy work on the part of your staff apparently. No follow-up, no hands on management of the process by your people. Asleep at the switch. Dozing at the wheel. No attention to detail. If I were you, Senator, I'd frankly pay a little more attention to what our state needs than to your admirable, if unrealistic, so-called reform proposals." Webster could be nasty, particularly on the eve of a fund raiser for his re-election bid sponsored by none other than the New GOP.

Bewildered, Jo could only say: "oh, of course, I'll get on it right away. Right away."

And Webster abruptly hung up. He had recently been supplied with the results of Hap Mandell's focus group and polling efforts in Vermont. The negatives about Jo that Hap reported bolstered his courage to confront his colleague. He would be the dedicated, hard working Senator. He'd get those funds if she failed. He'd deliver.

****

In the midst of this growing logjam, I wearily caught a cab on a crisp Fall evening and returned to my apartment just to forget about things and watch the Redskins game on television. By this time, Dawn was practically living at my place.

"Hi," I said as I threw down my coat.

"Hi," she answered, staring at the television set, mesmerized by Sleazy 55.

"What's up?" I asked somewhat cheerily. "Any food?"

"Nothing up and no, there isn't any food. If you want something call out for a pizza or look in the refrigerator." Always staring at the TV, the remains of a salad and a glass of white wine on the coffee table.

155

"You're a big help," I replied.

"What do you expect from me?" she suddenly shot back at me with, I recall, very little provocation. "I've been working all day too."

"Fine, no problem," I hastened to reassure her. "I'll find something. Really, don't worry about it. Turn on 6, would you? There's a ballgame on."

"I got a video," she said. "A movie I've been wanting to see. I'm going to watch that."

By now, I was getting just a little bit irritated. "Can't you watch it later?" I asked. "I really would like to see the game." By now, I had my coat and tie off, kicked off my shoes and mixed a martini. That was all I needed to get me started.

"No, I can't watch it later." She was expressionless. "I'm watching it now."

For just a moment, I had this enormous temptation to give her a swift kick but controlled myself. Best to disappear, I thought. Get out of here now. Something's wrong and I don't want to exacerbate it.

So, humming (to be noticed) "Dawn Go Away," I put on my shoes, straightened my tie, slipped on my coat and said, "okay, see ya later. I think I'll go over to the bar at the Four Seasons, grab some food and watch the game. You are being totally impossible!" I yelled as I slammed the door.

Still expressionless. It didn't matter to her. "What a world," I said out loud.

Moments later, as I sat at the bar, I was realizing that things were coming to a head. Something had to be done. I started on the road to this conversion months ago in Florida. I had become chummy with Josephine Stephenson. In fact, I had to admit to myself, I thought I was in love with Josephine Stephenson. It was all I could do to avoid taking her in my arms that night she was mugged. She sidestepped me nicely and I guess that was all for the best. That's all we needed to really complicate this deal.

But something had to happen. She had to make a breakthrough. The bills would go nowhere. I knew that. And I knew I had to stop playing both ends, pretending to be one of the boys while trying to help her out. It was not going to work. I was the Daniel Ellsberg of domestic politics without the psychiatrist. The hearings, the hearings. Get something to blow them wide open. I had something but I had been too cowardly to use it. The time has come, Charlie, I said to myself. The time has come. You've got to do it. So you rat on the boys. You've got to do it. As I tortured my psyche while bending my elbow, I noticed an item in a copy of the Post that was left on the bar. Oh my God, it's fate, I said. It's fate! Christ, there's no turning back now.

CHAPTER 13

THE BIG HYPOCRITE

The story in the Post was about the sort of event that Josephine Stephenson would not be invited to. Annually, in September, the National Gallery held the "must" gala of the social season. With full credit to its Director, Walker Green, the celebrated museum of the visual arts created a fund raising gimmick which became the envy of all such institutions throughout the country. Real big time. From the very pinnacle of the International Fortune 500, the National Gallery each year invited a major corporation to underwrite a $25,000 per couple white tie extravaganza and subsequent exhibition of great art from a foreign country of its choice with a table of ten at a 10% discount.

CEOs stumbled over each other to attach the corporate logo to the event. As the years went by bidding for the underwriting privilege became so extravagant that most recent galas were sponsored by foreign corporations which had lately adopted the charitable habits of their American counterparts and perhaps most importantly could afford to pay the bill. They too could be, as the pitch went, "proud sponsors." As reported by The Post, the current affair would feature art from Florence, Italy courtesy of the International Bank of South Korea which announced the coup of the century. For the first time in history,

Michaelangelo's David would leave its pedestal at Florence's Gallery of the Academy of Fine Arts and be transported to a foreign location together with other priceless works of art by Leonardo, Giotto, Botticelli, Lippi and Titian.

The David prospect created astonishment according to The Post. It would be packaged, bound and barged to America like King Kong. I could just see it. Every dip of the ocean which might dislocate the work would be meticulously and nervously noted by the media. Its safety would be guaranteed to the billion dollar level by the insurance company which controlled Caesar's Palace Gambling Casino, surrounded by Italian security police, and with the Pope solicitously dispatching a battalion of the Swiss Guard to provide colorful, ancient and camera ready round the clock surveillance. Already, the President was inspired by his speechwriter to note the symbolic importance of the moment. The David, he said, was sculpted as Columbus and Amerigo Vespucci were making their historic discoveries. It was then celebrated in Florence as a symbol of freedom and resistance to the tyranny and domination embodied in the Goliath story.

The only glitch reported, the one fly in the ointment as they say, was the staunch opposition to the David by Senator Joshua Mims and his fundamentalist following on obscenity grounds. Mims threatened to cut off funding for the National Gallery if "frontal nudity" were permitted to be shown. His followers also announced that they would picket the exhibit. But the protest was being balanced by various Italo-

American fraternal groups which were taking issue with the fundamentalists and, since those groups were predominantly Catholic and conservative, the frontal nudity issue, I rightly suspected, would give way to ethnic pride and Catholic tradition. I was convinced that, calculating the relative voter impact from Queens to Cleveland, the President would be reassured that any downside created by fundamentalist reaction would be more than offset by the gains to be made among Italians in key swing states, a judgment subsequently confirmed by several polls taken by the White House and the media. And since David had indeed been a King of Israel, all leading Jewish organizations came quickly to its defense.

I couldn't quite figure out the Korea-Florentine connection except to conclude that "money talks." But here was the kicker that got me going. In a bid for domestic respectability, the Koreans had asked Senator and recent Presidential candidate Wilson McAdams to serve as Honorary Chairman of the event. Widely regarded for his progressive views and integrity, McAdams had managed to survive the turn of the tide against liberalism and had become a genuine repository of admiration throughout the world. A frequent visiting lecturer on Ivy League campuses, writer of prescient bestsellers on foreign affairs and inspiration to a new generation of political activists, McAdams' hair had, over the years, turned statesmanlike gray flowing fashionably and sagely to the shoulder. Age had potbellied his formerly lean bearing. The few cynics known as "McAdams watchers" were quick to point to his late night drinking bouts at various select Beltway boites, his hushed up divorce, his pursuit of Bunny waitresses and his two Presidential defeats as proof of his vulnerability and humanity. There were even some who claimed that he ran the last time for the Presidency because his speaking fees were declining. "Mere Senators get $2500 plus expenses," wrote one gossip columnist. "But every time the Silver Fox runs for the Presidency he gets ten times that amount immediately after the New Hampshire Primary." Not only at home but abroad McAdams saturated the lecture circuit. "Them foreigners think that because you once ran and lost for President you're a big deal," remarked one McAdams watcher. "And old Wilson knows it all too well," he sneered. "Christ, don't those stupid bastards know that there's nothing deader than a defeated candidate?"

But the McAdams "thing" was difficult to deny. To the environmentalists he was Senator Ozone Layer. To the third world, he was Gandhi in a three piece suit. To the inner city he was Martin Luther McAdams. To Eastern Europe he was Wilson Walesa. He was, in the opinion of the cognoscenti, "Nobel Prize juice." And to us boys in the Beltway he was a predictable and malleable ally to numerous clients seeking entree, wisdom, access and respectability, a tall order for even the most resourceful of politicians.

As it happened, I had the goods on McAdams and what I had would lead directly to Controller. While consulting on his re-election campaign just a few years ago, I was privy to a really sordid transaction between the two of them and an energy company executive in McAdams's home state of Michigan. At least I thought I was. Once in a drunken state of relaxation, Controller had told me in absolute seriousness and delight that he and McAdams had split up $1 million in cash, a payoff the company exec had made in return for their help in getting some environmental restrictions relaxed. This was it! Of course, I couldn't prove it but the company, Global Cleanliness, had poured so much soft money into the coffers of Senators and Congressmen across the country that it certainly seemed plausible.

If you have any balls at all Coons, I said to myself, do it and do it now. No time like the present. McAdams' new found notoriety would only heighten media interest in the exposure and Jo could drag them all before the committee. To the phone: "Pete, I've got it. I've got to see you and Jo right away tomorrow morning. Yes, it's something big. And yes, I'm risking a lot. But you've got to hear me out and we'll take it from there. Believe me, you're gonna love it."

Nervous as a cat, I had another drink and walked home, shaking all the way. Damn Dawn! When I got there, she had indeed gone away.

****

Small wonder that Jo didn't want to do this one. "Pete, Charlie, it just kills me," she said, exasperated at the situation. "Wilson McAdams stands for just about everything I believe in. My God, I rang doorbells for him across the state line in New Hampshire twelve years ago. I just can't do it."

"Well, you really don't have much of a choice," I said with uncharacteristic finality. "I already gave the story to The Post." (I had not but I didn't let on). "They're going to run with it on Sunday. It is now Thursday. Tomorrow will be Friday. The day after that will be Saturday. Time is running out. They'll want you to say something and if you don't they will accuse you of covering up. They will call you a hypocrite, going after corrupt members of Congress only if they are your ideological enemies and trying to bury the facts about your friends."

"But goddamnit, he's a highly respected Senator. Do I have to take on everybody around here? Pete, this is really getting me down," she pleaded. "Tell Charlie to stop pushing."

"Senator or not, you're the one who has the information and you got it because the person who gave it to you, Charlie here, thought you were the only member of this Congress honest enough to do something with it," Pete retorted. "Right Charlie?"

I nodded as Jo blurted out, "but I am doing something about it."

"What?" I demanded.

"I'll turn it…" She paused, then continued. "I'll turn it over to the Attorney General…in confidence."

"Hah, a lot of good that will do," I shot back. "And besides, it's too late for that. The Post runs with it on Sunday. They've already talked to the Global guy and he's confirmed the so called contribution. And we have his affidavit. Perfect!"

As the two of them sat there at a loss for words, I reminded them of one missing factor.

"All but the Controller piece. The Global exec can't prove Controller's involvement and neither can I. But I know it."

Jo was exasperated. "You Charlie, you set up the whole thing. Can't they hold it? Do they have to go on Sunday? That Gala at the National Gallery is Saturday night. You know, the David thing that Wilson's Chairman of. Can you imagine how embarrassing it's going to be?"

"Frankly, my dear, that's the beauty of it," said Pete. "Just what these sons of bitches need. No, they won't hold it because the Times will get wind of it and the name of the game is scoop, baby, scoop. Exclusive. Breaking news. You know the rules."

"Yes, and I'm about to get fried by them. Okay, okay, what do you want me to do?"

Continuing to be surprised by my own hard line position, I told her just what she had to do.

"Listen, before another minute goes by, I want you to call a press conference for this afternoon and get this thing out and preempt the Post. The hell with the Post. It's your integrity that's at stake here. Let the world know. Let the networks know. That's what's important. If you're going to be pure, then you'd better be pure on CBS, ABC, NBC and the cable networks. You set this standard and now you'll have to live by it. If you go with it at 3, then Sleazy 55 will run with it at 4. Pete already told Mug that something may be coming. He's standing by." Pete nodded in affirmation and suddenly I was getting antsy. That goddam Mugger connection of Pete's continued to make me nervous.

"Oh, that smarmy vomitacious person," Jo declaimed. "Your roommate," she said to Pete. Then sighing a deep sigh, she rubbed her eyes, buried her fingers in her hair, bowed her head and said simply: "Three o'clock."

Pete jumped up, raced for the phone and the drama began. In the meantime, I ran out to tip off Controller and maintain my cover. I would continue playing both sides. I knew what I had to do.

****

Much to my amazement, Controller appeared to take the news calmly. And even more amazing, he asked me to get over and be with McAdams when the news broke. If he only knew.

Four o'clock. I was waiting in the lobby when Wilson returned to his Watergate apartment, rushing to change for the seven o'clock preview reception at the National Gallery. He had begged off an entire day of ceremonial events surrounding the unveiling of the David because of the press of Senatorial business. I told him I needed to talk to him. He said he was too busy but to come up anyway. I told him to turn on "Sleazy 55" as he mixed himself a double martini – a "see through" he called it. He proceeded to loosen his tie and turn into a basket case.

"Good afternoon everyone," intoned the Anchor Man. "A bombshell was dropped today in the

Capitol as Senator Stephenson of Vermont announced the first major discovery in her series of inquiries into Congressional ethics. And this one has shaken the Capitol to its foundations, big time. It involves none other than Senator Wilson McAdams. We'll be back in a minute to bring you the complete story."

And then the jingle, "Sleazy 55, Sleazy 55, hardly a man is now alive, who doesn't watch our daily run of murder, mayhem, rape and fun." McAdams retched and rushed for the phone. Calling his office, he reached his press secretary on a direct line. The young man, unaccustomed to news of this nature, replied in a shaking falsetto: "Yes sir, we've been bombarded with calls for reaction. I, I left a message on your voice mail. Did you check it?"

"No, I didn't check it. What are they saying," McAdams asked anxiously.

"It's coming on television right now, Senator. I think you'd better watch it. Then I'll call you back."

"So this is why you're here, Charlie. Tell me what's going on."

"Be quiet and listen," I replied as I turned up the sound. The report continued:

"Senator Josephine Stephenson of Vermont, Independent Chairman of the Senate Special SubCommittee on Ethics, announced this afternoon that she has received confidential information that Senator Wilson McAdams, the long admired progressive conscience of the Senate, last year demanded and got a payoff of $1 million in cash from an executive with the energy corporation Global Cleanliness in return for his help in softening environmental regulations in legislation pending before his subcommittee. The energy executive, Gregory Marshall, recently fired from his position, confirmed the transaction to Senator Stephenson's staff, claiming it was requested by Senator McAdams as a soft money campaign contribution. According to Mrs. Stephenson, Marshall said he first considered filing a lawsuit against his former employer but, when approached by Stephenson's investigative staff, decided to cooperate with her committee because he felt she would investigate the situation in an uncompromising fashion. The Senator said she would immediately subpoena McAdams, Marshall and other witnesses to a hearing on Monday morning. We'll keep on top of this fast breaking story as the evening goes on. So far, attempts to reach Senator McAdams have been unsuccessful. We'll be back in a moment. But before we go, remember, Sleazy 55 is the station that goes to the airport to cover crashes, not landings!"

"Breaking news! Breaking news!" intoned the jingle artist on Sleazy 55 just before the first commercial appeared.

McAdams crashed, not landed, in his easy chair, drink in hand. "What a goddam rotten thing to do. That bitch," he spit out as he stared at the television. And as his brain swirled he saw bars on the dog food ad, headlines of impeachment, rejection by voters, disgrace, the fall from eminence made all the more horrible because it came from such heights. And, of all things, a scoop on Sleazy 55!

"What to do, what to do, Charlie. All those Koreans and Italians. The David. The National Gallery. The President. Allenwood. That sleazy bastard Marshall. Revolting. Disgusting. Only did it for Ludwig. Didn't even want to talk to him. He insisted on that money. It wasn't me. How will I handle this? Another martini." And then the ringing of the phone. I stood by speechless, not knowing what to do and finally blurted out the all time political cliché: "Senator, I'm shocked and appalled at this irresponsible smear!"

Terrified to pick up the phone, McAdams waited for the voice mail and put in on speaker. Maybe it's Pat the Press Secretary. No, what relief!. It's Ludwig. "Ludwig, wait, don't hang up. It's Wilson. I need to talk to you."

"Wilson, be very careful," Controller cautioned in a steady voice. "The phones, Wilson. Talk to no one. Not even your office. Just wait to hear from me. Is Charlie there? Good. Tell him to wait." The phone clicked, McAdams drank, perspiration began to strain down his back, he looked out the window and waited. Messages, messages poured through the machine. Pat in the office, media people who had his number, fellow Senators, drinking buddies and one girl from the Bunny Club.

Hiding behind the curtain, he watched as Controller drove up just before the television vans, photographers and reporters began assembling. "Don't let them in, don't let them in," he ordered the doorman over the service phone. Before he could lose even more control of himself, I grabbed the phone. "Dr. Controller, yes, let him up, now, right now," I ordered.

The phone kept ringing incessantly. Finally, as the doorbell buzzed, I took it off the hook, peered through the door and opened it for Dr. Ludwig Controller.

"Stick around Charlie," he ordered. "And Wilson, there isn't much time," Controller began with soothing strength in his voice. "Now sit down, Wilson and listen to me. We are not – I say not – going to discuss this matter in detail. We are simply going to learn again how to lie."

Again? I asked myself. Again? These guys have been lying for so long they don't even realize it.

But Controller's admonition produced the desired effect. For the first time since the television set went on, McAdams calmed down. He looked directly at Controller, the comforting darkness and silence in the room adding to the atmosphere of reassurance.

"Yes, Ludwig," he said. "Whatever you say."

"First, Wilson, put down that martini. You are not to drink again until the Gala is over tomorrow night. Do you understand?"

Down went the martini. "Yes Ludwig," he said.

"If you betray one iota of concern through speech or body language, it will all come apart. So tonight, you are to dress impeccably, smooth back your graying locks, pull in that gut and summon all the poise and confidence in your being."

"Yes Ludwig," McAdams responded.

"Isn't that right Charlie?"

"Yes sir," I snapped.

"Then I want you to reread those sections of the 'Seven Forms of Political Illness' which have to do with adversity, paranoia and guilt. Fuck them, Wilson. They don't know what you know. They don't know anything. That woman from Vermont doesn't know anything. All they know is what that disreputable sonofabitch Marshall told them. Did you ever tell anyone about the cash?"

"No."

"Did you tell anyone you kept it?"

"No."

"Did anyone else, to your knowledge?"

"No."

"Does anyone else except you, me and Marshall know about the cash?"

"I…I don't think so."

"Why do you hesitate?"

"Because you never know. You know that Ludwig. You never know. No secrets, isn't that what you say? No secrets. Didn't you tell me once you told Charlie? And now he knows anyway."

Uh oh. But Controller chose to ignore the question as I feigned puzzlement.

"Stop it," Controller demanded. "Nobody knows but you, me and Marshall. And Charlie heard nothing right now, did you Charlie?"

"Not a thing, Doctor, not a thing," I blurted out. "And even if I did, it's hearsay. But I didn't. I was listening to the TV."

"Okay. So, Wilson, you deny it. It is now 5.30 P.M. For the next half hour I want you to re-read that section of my book, Seven Forms of Political Illness, dealing with Adversity, Guilt and Paranoia. Then, I want you to run that positive reinforcement tape. I then want you to take a shower, dress and go to that reception. I will accompany you and we together will attend. Meanwhile, Charlie here will call your Press Secretary and dictate a statement. The statement will deplore this unpardonable smear, deny the million dollar business flatly, admit knowledge of Marshall, but say that the talk of a contribution was something he kept insisting on and which you resisted. It will end with a reaffirmation of your integrity and a charge that all of this is being done to smear you because you are a symbol of enlightenment in this rotten political world. You are being persecuted for your beliefs and you will call upon all of your friends from Washington to Warsaw to express their indignation at this unconscionable smear. Do you understand, Wilson?"

"Yes, Ludwig. Let me go into the bedroom and get the book and the tape. I'll listen to the tape while I shower."

"In exactly one and a half hours, we will leave this place and go to the National Gallery. Be ready."

McAdams stared blankly at Controller, painfully raised himself from the easy chair and walked rigidly into his bedroom. Controller ordered me to go immediately to the phone, dictate the statement to the press secretary, call the National Gallery and tell Walker Green that of course McAdams would be present and to tell the people involved with the exhibition that it was all an outrageous lie and that they would be prouder than ever of McAdams as Chairman when they read his statement.

That evening, McAdams did indeed summon up all his powers of statesmanship, self worth and the automaton-like mechanistic motions so common to his ilk and got through it triumphantly. The Koreans, the Italians, the art world media, even the President, rallied around the gray haired eminence in a mixture of relief, pride, admiration and sympathy as the media counterattack took over the airwaves. Not one drink passed his lips. Not one miscue dogged his performance. With Controller at his side, he alternately held his head high, exhibited just the proper amount of hurtful indignation and stood there, before the statue of David much as Caesar held forth in the Senate of old. But then there was still the Saturday Gala to get through. I was prepared to follow this through to the end. I had cast my fate to the winds of Josephine Stephenson and, double agent though I may be, I would risk the consequences.

And Saturday dawned gloomily in her psyche. Had she screwed up? Shot too fast from the hip? Loose cannon on the deck? Flake? Ditsy broad? It's Pete, that compulsive assassin. And Charlie. Maybe tricking her? Did she trust too much? In several phone calls, I assured her of my devotion and determination.

When I finally arrived at her apartment, she was staring at the headline in the Times as she sipped her morning coffee:

CASH TO GO SOFT?
MC ADAMS DENIES CHARGE
CALLS STEPHENSON LIAR
GLOBAL CLEANLINESS EXPRESSES SHOCK

"Look Charlie, I don't like being called a liar," she shouted at me as she got on the speaker phone with Pete.

"Where are you Jo?" he asked.

"Where do you think I am? I'm in my apartment reading the Post and the Times. Both are giving Wilson the benefit of the doubt. To say nothing of the networks. The only one that's really nailing him is The Mugger on Sleazy 55. Did you see his late editorial? And did you see Wilson framed against the David, almost crying with hurt and indignation? And that creep Controller standing by his side? And the President wrapping his arm around him? Christ, what a scene. I'm getting murdered and it's all because you and Charlie are shooting from the hip. I can't take it anymore, Pete. I know you mean well and I think your head's basically in the right place but I just can't take it anymore and I think that this time we really screwed up. We really did, Pete. And that goes for you too Charlie," she snapped at me.

"Will you be there for another hour?" Pete asked calmly.

"You don't think I'm going to the office, do you? You don't think I want to run into the media at my front door, do you? Maureen went in about half an hour ago and I told her to tell them I was held up by some family matters."

"I'll be right over, okay?"

"No, it's not okay. It's bad enough your friend is here. Pete, I just don't want to see you and deal with this right now. I really don't."

"Yes you do, Jo. Believe me, you do."

"What are you talking about?" she asked.

"Not over the phone, Jo. How about fifteen minutes from now, okay? Tell Charlie to stay."

Jo paused. What was going on? "Charlie, I hate him. Gave me the wrong advice. Playing a double game." Then a moment of silence and "okay, in fifteen minutes but I really have to be left alone. I really do."

"No you don't," Pete reassured. "No you don't."

As Jo slammed the phone down, I stared at her, hurt and uncomprehending.

"Hate me! What do you mean you hate me? Except for Pete and Maureen, I'm all you've got and sometimes I wonder why. I think I'll just get out of here."

"I'm sorry. I'm sorry, okay?" Jo replied. "God, I don't know what's going on and who to trust. Please don't go. I...I need you. And no, I don't hate you. You know that. You do, don't you?"

There was nothing more I wanted to say. Obviously I wasn't leaving. I simply sat down with a wounded puppy dog look on my face and shrugged my shoulders. Besides, I had to wait because I knew that

Pete had something that would break this wide open. I knew because I gave it to him.

I could imagine that everybody was tense and hiding out that morning. How did it play, McAdams would wonder, staring out his Watergate window. Will it hold, Controller would ask himself, for once not in control of the situation. Staffers will be wandering around Congressional offices, reading the paper, catching sound bites on morning television, exchanging e-mails. Reporters would be watching all doors. Predatory. Waiting for the first piece of meat. For the moment, McAdams was out front, gaining the automatic sympathy granted to statesmen. People with signs outside The Watergate: "Free McAdams," or "Stop Slandering Our Hero." But one never knew whose the next move would be. Would it be Marshall? His lawyer? Couldn't be. The creep was one of us, member of the New GOP, Controller must be sitting over there reassuring himself over and over.

Momentarily, Pete was at Jo Stephenson's door, having slipped quietly in through the apartment house parking garage. We quickly went over to the dining room table. I had found it and given it to Pete who had it in his inside coat pocket and took it out. Jo, who hadn't smoked in years, lit one up as she looked at him with a combination of curiosity and exasperation.

"You've got something there. What is it?"

"It's the copy of a letter," Pete replied.

"Let me see it," she said, excitement building.

"No, let me read it to you," Pete said, not smiling, not smug, just dead serious.

"This, my dear, (she hated that my dear business), is a letter dated January 16 of last year on the private stationery of one Wilson McAdams to a Mr. Gregory Marshall concerning a certain piece of legislation being considered by the United States Senate.

"I don't believe it," Jo blurted out.

"Believe it," I said confidently.

"You haven't even heard it," Pete darted back as a slight smile crossed his mouth. "Now listen, just listen. It's an authentic copy of a letter."

Pete and I could by now barely contain ourselves. Summoning up his best officialese, as if he were announcing some diplomatic agreement in the White House Press Room, Pete pronounced:

"Dear Gregory:

(Get that, Dear Gregory, old buddies, not Mr. Marshall)

"This is to let you know that I have talked with several colleagues and staffers on the Environmental Subcommittee about your concerns with the pending legislation. They have informed me that, in light of their pressing need for contributions during this election season, they would be pleased to accept any and all offers of financial support, consistent, of course, with doing the right thing for the American people. And I want to thank you especially for that impressive seven figure corporate contribution to my party."

"Oh I don't believe it!" Jo blurted out.

"It gets better," Pete shot back emphatically.

"While they emphasize that these generous gestures would in no way guarantee favorable action on your proposed amendments, you will be afforded access, consideration and a fair and equitable hearing as they begin their deliberations.

"I shall call you tomorrow to make appropriate arrangements for your most generous contribution" and it's signed "Wilson McAdams, The Watergate, Washington, DC."

Jo collapsed on the sofa, extinguished the cigarette and stared in disbelief. "Let me see it," she demanded and soon was reading it herself.

"This is unbelievable, crazy. Is he nuts? Putting that in writing? Could it be a fake? All we had earlier was Marshall's affidavit. Where was this?"

"No fake, Jo. I found it this morning," I finally said. "Forgot I had it. Never write a letter and never throws one away, right Pete?"

"Right," Pete said triumphantly.

"Why, Charlie? Why would you, of all people have it?" Jo demanded.

"When Controller told me about it, he handed me a copy of the letter because I just didn't believe him. And I didn't give it back. He was drunk. The only time in my memory Controller made a stupid mistake."

"But Pete, Marshall didn't get what he wanted and now he's fired. He's just a disgruntled fixer ratting on the politicians. It's not because of the money, it's just because he got double crossed.

Where's the money? Do you really believe, could you really believe, that Wilson kept it?"

"Come on, Jo," I shouted.

"No, I'm serious. I'd sooner believe they found him with a little boy than this. I mean, we knew about the request. But Marshall hasn't talked about the exact disposition of the money."

"Jo, there is not a single member of the subcommittee ready to corroborate McAdams' story in that letter. Not a trace of a request. Not an iota of evidence that they even considered Marshall's proposals. Not even a favorable response in writing. If anything at all happened, it had to be between Controller and the members. Or McAdams and the members."

"You mean, McAdams may have fabricated the whole thing about subcommittee consideration?"

"Don't know. But the letter exists. And the only people who know about it are you, me, Marshall and Charlie," Pete responded.

"And Controller, if he remembers," I interjected. "And he surely does although he chose to ignore McAdams's reference to it last night. But what was he doing involved in it for that kind of money? It's not much for him. I don't get it."

"Does the Post have the letter?" she asked.

"Of course not," I replied. "They're running entirely on speculation. But Pete's already given it to The Mugger. Once he chews it up, we're on Cloud Nine."

It was sinking in. She could see it all now. Saved. Out of the depths. Massive relief. Yes, cloud nine, an unreal condition that I never permitted myself to succumb to.

CHAPTER 14

THE BIG MISSPEAK

It did not take very long for the word to get out. By 10 A.M., Pete was back in the office. Jo didn't go with him. And I ducked because I didn't want to be too visible, still playing the double game, joining Controller for the next round. Although she was now on Cloud Nine, she still had not shaken the atrophy of the past few days and besides, Pete knew what to do. He had the letter and it spoke for itself.

And speak it did. This wasn't just the dropping of the next shoe. It left the entire political world shaken, wondering where it would all end, with observers and sideliners commenting to the press that they were "trying to make sense of this thing."

I never understood that ridiculous phrase, I mused as I watched the 11 A.M. cable news. It's like what the reporters say about all of life's absurdities, tragedies, natural disasters and follies. They always go around saying people are trying to make sense of this thing. What sense? There is no sense. Earthquakes make no sense. Mass killings make no sense. Terrorist attacks make no sense. Airline crashes make no sense. And Wilson McAdams makes no sense. Christ, this whole goddam business makes no sense. So why do they keep saying people are going around trying to make sense of this thing?

Not to speak of the fact that my getting involved in it made less and less sense to me the more dangerous it became.

Sense, no sense or nonsense, McAdams was by this time hiding in the Rock Creek Parkway psychiatric office of Dr. Controller, having heard the flash about the letter on the radio as he drove to his office. And once again Controller insisted I be there.

"Senator," Controller intoned, his demeanor becoming more chilly toward his old ally. "Senator, did you ever read page 13, paragraph two of my book?"

"I, I don't know, Ludwig. I don't know if I ever read it. What am I going to do? It's the end. I know it." McAdams on the brink again.

"Senator, page 13, paragraph two of my book teaches a valuable lesson in political conduct. The headline is 'Never Write a Letter; Never Throw One Away.' Why did you write that letter, Senator?"

"I don't know, Ludwig. I don't even remember it. Maybe I just didn't want to forget. Maybe I wanted to get the thing over with. I don't know. I have no explanations. I have no excuses. It is the end. I know it."

The truly venal thing about Controller was his denial ability. He had either forgotten, which I very much doubted, or refused to face up to the fact that it was he himself who carelessly tossed a copy of that letter to me. And now he was counseling a broken man on how he should conduct himself in the future.

"The future? What future? There is no future. Why don't I just own up and take the consequences?"

Controller stared at me and asked me to leave. But he could still be heard clearly from the outer room. "Because I am involved, Senator. That's why. Because some of that money will be traced to me, Senator, to me and I am numero uno around here. Whatever may be your current frame of mind, I can assure you of my current frame of mind and it does not include the element of candor."

"But what is there to do," McAdams implored. "This is the end. I can see it. There's no lying anymore."

"That's correct Senator. No more lying. The last lie was that letter." Controller was warming up to it.

"The letter a lie? What do you mean? I mean, I know it was stupid to talk about Senators needing money. But I couldn't carry the day alone. I needed some help"

"I'm not talking about them and their stupid contributions. You took $1 million in cash, Senator. As I told you yesterday, three people knew about that money, you, me and your Mr. Marshall. That was twenty months ago. The money is long since untraceable as far as we know, unless the son of a bitch did what I don't think he did."

"No, he didn't. In fact, he had the cash in a safe deposit box. No traces at a bank. Didn't distrust me. No reason to." McAdams was also warming up to it.

"So there is no money, Senator," Controller continued.

"But what about the letter?" McAdams asked. "You can't deny the existence of the letter. There's nothing there to lie about."

"No, no, no, there is an explanation for the letter, Wilson." Controller's return to McAdams' first name indicated clearly that he now saw a way out. Buddies again. "You didn't lie. You won't lie. You misspoke."

"Misspoke?"

"Yes, Wilson, misspoke. Not a lie. Misspeak. Misspeaking is a device designed to help one, do a favor. You were doing Marshall a favor by misspeaking."

"A favor with a misspeak?"

"Yes, Wilson, a favor with a misspeak."

"So I actually did him a favor by misspeaking. Something like a mistruth."

"Yes, Wilson. You misled him with your letter to keep him from doing something worse. Global Cleanliness is a very pushy, aggressive outfit. Big time. Always paying their way. Wanted to shower the nation with greenbacks to buy tawdry legislative and regulatory favors. Thought that was how it was done. You tried to persuade Marshall otherwise. Begged him not to do it. He kept upping the ante. Talked about a million. Wouldn't take your advice. Finally, to keep him from doing something worse, you wrote your letter. Deliberately put it in writing so it would be clear that this was the limit. To prevent him from doing something really crazy. After all, what's a million these days? You were trying to rein him in, for his own sake, to avoid his voracious appetite for buying the body politic which you have always kept pure.   You weren't serious.   It was all a ruse, a...mistruth as you say."

"But, but what about the money, Ludwig?"

"You never saw it.   Don't know what, if anything happened.   You never talked to anybody. Nothing happened.   No doors opened.   No favors.   No access.   No payments.   No records of contributions, no staffers admitting any contact with you or with him. And it's all supported by the fact that his original complaint is merely that of a disappointed lobbyist. You didn't intervene, he didn't pay and your letter stopped him in his tracks.   You were actually trying to derail him and do him a favor all at once through the device of a mistruth."

"And you think we can contain this?   I admit that, in my own indifferent way, I never bothered to influence the subcommittee.   But will they really believe me?"

"If you stick to your story, Wilson.   I have already arranged for a half dozen New GOP lawyers to begin throwing roadblocks in the path of any possible charge or indictment.   They are totally experienced in the art of legal misspeak.   The only loose cannon on this deck, Wilson, could be you.   Unless, of course, you want to save your reputation and your career by carefully remaining within the confines of what I just said."

"Ludwig, could you write it down?"

"Now what do I say in my book, Wilson? Never write a letter, never throw one away.   I write nothing."

"Then why did you insist on this in the first place?"

"Oh, for God's sake, Wilson, if you must know, it's bigger than the money and you'd better know it. I've got millions in stock options at Global Cleanliness. It's the options, Wilson. You won't find my name on the documents but I was an early and principal investor. Get it, Wilson? I've raised millions for key legislators to make one of the nation's largest industries a success. Campaign contributions mostly. In the name, of course, of jobs. Jobs and taxes. And I'm going to get every penny back through those so called corporate executives who will make millions in return. Understand now, Wilson? You'd better stay with me on this one. This isn't nickels and dimes. This is real big time. You too can be a rich man. If you're alive to collect."

This was really getting scary. The implications for McAdams, Controller and Global Cleanliness were enormous. And God only knows who else is involved, how far this reaches. I felt trapped in a box of my own making. Smart ass. Know it all. And all for a woman I admired and thought I was in love with. I ought to disappear and get the hell out of town.

Somewhere it's written that there are four standards of decent human conduct. What were they? Honesty. Yes, honesty. Is anybody honest in this town? Can I be? Do I dare? What are the others? Loyalty. Loyalty to whom? Controller or Stephenson? To thine own self be true said Polonius. But I don't even know what the truth is. I like the third one, it's forgiveness. Boy, I hope somebody forgives me

185

before this is over.   And maybe even forgets me.
Finally, self discipline. I don't think I've ever had it.
Charlie, the issue is clear, you jerk.   Steel yourself.
You'll survive. And maybe even prevail.

CHAPTER 15

DEATH BY GALA

No one in the Beltway community knew exactly how to respond to Wilson McAdams' latest explanation. Some members of the press grimaced. Eyebrows were raised. Most couldn't figure it out. It all depended on one's definition of "misspeak," commented the President. But there McAdams stood, in the media center of the United States Senate confessing to a mistruth and a favor neatly tied together by Ludwig Controller, his lawyers and his army of media consultants. Several of Controller's most trusted lieutenants began to call key contacts in the media to spin the situation further on deep background. There were many brunches and lunches that day as reporters, opinion makers and key political operatives mused about McAdams over Bloody Marys and light luncheons of salad and seafood.

And as the day wore on, it appeared as if, in the end, nobody would give a damn. It was all too confusing, too typical and too bothersome. No money, no story. No story, no investigation. No investigation, no television. No television, no polygraph test. No polygraph test, no grand jury. No grand jury, no trusted aides testifying with immunity. No betrayals, no indictments. No indictments, no convictions. No convictions, no Allenwood. No Allenwood, no early parole. No early parole, no bestseller. No best seller, no talk shows. No talk shows, no anchor opportunities on public affairs programs. Just another Beltway bomb.

Except that Marshall, the fired executive, was saying nothing publicly. And Jo and Pete couldn't be found, adding to the impression that maybe, just maybe, McAdams had defused the situation. Still, as always, Washington had its skeptics. But they would wait until next week and by then the David would be gone, the Koreans would be spared further embarrassment and the evening's grand opening would probably go off without a hitch.

In Pete's office in the bowels of the House Office Building, however, Marshall reaffirmed the transaction in my presence to my everlasting relief.

"It's true," he insisted. "The son of a bitch took that money. I walked it over to his office and personally handed it to him, in cash! In a big box with a ribbon on it."

"Prove it," I demanded in desperation.

"I can't right now but if you give me a little time I will. Right now I can't get into the Global Cleanliness financials," he responded.

"We don't have any time," I shot back. "By next week, I'll probably be dead, Jo Stephenson will be ousted as subcommittee chairman and you'll be under investigation yourself for attempted bribery."

"I didn't bribe anybody," Marshall shouted. "He extorted that money from me. It's not bribery but extortion. And conspiracy too with that insane Ludwig Controller. And obstruction of justice and perjury and tax evasion and all those other things politicians are guilty of."

At the mention of tax evasion, the phone rang. Pete picked it up and began to take notes. Putting the phone down, he turned to Marshall and me and said, "excuse me, I've got to go. It's about the McAdams thing and it's confidential. Charlie, come with me."

Practically flying out the door, we raced to his car and drove to the VietNam Memorial. There, among the tourists, mourners, soldiers and flowers, we saw a face we knew, the face of the man on the phone. We met and walked a short distance, scanning the area for people we recognized but knowing that this was one place the Beltway crowd rarely frequented.

"I'm going to tell you this once and once only," the other man said. "Last year, Wilson McAdams reported on Schedule C of his 1040 Federal Income Tax Form $1, 127,000 in royalties, speaking and consulting fees. In his own records and those of the IRS, there are 1099 forms or other documentation for $127,000. There is no explanation for the million except the fact he had a huge tax bill which he paid. The IRS picked it up because the total amount is far in excess of the amount allowed by the Senate for fees and royalties. It's on his tax return but not on his disclosure form. The IRS further believes that the million is the amount in question with Marshall."

"What, is he crazy," I asked, astounded by the revelation.

"The IRS doesn't respond to questions about a citizen's state of mind, only about his taxes," came the matter of fact reply. "What I tell you is the truth. Use it as you will."

With that, the conversation ceased, the other man vanished into the crowd and Pete and I stood there trying to absorb what we had just heard. We started walking. We walked all the way to Jo Stephenson's apartment, bewildered for once and incapable of immediate action. Incredible. Ridiculous. What an idiot, I kept murmuring on the way. Even I, the Beltway Boy incarnate, found it hard to believe.

Not so ridiculous to Ludwig Controller for he too had his other man and he too by now had the story. It was 4 P.M. on the day of the Great Gallery Gala. McAdams was in his Watergate apartment once again, hiding from the world, listening to his tapes, refraining from see throughs and hoping to get through the evening. The buzzer rang. It was Ludwig, once again accompanied by me. In minutes, we were together again.

"Charlie, how's it playing in the media," McAdams asked calmly once they had sat down.

"We won't know until tomorrow for sure," I replied, "but the early radio reports aren't bad. 'McAdams Admits to Mistruth' is the all news radio lead. 'Favor for a Friend' is the subhead. At least we'll get through tonight without a blowup. But Wilson, the Doctor here wanted to ask you about something else."

Weary but passive McAdams flatly replied, "yes Ludwig, what is it now?"

"Did you..." even Controller, who always had his wits about him, faltered at this one..."did you, uh, did you...last year...on your income tax"...and then he blurted it out…"did you report a million dollars in non-documented income on Schedule C?"

McAdams reddened, his face glowing amidst the white locks. "Yes," he answered calmly.

"Was it the Marshall money?"

"Yes," he said again.

"Wilson, why did you do that?" asked an increasingly anxious Controller.

"You didn't want me to lie to the IRS did you? Oh no, when I sign that form it says I do so under the penalties of perjury. You didn't want me to commit perjury did you? Me, a United States Senator? Me, respected around the world? And I paid every penny in taxes too." McAdams was becoming granite faced, crimson, embarrassed but not twitching, not mumbling, not nervous around the lips, not perspiring. Just as matter of fact as he could be.

"Uh, no, Wilson, I would never suggest you lie to the IRS. Or commit perjury. Never Wilson," said Controller, the world suddenly closing in on him. "But half of that money went to me. Why did you report my money?"

"Well, I knew you wouldn't. Or at least I suspected you wouldn't. And besides, it was given to me, not you. It was my income as strictly defined by the Internal Revenue Service. Or at least I thought it was. Ludwig, I have always been very conscientious about taxes. Once the IRS is defied by a United States Senator, the people will lose their trust in the system. We can't let that happen Ludwig. I recently gave a speech on the necessity of voluntary compliance with the tax laws. Why, I would be a hypocrite if I violated those laws myself."

"Yes, of course, Wilson. Of course," Controller interjected, rolling his eyes in amazement at the sheer stupidity of what he was hearing. He now realized he was dealing with someone on the edge, someone about to either do something violent or mentally pass away altogether.

"Okay, okay," he continued. "Let's get through tonight. We'll think about this tomorrow. Chances are no one else knows. Maybe we can keep it that way. Everything will be alright, Wilson. Get ready. I'll have someone pick you up at six. We can't keep the Koreans and the Italians waiting. No, we can't keep them waiting."

Controller drifted toward the door, turned, looked wide eyed at McAdams who was wide eyed too, slowly began leaving the apartment, turned, and asked, "Do you have copies of your returns?"

"Yes, in the office," McAdams replied.

"We will stop there on the way to the Gala. Do you have a shredder?"

"Yes, I have a shredder."

"You will shred the Forms," Controller continued. "Maybe the IRS won't surrender it to her committee. And if they subpoena yours, it can't be found."

"Yes, yes, we'll do that. But Ludwig…"

"What is it, Wilson?" Controller asked impatiently.

"Is shredding better than deep sixing?"

"Definitely better, Wilson. Definitely better."
And he quietly closed the door.

McAdams reached for a glass. It was time for a
see through.

****

Five thirty. It was surreal, as if the whole
world was waiting breathlessly for something to
happen. I could envision the entire scenario. Jo
standing at the window of her high rise apartment,
looking at the limousines slowly winding their way
down the Great White Corridor of Massachusetts
Avenue, all bound for the Gala, saying nothing.
Behind her, Pete would be finishing off a double
scotch on the rocks, his first of the early evening.
There would be more to come. I was all decked out in
formal attire, having scrounged an invitation from the
Speaker's Office through Dawn. That, of course, was
well before she walked out on me.

And the scene would shift to Ludwig Controller
leaving his McLean mansion, staring directly ahead,
resplendent in white tie and tails, as expressionless as
the face on a dollar bill.

At the Watergate, Wilson McAdams would be
finishing his fifth silver bullet, staring at himself in the
mirror, noticing that he was uncharacteristically jowly
and seeming very old. At the buzz of the buzzer, he
would start downstairs for his long and agonizing trip
to the Gala with a short detour to his Senatorial office.

As I stood on the steps of the Museum, others
began arriving at valet parking as the sun went down in

the West. Fat men, uncomfortable in their tails, skinny women coiffed and plastered with diamonds. Unhappy faces in the crowd, Mims pickets rudely jostling and heckling the guests, the march up the steps, the final movement in a month of fretting and preparation. Nervousness abounded, smiles forced, irritation with detail apparent in the demeanor of many.

"This is my fifth goddamn formal event in ten days," grumped Senator Forrester of Ohio to the Secretary of Defense. "I missed one the other night and somebody asked in amazement why I didn't show up. I said if I had shown up, it would have been my last engagement. I'm experiencing a new disease. It's called 'Death by Gala.'"

They both laughed and moved into the main gallery where the David commanded the room in Renaissance splendor, proud, defiant, casual, amazing and delighting us lesser bodies.

"God, he's gorgeous" blurted out Willa Schramm in a moment of unusual earthiness. "I wish we had a few like that around here."

"I think the one in Caesar's in Atlantic City is better," complained a disappointed fast food chain founder.

Cameras flashed. Drinks abounded. Champagne cascaded from a dozen Florentine fountains. Koreans bowed and Italians smiled as the President inspected the works of art.

And then, to the curiosity of everyone, Wilson McAdams entered the room, jittery after his stop at the office (anyone see us?) and oddly encouraged by Controller to have another, then another in the limo ("let me freshen your drink, Wilson") before arriving at the Gallery. They know, he said to himself as he began to walk among the patrons. They know what I know. They know what Ludwig knows.

"They don't know" whispered Ludwig, guessing at the mental condition of his ally. "They don't know. So get through this, do you understand? And grab something to eat." Controller spotted me on the edge of the crowd and, before I could duck behind a partition, gave me a suspicious glance which indicated to me, for the first time, that he was beginning to put two and two together.

Wilson attempted a smile, said hello to hundreds and headed for the bar. He couldn't stop. He had one see through and then another. Then he began to call them silver bullets again and had a third. He was approached by the museum officials. Time to get ready for the ceremony. The Koreans and the Italians were waiting. Uncomfortably, perhaps, but they were waiting. With the President too. There he is, across the room, smiling at me. He knows too. He's one of us, isn't he? The same guy, only he's got Secret Service.

"Just a moment, my good man," he replied to the courier. "Just want to get something to eat. Starved. Just a few hors d'oeuvres."

His stomach was churning. He coughed a little and dove for the small roast beef sandwiches. By now most of the room had turned to watch as Senator McAdams alternately guzzled his martini and stuffed his mouth with small roast beef sandwiches. Suddenly his face turned beet red, he coughed and splattered some chewed roast beef over his white formal shirt.

"Sorry," he said to no one in particular. The martini quaked in his left hand, the rocks tinkled with an alcoholic's rhythm. McAdams casually turned, grabbed another roast beef and stuffed it in his mouth. He choked again. It was a piece of gristle. The glass fell from his hand. I rushed to slap him on the back. Women screamed. Men said "Oh my God." Wilson McAdams was literally choking to death before their very eyes. He pushed away would be helpers, staggered across the room, hand to his neck, going straight for the jugular as he had so many times in politics and fell, slobbering and ignominious, at the base of Michaelangelo's crowning achievement. He was choking on his own tongue as I raced to his side and tried to grab it, sticking my fingers into the gin soaked interior of his mouth. "Help me, somebody," I cried out. But no one could or would move. Bunch of goddam hopelessly useless empty suits, I thought.

And then it was too late. The gurgling and slobbering stopped as I desperately didn't know what to do next. Only Controller stepped up – after the messy part – to give me a hand. And then only when the cameras came upon the scene.

At my side, the onlooker Secretary of Defense turned to the on looking Senator from Ohio and said, "what was that you said about Death by Gala?"

CHAPTER 16

BIG DAY IN THE COMMITTEE ROOM

"I want my soaps!" screamed the typical American housewife to Lenny Lordan talk show host. But she was not to have them. The network decision to cover the Ethics Subcommittee's hearings into the McAdams affair was, of course, fueled by his untimely death and vague hints of sexual scandal involving a member of a Senator's family, no doubt a reference to the Raymond incident in L.A. No sooner had the McAdams body been cold than ratings began to soar during market tracking news reports of the events in the nation's capital.

"Nothing like a political death to get the public interested," said the Mugger to Pete O'Connor.

Some in the media were less than kind. Talk shows filled the airways with paranoid suspicions of dirty tricks. No friend of Wilson McAdams, Lenny Lordan nevertheless defended the "statesman," as he put it, because he hated Josephine Stephenson more.

"The woman has no shame," he declared to a shocked caller. "Sent him to his death as sure as if she had stuffed that gristle down his throat. Now I didn't always agree with McAdams," he assured his audience. "But the man had a record and that's more than I can say for this arrogant newcomer. Rest assured, ladies and gentlemen of America, there'll be more uncovered about this situation than we've seen already and it's not going to look good for Mrs. Senator Stephenson."

"What's he talking about?" Pete asked me as we drove together to the Capitol.

"The kid, I'll bet," I replied.

"The kid? What kid?"

"Pete, I told you months ago. Around the time Jo was inaugurated, her son, Raymond, at UCLA, became acquainted with the TEEN TEAM sex and drug crowd in Hollywood. Don't you remember? I told you Ludwig got the tape. I told Jo. Nobody wanted to think about it. This is all very irritating. It's bad enough when you don't know the time bombs are about to go off. But when you know about them it's inexcusable."

"Oh yeah," Pete replied uncomfortably. "Well, what will be will be. Can't think about that now. Got these hearings to get through."

We had spent hours preparing her for the big event. What to say. How to say it. How to be in command, take charge. We had also warned her that anything could happen, given the unpredictability of this sort of thing.

I shook my head and stared out the window. When we got closer to the Capitol, I got out of the car and went in a different entrance, still playing undercover. It would be okay if I went to the hearings but not so okay if I actually showed up with Pete O'Connor. Despite my heroic resolve that night in Florida, courage had a way of slacking off, so what was to happen to me when my involvement in all this came out still worried the hell out of me but I found that the best therapy was not to stop. Just keep going. Go with the flow. I noticed my hands were shaking a little more than they used to. Probably the booze. Can't take it anymore. Getting old.

What a spectacle as I walked down the corridor to the Ethics Committee Hearing Room. On one side were the distinguished members of the media, lined up with cameras, microphones, pouty faced male reporters and wild eyed stylish fringies, shouting unanswered questions about murder and bribes at individual Senators. On the other side were the legions of lobbyists hoping to get a chance to buttonhole Bushey, Bagot or Green, the real powers in the upper Chamber, on a tax bill currently before the Senate Finance Committee. More pouty faced males and wild eyed fringies but this phalanx armed with fact sheets instead of microphones, press releases in place of cameras. Sullen but knowledgeable staffers stood in the background, the real powers, the committee pros who write the bills and run the government. I know what you're thinking, I said to myself. These asshole runners for lobbyists, if they knew any better, would be talking to us. The Senatorial robots don't know what's going on. We do, you fools! I saw a few I knew, flashed my wry knowing grin as they nodded and flashed back their own. Boy, it's neat to know what's really going on.

When the session convened (I barely got a seat in this standing room only chamber), the Chairman (in this age of laxity on political correctness, we began gingerly to dispense with the "person" business), Senator Stephenson of Vermont neatly defined the parameters of the investigation. Although he was tragically quite dead, the hearings were necessary to try to get to the bottom of the charges that had been made and, if at all possible, clear the good name of Wilson McAdams. Come on, Jo! We didn't rehearse anything like that. On the other hand, she continued, if there is truth to the allegations, then the truth should come out and any possible conspiracy uncovered. Good for you, Jo!

Then bombshell number one: the Senator from Vermont introduced into the record an affidavit from the security guard at the Russell Office Building who testified that, on the prior Saturday night, Senator McAdams and another individual in white tie and tails had hurried into the building. McAdams had a manila folder in hand. And the guard swore in his affidavit that the other man had asked the Senator whether he was sure the shredder would operate during off hours.

Bushey, Bagot and Green began to squirm and turn pale. Murmurs filled the room. Cameras moved in for a closeup of Jo Stephenson who moved quickly from the affidavit to calling the first witness, a Senate Office Building cleaning lady named Thelma Wicker.

Mrs. Wicker, sixtyish in a flowered housedress with the determination of a Mother Superior, strode resolutely to the witness table, alone, without benefit of lawyer. Evasion, obfuscation, lying and memory loss were unknown to this gothic American. And, as Senator Stephenson asked her to tell the committee, in her own words, what transpired on that Saturday evening, she looked directly at the Senators, especially Floyd B. Green, and began.

"Well," she said, "it was about seven o'clock and I was vacuuming the rug with the flag of the state of Michigan on it when in walks the Senator and this other fella all dressed up in white tie and tails. They looked pretty fancy to me. Now usually Senator McAdams is – or I should say was – a fine gentleman. He'd always say hello, how's the family, anything I can do for you, and all that. But this time – I don't know – he looked almost frozen. And the other guy looked liked something out of a vampire movie. Anyway, they don't even give me a nod but just keep goin' right into the room with the xerox machine and all that other stuff. Then I hear this machine goin' and it's like they were using that shredder they got in there."

"Excuse me," Jo asked politely, "when the two gentlemen came in were they carrying something?"

"Right," Mrs. Wicker testified. "Right. The Senator was carryin' an envelope, one of those big Senate envelopes and it looked like he had documents in it."

"My...my, Mrs. Wicker," Floyd B. Green interrupted. "I believe you're a fine upstanding citizen. Yes ma'am. A fine upstanding citizen. But did you actually see the documents? In fact, did you have any other reason than your own suspicion to believe there were any documents?"

Mrs. Wicker for the first time hesitated. "Well, no, Senator. But I never seen Senators like you and Senator McAdams carryin' around envelopes that didn't have somethin' in them."

Laughter filled the room as the tension lightened for just a moment.

"Like greenbacks," came an audible whisper from the media congregation.

"But I'll tell ya what I heard," she added, with silence once again descending on the committee room. "I heard that other fella say, and excuse me, but I heard him say directly, 'Wilson, goddammit, you've got the 1040 Form but you forgot the Schedule C!'" Gasps of amazement filled the room as Mrs. Wicker continued. "And then the Senator said, 'not so, it's right here in the envelope. I just forgot to staple it to the form.'"

"And who was the other gentleman," Jo asked excitedly.

"I don't know, Senator," Mrs. Wicker answered. "I never seen him before."

And then Floyd B. Green took over.

"Madame Chairman," he declaimed, "just one question of this witness if I may?"

"The Senator from Texas has the floor," she replied. Stupid! Stupid! Once surrendered, he'll never give it up. And Jo, you're not on the floor for God's sake! I glanced at Pete and could see that he shared my sentiments.

"Now Mrs. Wicker," Green began. The barracuda was about to devour his victim. "Did I hear you say that it was about seven o'clock when you saw Senator McAdams and this other gentleman?"

"Yes sir," Mrs. Wicker replied. "I was just finishing up."

"Mrs. Wicker, what would you say if I told you that I personally greeted Senator McAdams on the steps of the National Gallery at 6.30 P.M.? What would you say, Mrs. Wicker?"

"Well, I…but that's impossible…I think." For the first time the poor woman was shaken.

"And what would you say if I told you that there are several hundred other people who will corroborate that timing?"

"But I always do the rug last," Mrs. Wicker insisted. "And it's always seven o'clock."

The whole room was swaying by this time.

"And Mrs. Wicker," Green continued in a very quiet voice, "what would you say if I told you that there is no record of sign in to the Russell Office Building despite this affidavit from the security guard?"

"What was that, Senator?" Mrs. Wicker asked, straining.

"Mrs. Wicker, do you mean to tell me we are just ten feet apart but you didn't hear the question yet you heard all that talk about tax forms behind a heavy wooden door while you were vacuuming the rug? Come now, Mrs. Wicker. Do you know what PERJURY is? Who put you up to this, Mrs. Wicker?"

Consternation filled the room, reporters straining, staffers rolling their eyes, Jo caught totally off balance. "Senator, that's going too far," she shouted. "I demand that this subcommittee vote to subpoena the tax returns for the last five years of Wilson McAdams. If we can't retrieve them from the shredder, then maybe we can get the truth from the IRS!"

"Not until we get the correct answers, Senator," he shot back. "The correct answers to two simple questions: WHAT DID HE SHRED AND WHEN DID HE SHRED IT! And there'll be no subpoenas and, Madame Chairman, I would caution you not to further malign the reputation of a man of the character of Wilson McAdams without further proof!"

Oh my God, WHAT DID HE SHRED AND WHEN DID HE SHRED IT, the one liner of the day, the ultimate sound bite. This is a fiasco! I kept mumbling to myself.

"That's it, Senator," he repeated, knowing he had the momentum. "WHAT DID HE SHRED AND WHEN DID HE SHRED IT!!"

Mrs. Wicker totally bewildered.

Jo caught utterly off balance.

Pete paralyzed.

The media having a field day.

And in that moment, Green once again filled the vacuum by calling immediately for a vote to suspend the hearings.

"Until we get far more detailed information and responsible staff work," he demanded, shooting a glance at Pete, "I move that we suspend these hearings indefinitely lest they, in their total irresponsibility, destroy the honorable reputation of a great Senator and return us to the deplorable days of...MCCARTHYISM!"

Jo began banging the gavel to restore order but it was too late. Bushey and Bagot quickly voted with

Green and the three of them didn't even wait until the hearing was formally adjourned by its nominal Chair. They just got up in unison and strutted out in indignation. The investigation was in shambles. Mrs. Wicker donned her coat and slowly went back down the aisle. She was history.

And unless something dramatic happened to alter the course of events, so was Josephine Stephenson.

CHAPTER 17

PEOPLE IN GLASS TOWERS

"This is interesting," I commented to Pete O'Connor with my feet up on his desk the next morning.

"What's interesting," he asked in his dejected frame of mind.

"The CEO of Vegetable Pizza is actually taking a 32% pay cut. Says so right here in the paper."

"No shit," Pete replied. "What does that leave him with?"

"He goes from $20.8 mil to $14 mil," I observed.

"Poor guy, I feel for him," Pete said. "Charlie, we're in the wrong business."

"Hey, there's an overnight poll in the Washington Post. It says that 23% of the American people believe McAdams did something wrong and 37% believe he's an innocent dead man."

"What about the other 40%," Pete asked.

"They don't give a shit," I replied.

"Ha, neither do the 60%," he said, managing a laugh.

"It also says here," I continued, "that – listen to this – 'committee staffers are scrambling around trying to cover up the embarrassment of yesterday's fiasco.'"

"Who wrote that, goddammit," Pete demanded.

"Sophia Driver, your favorite political analyst," I replied.

"Get her on the goddam phone," Pete ordered.

"I don't have her number," I said.

"Well, I do, and I want you to hear what I'm about to tell her," he remarked, lunging for the phone. "Sophia," he practically shouted, "what's all this bullshit about scrambling?"

Think before you pick up the phone, Pete, think!

"Who the hell is this," she asked in her throaty tone of superiority.

"Pete O'Connor. You know who it is," he answered.

I had always defined Sophia as one of those media types sent down from the established bastions of privilege, money and celebrity to spy on us ordinary mortals schlepping around the world of realpolitik. She also had a weekly segment on a network television documentary where, armed with a multi-year multi-million dollar network agreement, she would travel the backwaters of America, microphone in hand, followed by a dozen obsequious production people, profiling some poor family without health insurance, in the meantime looking and sounding like she just dropped off the top of the Waldorf Astoria, having been styled and outfitted on Rodeo Drive.

"Well," she began, clearly resenting the arrogance of this politician, "isn't that what you people always do when you get into trouble?"

"No it isn't as a matter of fact," Pete shot back. "I'm sitting here with my feet on the desk, having my coffee and scanning your rotten newspaper. I am neither scrambling nor embarrassed and I would appreciate it if you would report the fact that the Senator and her staff are confidently looking to the future and determined to get to the bottom of this and a helluva lot of other rotten things in this rotten Capital of the free world."

"Indeed," Sophia replied. "Tell me, are you prepared yet to answer Floyd's question: what did he shred and when did he shred it?"

"You people never get it right. You never get it right. That's not the question, Sophia. That's the diversion. And what's this Floyd business? Are you on his payroll?"

"Senator Green is a longtime friend of my family, Peter, and I resent your allegation. So then, what, may I ask, is the question, Peter?" she asked in her wearisome tone.

"The question is about the $1 million in cash, Sophia. That's what the question is," Pete went on.

"Cool it, Pete. Cool it," I whispered. God, he was beginning to blubber and blah all over the place.

"I hate that word, cool. I hate it," he shot back at me.

"What do you hate, Peter," Sophia then asked.

"Among other things, you!" he shouted.

"Let me tell you something, Mr. O'Connor," she broke in. "When you trace the phantom million, give me a call. Until then, I'd appreciate it if you would end the abuse which I will do you a big favor with and leave off the record even though you didn't say so. And don't call me again until you have something substantive."

The next thing I heard was the dial tone.

"Can't you control yourself?" I demanded.

"Oh yeah? How about you? Can't you commit yourself? I've just about had enough of you lurking in the background, giving advice and dodging the bullets," Pete shouted. "You'll probably call Sophia up and tell her I'm deranged."

"You know that's not true," I quietly replied. "You know the risks I'm taking. And you wouldn't even be here without me."

"Thanks a lot Charlie. Thanks a lot. And I'd probably be better off. Maybe it's time for you to confront your mentor and show some guts." At that point he curtained me off with The New York Times.

Thankfully this little dialogue was finally ended when Jo walked into Pete's office, looking as if she hadn't slept in days and slouched in an easy chair.

"Where do we go from here?" she asked. Funny, but she didn't seem particularly stricken. She only looked it.

"Your guess is as good as mine," I replied.

"You started this, Charlie," she reminded me. "You told me about Controller splitting that money with McAdams. Suppose we subpoena you to tell the truth."

"Fine," I said, feeling a little queasy. "Except that I don't have any more evidence than Thelma Wicker. And what's worse, I haven't the slightest idea where to find it. Besides, you don't have the votes to subpoena me. Bushey, Bagot and Green are my friends. Remember?"

"Look," Pete interjected. "We know we're solid at the core. We know that all of this is true. The media can rant and rave all it wants. People like Sophia Driver can sit in judgment. Floyd B. Green can rent his garments. Controller can duck. But sooner or later, we're going to get to the bottom of this."

"Make it sooner," Jo observed. "You know what?" she continued. "I don't care. I don't care if I look like a jackass in the press. I don't care if momentarily even the people of Vermont think I'm stupid and amateurish. And I'm not sure they do. I'm convinced that McAdams took that money. I'm also convinced that Controller split it with him. So what if I can't get the subcommittee to move. I just know that, if we keep our cool, and stay on top of this, we'll find it in the long run. And Charlie, I think it's about time you stopped this double game and came on board."

"You too. I just had that sermon from Pete. I don't know," I replied. "I just don't know. Maybe you're right. Let me think about it." Obviously what I had to think about was, among other things, that bi-weekly check from the think tank being cut off and me in the unemployment line.

As we spoke, Pete had taken a phone call and, when it was finished, looked at us dejectedly again.

"What was that?" Jo asked.

"One of our investigators. Showed Controller's picture to Mrs. Wicker and the Security Guard.

Neither identified him. But our guy will swear they knew the face as soon as they saw it."

"Terrorized into silence," I observed.

"Poor woman," Jo said. "Probably supports four kids on a cleaning woman's salary. I can't blame her. She certainly was courageous enough. But we couldn't back her and now we can't protect her."

At that moment, Frankie Phillips picked up the phone and called Jo Stephenson. He had been following the events with the fascination of a fellow player of the political game. Team player though he may be, one of "theirs" though he had allowed himself to become, he seemed to feel a deep and very personal concern for his former classmate, alleged onetime lover and friend. He understood just as clearly as we did that the tragedy of the McAdams business was its lack of finality.

"Jo, I've been thinkin'," he said, getting to the point immediately. "Do you remember Roger Moss from Business School?"

"Of course, I remember him," Jo replied. "I even got a congratulatory note from him when I was elected. Very successful on Wall Street, isn't he?"

"You better believe it," Frankie answered. "Millions. I mean real millions. Hundreds of millions. Mucho bucks. Chief Honcho at Mirrors, Kiddem and Flease, the brokerage house. I don't know how those guys do it. In fact, I don't even know why those guys do it or how they get away with it, but I'm telling you, big time, big bucks."

"So what's this all about, Frankie?" asked Jo, beginning to get impatient.

"Well, I figured that, with all the complications you've got right now, he may be able to help. Now I know you don't like the big money boys but this is different. These guys aren't really into the lobbying racket. Don't need it. They're all over the world. But they've got clout and influence. Operate on a higher plane. Definitely a cut above. They don't just have annual meetings. They go to London or Tokyo. Arrange for speeches by royalty. I mean, they're really in a different world. I thought maybe, if you reestablished that friendship, you might enlist some powerful allies and, frankly, Jo, you need allies right now."

"What do you suggest," Jo monotoned.

"Well, I took it upon myself to talk to Roger and he said he'd love to see you again. Very impressed with your – I think he used the word – celebrity. Likes what he sees. Said he'd love to get together sometime when you're in New York. I'm telling you, it could be an opening to the power crowd on Wall Street. Why don't you give him a call?"

"I can't imagine why, Frankie," Jo replied. "It's inconceivable to me that he would have the slightest interest in what I'm doing. International finance and the world I have to live in just don't mix. At least I don't think so."

"You never know. You never know," Frankie intoned. "Look at it this way. At least, you'll make a contact which may be worth a lot of clean campaign dollars when you run again. These guys love to rub shoulders with prominent politicians, quid pro quo or no quid pro quo. It goes with the territory. If they can't get Presidents or Vice Presidents, they'll take Senators."

Jo hated to admit it but the thought of some alternative source of support and substantial money tempted her. "Okay, Frank, I'll be in New York next Friday before I go back to Burlington for the weekend. What should I do, just call?"

"Absolutely. I tell you, he's waiting by the phone. He'll love it. Jo and Roger together again. An item for the Wall Street Journal," Frankie quipped.

"Or the New York Post," Jo retorted.

As she hung up the phone and informed Pete and me about Frankie's message, she asked: "anybody know the firm of Mirrors, Kiddem and Fleece?"

"Of course," I said. "They're part of the network. I know several guys there."

"Well, if you could find an excuse to go to New York next Friday, maybe you'd join me. I'm seeing Roger Moss."

"Sure," I said. "I'd like to get out of this town anyway. Why not."

Actually I didn't so much want to get out of DC as to revisit New York. Hey, maybe we'll see a few plays, have a couple of four star dinners, do the celebrity circuit. In any event, we were off the following weekend on the metroliner and very soon thereafter viewing the skyline from the 58th floor of the ultimate glass tower.

Mirrors, Kiddem and Flease was not just Wall Street. High above lower Manhattan, it was aged in wood, mirrored in tradition and blanketed with some of the world's most sought after art.

"Jo Stephenson! I can't believe it!" came the silken but emphatic welcome from Roger Moss. "What an honor! And Charlie Coons, no less. How'd they let you out of the Beltway?" The benign smile that only the absolutely insulated can conjure came from this polished, impeccably dressed apparition in horned rimmed glasses. Get the handkerchief in the pocket, I thought. "I'll need a gas mask to get out of this place," Jo murmured to me.

"Hello Roger. Good to see you. It's been too long," she replied politely.

"Hi Rog, me too," I added.

"Well, come on in. Come on in," Roger fussily continued in a manner which suggested that we were welcome and should feel comfortable where few dare to tread. And then that awkward reception room kiss cynically observed by the smiling woman behind the desk.

"Now before we have our little chat, I hope you'll do me a favor," he implored, knowing all along that he could not possibly be turned down.

"Roger, my morning is yours," she answered obediently.

"In the past few years, we've really done a job of recruiting professional women, absolute financial wizards from the Ivies. You know, just like some of the gals at Wharton. But lots more. Boy, the world's changing, Jo. These kids really have something on the ball. And do they know how to make money."

Continually walking down the endless corridor.

214

"Anyway, when they heard you were coming, well, wow, I turned into the most popular guy around here."

Cut the false humility, Roger, Jo thought. You're the most popular guy around here anyway and it has nothing to do with me.

"Several of them were dying to meet you. I mean, you're their idol. They worship you from afar. I was hoping you'd take a few minutes and meet with them over coffee in the board room."

"I'd love to," Jo replied, beginning to be impressed by her celebrity.

The great mahogany door opened to a burst of applause and expressions of delight from a dozen young women who had to be among the best turned out specimens in the world, attractive, fashionable, exquisitely dressed, meticulously coifed and affluent, each introduced by Roger in a manner one could only call courtly.

"Oh God, this is a real honor!" exclaimed Betsy Bolger.

"Boy, do I admire you," oozed Liz Weatherby.

Roger beaming in the background. Me? Just kinda sizing up the girls.

As she shook hands all around, Jo brightened up considerably. Oh what a world, she seemed to be thinking. I could read her mind: "What am I, nuts? Struggling in the Senate, embattled in Vermont while this crowd jets around the world making millions?"

"I'd give anything to be you," gushed Mimi Marker. "When I was at Smith, you had just decided to run for the Senate and I've followed every move you've made!"

Several had come in late, tossing their minks on the boardroom easy chairs, obscuring the gold plated names of the principal partners of Mirrors, Kiddem and Flease. Roger maneuvered everyone to sit down and, smiling broadly, introduced his catch.

"Senator, I can't tell you how honored we are that you're here," he intoned, adopting a more formal manner. "Of course, being an old friend from Wharton days helps. I can now say that I know a famous person!" What humility. "I don't intend to use up our precious time. And I don't think I need to make a formal introduction because the Senator needs no introduction. Indeed, I could go on and on and on about her incredible career. But, to make a long story short, she's really turning Washington upside down. Without further ado, Senator Stephenson of Vermont!"

Enthusiastic applause and a couple of whoops of feminine pride followed. Jo spoke very briefly about her goals and ended with a short retrospective on the McAdams affair.

"I was deeply shocked by the untimely death of Wilson McAdams," she concluded to a hushed room. "It certainly was not my intention to see it end this way. In many ways, I admired what he stood for. But, in my position, I just couldn't let some very serious allegations pass without pursuing them. Unfortunately, now we may never know what really happened. But I'm convinced I was right and I'm determined to do what I can to clean up this system. And I can't possibly describe how difficult it is to get to the bottom of a system that is thoroughly corrupted by money, power and influence. Now, any questions?"

"Isn't it difficult because you're a woman?"

"Not really. It's just difficult, period."

"The only issue I'm really interested in is choice. How long will we women continue to be threatened by the neanderthals on the right?" Applause.

"I think – and I hope – that the country's reached a consensus on the abortion issue. Whatever your personal convictions, I keep telling people, it's not a matter for the federal government."

"Are you running for President?" Cheers.

"God no!"

"Some of my militant friends in the women's lobbies in Washington tell me you're not always responsive to their agenda."

"That's really not so," she replied with a note of irritation beginning to show. "But my own agenda is simply broader than theirs. It's true that I don't jump every time they call. But I need them to support me too, not just on their issues but on the bigger ones."

To this group it was apparent there were no larger issues.

"Most of us fly all over the world. Can you get the federal government to lean on the airlines and get better and safer international service?"

"I haven't thought about that. I have enough trouble getting back to Burlington." Laughs.

"Do you know the Governor of Vermont?"

"Yes, why?"

"Well, I'm in our municipal bond business and I need a contact for their next big highway issue."

Jo, restraining a scream, "call Maureen Sullivan in my Washington office. Being an independent, I'm not exactly the Governor's favorite Senator but I can get you a hearing."

"One last question," Roger interrupted, just a bit embarrassed by the level of the questions. "Mimi Marker?"

Giggles. "Can I get your autograph for my boyfriend? He thinks you're really neat!"

Laughs all around. Jo smiled and said "of course." Then everyone ran up to get an autograph. Finally, Roger rescued her and transported us to his office overlooking uptown Manhattan, lined with framed photos of Roger and Kissinger, Roger and Tony, Roger and Vladimir and, she thought, Roger and Ludwig Controller. And the art, the oriental rug, the spotless desk with the family picture, those two healthy and handsome sons and Eleanor, smiling serenely by Roger's side.

"Sit down, sit down and relax," said Roger. "Gee, I'm glad you did that. Real inspiration to those gals. It'll be the talk of the firm for weeks. And you made me a hero."

"I'm not so sure about that," Jo replied. "It looks to me like you're a hero already."

"Listen, Jo, heroes don't have my problems," Roger commented, easing into his leather swivel chair. "I spent all morning, until you showed up, trying to get my new Rolls out of the repair shop in East Hampton. Can you imagine that? I just bought the thing for a sinful amount of money and it broke down on the Long Island Expressway, of all places. And I've got to fly to Zurich tomorrow morning and won't be back for two weeks. I can't get Eleanor to pick it up because she's on her way to Bar Harbor tonight. And the kids are back in school."

"I'm sure you'll find a way, Roger," Jo reassured him. "What's going on in Zurich?"

"One of the most complex financial deals we've ever done," Roger answered. "But if we pull it off, it's worth millions. Everybody involved. The Japanese, the Germans, the Arabs, some of the biggest banks in the world. Jo, I spend half my life in first class and the other half in board rooms. But, I am telling you, it's paying off. I'm faxing a document over there today that will make their eyes pop out. And I've made some very valuable friends abroad and that makes it a lot easier. But what's with you? How can I help?"

"I don't know, Roger," Jo replied thoughtfully, clearly a little intimidated by the distance placed between them by Roger's prior comments. "I don't think you can. We live in such separate worlds. I was hoping to put together a group of influential people who would publicly support my reform proposals in the Congress. But what's really in the back of my mind is to get in the forefront of some legislation to help the cities and attack the crime and drug problems that I believe will destroy us if we don't turn around

219

the domestic economy and find jobs and hope in the inner cities."

"Hey kid," Roger quickly retorted, "you're beginning to sound like Jesse Jackson. Remember, you're from Vermont and the one thing I love about Vermont is the skiing. Come to think of it, I haven't been up there in years, what with the place in Aspen and the invites to Kitzbuehl. Look, I'd love to help but I'm really stretched. I'm never here. Sure, I live in New York and the situation on the streets makes me nervous. But it's far too complicated for me to make a difference. And besides, that's not where my bread and butter is. I'm more likely to be in Paris than on the upper West Side or Queens. I haven't been back to Queens since I was eighteen years old. As for political reform, the system doesn't treat me so badly. Or the firm. Now if you're going to get involved in the next tax or trade bills, there's something I could think about. But right now, my head's in Zurich and it's awfully hard to refocus on grass roots stuff. Charlie here understands, don't you Charlie?"

"Sure do," I replied. Man of few words on this trip.

"Of course, I realize that," Jo retorted. "But we all have to live here."

"I'm not so sure about that anymore," Roger responded quickly. "Frankly, I could live anywhere and run the business from anywhere. All I need is a fax machine, a desk top, e-mail, cell phone and the proper equipment. And we could take this firm anywhere. The taxes get too high, the crime too bad, we could be in the Rockies tomorrow. Or the

Caribbean. Look, I'll let you use my name. But I can't get out in front. And I don't have the time to recruit anybody else. But if my name will help, you got it."

"Thanks, Roger, I really appreciate that," Jo said.

"And here's something else," Roger continued, opening his desk drawer and taking out his checkbook. "Here's my own personal contribution to The Jo Stephenson Committee. What's the limit? Two thousand dollars? There it is. And I'll send a note over to our PAC and see if I can get more."

"Thanks again, Roger. I can take the personal check but I don't take PAC money."

"Okay, okay," Roger replied. "And if you ever run for President, there'll be more. We could use a Treasury Secretary and a Trade Rep who really understand what's going on in the world."

Roger was getting restless. Glanced at his watch. Passed the check over the desk. I felt like throwing it at him. But took it. He stood up. Smiling broadly. Warmly. In moments, Jo, holding my arm, was ushered to the elevator, once again profusely thanked for the honor of her presence.

"God, it was good to see you! And boy, were they impressed. Keep in touch and let me know how it goes. I wish we could have gotten together for lunch but I have to be uptown at Perigord with some clients. Wait'll I tell them I spent the morning with Jo. Like me, they've been reading about her in the Times! Oh, by the way, I didn't want to mention it while Jo was here but I've got a great tip for you. Buy some Global Cleanliness. It's going to $70 and you can pick it up now for $20."

"Global Cleanliness? Are you sure," I asked. "They could be tied up in the McAdams scandal Jo's been pursuing."

"Penny ante stuff," Roger said dismissively. "They've got the access, the power and the money. That's why we named it Global. Get it? World Class. And we're in the perfect position of recommending the stock and handling their money at the same time. Bound to take off. Well, anyway, great to see you. Gotta be movin' along."

Thanks again, Roger, you shit, I said to myself.

That night, Jo and I stayed over in Manhattan prior to her return to Vermont. We had dinner, a very special unwinding dinner. And that's it. I'm not going to tell you anymore about that night. Suspect what you will.

CHAPTER 18

THE CANDIDATE

By Sunday, I was back in Washington checking in with my mentor, Ludwig Controller, hoping to get some clue as to what he would do next. He had weathered the storm. In fact, having been seen at the side of Wilson McAdams turned out to be a net plus. Beltway observers and insiders admired his loyalty to his friend, the way he walked into that reception shoulder to shoulder, the manner in which he helped me as the strangling statesman drew his last breath, and above all his accompaniment of the expiring McAdams in the emergency vehicle.

There were cynics, of course, those who commented out of the side of their mouths that his concern for the corpse was more a need to be reassured that he was really dead. But on balance, the Doctor was looking good and looking good was the name of the game.

And so, as the David departed for Florence in a flourish of fireboat spray, and as Wilson McAdams was being laid to rest in his native soil, Ludwig the Survivor sat contentedly, in his easy chair, watching his latest recruit for the Ass Kissinger Society, the distinguished Senior Senator from the Lone Star State of Texas, Floyd B. Green, obscure the facts on a Sunday morning public affairs show while we waited for the arrival of his favorite pollster, Hap Mandell. I told him nothing of consequence but just enough to titillate his interest, little insider vignettes of Senator Stephenson looking haggard and worn. Just enough to mislead him. Not enough to go on.

"On the one hand, we must be very careful not to condemn a dead man prematurely," commented Floyd B. Green in all his authority. "On the other, there were obviously some things which required ethical scrutiny. But, then again, you have to realize that, on one hand, Wilson McAdams was a highly regarded statesman, while, on the other, he was required to function within the American political system."

Controller roared. "What a joke!" he hollered. "So help me, old Floyd is turning into the best Ass Kissinger in the business. He's ass kissing the assholes. They're looking at him like he's saying something profound. I can't believe he's getting away with it."

"But Senator," said the puzzled moderator, David Shockley, "the fact is we'll never know the truth unless that alleged bribe can be traced. Is anybody going to do something about it? Where will you and Senator Stephenson go from here with the investigation by the subcommittee?"

"Well," said Green solemnly, "on the one hand, we could call for an Independent Prosecutor. But that path died with the expiration of the enabling legislation. Besides, it's now exclusively up to the Attorney General and you know the story there. Why, just the other day you saw where there was a demand in the Senate to revive the statute and for an

Independent Prosecutor to investigate the activities of a prior Independent Prosecutor! On the other hand, we could hold more hearings ourselves and get people under oath. But frankly, David, that session the other day was a fiasco and we have no one to blame but our inexperienced Madame Chairman and her incompetent staff. Besides, I think the United States Senate has more important things to do than investigate the alleged misconduct of a dead man. Why, for heaven's sake, next week we've got half a dozen Senators preparing three hour speeches on health care. And the other ninety four will probably focus on social security, prescription drugs and homeland security. So, you see, we've got a lot to do for the American people. That's what the American people want."

Pure bullshit, I thought. But he was getting away with it, much to Controller's delight and my discomfort.

"Senator," snapped Wally Blunt, syndicated Washington columnist, "on the floor of the Senate yesterday, Senator Stephenson was quoted as saying that she still intended to pursue the McAdams incident and other leads which have come to her attention with the full powers of the subcommittee. Would you care to comment on that?"

"Now, I do indeed admire the Senator and her tenacity, not to speak of her convictions," Green replied, noticeably annoyed. "But I doubt that the Committee will support such a move. Senators Bushey and Bagot have already informed me of their extreme reluctance to pursue this matter any further. And they are men of great experience and proven integrity. I must say I would be inclined to go along with their judgment. I did not, sir, make that comment about McCarthyism lightly. Indeed, that speech the Junior (with emphasis) Senator from Vermont made on the floor of the chamber the other day was made to an empty Senate and an empty media gallery. It was hardly a significant event."

"An empty Senate and an indifferent media are no barometers of public policy," Shockley shot back.

Controller hit the button, causing the television image to vanish in an instant. At once satisfied and uneasy, I knew he would never rest until the woman from Vermont was out of the way. Loose cannon on the deck, he murmured. Unpredictable. Dangerous. Most definitely not one of ours. Not a team player. Got to be beaten.

"But Doctor," said Hap Mandell, Common Good's exemplary pollster, after having been escorted through the door personally by his mentor on that quiet Sunday morning, "she'll self destruct like all reformers if given enough rope. She's not getting anywhere anyway. Oh, hi Charlie, good to see you."

"Hap, I'm telling you, if we don't start now this thing will grow," Controller responded. "It could destroy us. Common Good, the New GOP, everything we've worked for. She's after the whole system. Fortunately, when she put in those three ill advised reform bills, every domestic and foreign interest with a piece of the government, panicked. There's more money flowing in than ever before. But the McAdams thing isn't dead. It's not going to die. She hasn't even scratched the surface but she stumbled on that one little thing that could open all the doors. All she needs, and that smart ass assistant of hers could pull it off, is to get the documentation on the money."

Open all of what doors? I knew but what Mandell did not know, and could not possibly comprehend, was the fact that the money led directly to the Doctor. And what agitated Controller more than any attempt to protect the system, was his own vulnerability. And more than the money, it was the options.

Exasperated, Mandell, one of the few who could talk to the Doctor on relatively equal terms, continued: "I don't know what that has to do with us. I see McAdams as an isolated incident. I don't see him as a core issue. We have a system to perpetuate. We've managed to turn this game into a finely tuned racket. Let's get out there and raise the money, tighten the network and elect more of our own."

Controller, lighting a cigar, totally avoided Mandell's suggestion. "Hap," he continued, benignly, "did anybody ever tell you you're getting fat? Look at those strained buttons on your shirt. And that walrus face. Too fat and too comfortable, young man. Now Charlie here takes care of himself. I think it's time you got back into shape by getting this Vermont thing under control. Hap, we start now," he continued, quickening the pace and changing the tone, cigar smoke swirling around the walrus like countenance of his favorite pollster. "I want that woman so goddam preoccupied with local problems that she won't be able to see straight on that committee of hers. I want her surrounded, outspent, outflanked, criticized, screamed at and investigated. I want the best opposition research team at our command to get up there and destroy her. I want Rick Brewster and Frankie Phillips to land her in bed with the cameras going. I want every lobbyist in town blocking everything she tries. I want to drive her to the edge of complete paranoia. I want her to be so unstable that she can't think straight or sleep at night. And if all that doesn't work, we'll have to take drastic action. I haven't forgotten about that kid in California."

At the mention of California, I froze. Even I had put it out of my mind. One of the things you try to bury. But Mandell was astonished. And embarrassed. California? He pulled in his gut and tried not to breathe. The buttons eased as he sat up straight in his easy chair. Never before had he seen Controller get so close to the destructive brink. "Okay," he stammered. "Okay. What do you have in mind?"

Controller stared intently. "You can't beat somebody with nobody. I already have our candidate."

"You already have a candidate?" Mandell asked, slightly amazed but no more amazed than I was. I had been taken completely off guard.

"Our candidate," Controller replied with emphasis.

"Who?" asked Hap.

"You won't believe it. His name is Ethan Allen Aiken."

"Ethan Allen Aiken?"

"Yes, a distinguished descendant of the original Green Mountain Boy and a more recent descendant of that great statesman, Senator George Aiken. We'll give them one of their very own, not some Ivy educated new woman from Burlington."

"Aside from the name, are there any other qualifications?" asked Hap.

"Frankly, my boy, I don't know that we need them but yes, he's a small town lawyer in Bennington. Six foot two, just like his great great great great granddaddy. Thirty five. Wife, two fine children, one girl and one boy. Good looking kid, too."

"And how did you find him?"

"He was an intern years ago in the office of our fine Senior Senator from the Green Mountain State, the Honorable James Webster. Webster tipped me off at his fund raiser last week. Doesn't want to get personally involved, of course. A little worried about Stephenson's appeal. We're already feeding the boy some nice legal business from Stratton, Berry and Snow. But here's the real kicker, Hap. The President has agreed to nominate him as Federal Attorney for the Northeastern District upon Webster's recommendation. He won't surface as a candidate immediately and in the meantime, he can convene all sorts of grand juries, indict a few people, keep an eye on Stephenson and her husband's law practice and make a name for himself as a ferreter out of corruption. By the way, he really means it. Very dedicated guy. Integrity. Determined to use all the tools at the federal prosecutor's command in the pursuit of justice as we know it." Controller had it all down.

"But what about Stephenson," I inquired. "Won't she see through this and block the nomination?"

"Why should she? Ethan Allen Aiken was her Bennington coordinator in the campaign! That's when he began to get the real itch for politics. The night she won, he stood there, staring at her, saying over and over to himself, 'that could be me, that could be me.' It was the moment his ego took flight. He'll do anything to win and he's determined to make the effort to do it. Honest, of course. But our honest guy, not hers."

Yes, of course, I thought. I remember him. One of the envious ones at the rally. Of course.

"And what role am I supposed to play in this?" Hap asked.

"You start now by polling the hell out of Vermont. Tommy Rock starts raising money for the 'Committee to Save Vermont' and we get Aiken into the Federal Attorney's Office. Meanwhile, Opposition Research begins and our phalanx of lawyer-lobbyists right here in the nation's Capitol mobilizes to tie up Mrs. Stephenson in legislative knots with the help of Bushey, Bagot and Green. Vermont federal aid money gets delayed. She gets blamed for it. We engineer some controversial federal project for the state and say she's behind it. This should be most interesting. And it'll be a two person race, the Independent versus the consensus candidate of the two major parties. We buy them both. What did George Wallace say? 'There's not a dime's worth of difference between 'em.' Smart politician, George. Maybe even Charlie here will see to it that we have a two man race. What do you say, Charlie?"

"Let me think about it," I replied.

"Don't take too long," Controller said, staring coldly at me.

Hap was uneasy. It all seemed too cute. But he was powerless to do anything about it. The money, the power and the influence Controller could bring to bear were too much to confront. And so he went along. And went along. And soon found himself, as I was, enmeshed in a confrontation of substantial proportions.

For me the moment of decision was imminent. I was never going to run that jerk's campaign. I hadn't even met him but I just knew he was a bad guy. He wouldn't be Controller's boy if he wasn't. And I was not going to desert Jo. I was not going to subordinate my conscience to cowardice. But I just needed a little more time.

....

"Mandell, what's going on here?" Controller shouted as he entered the Application of Rapid Technology think tank not far from the CIA headquarters in McLean, Virginia. Mandell had begun the think tank as the ultimate advance in campaign methodology.

As Controller and I walked in, we entered a large hall with two hundred computerized work stations, all manned by average American citizens. The strange thing about the scene, however, was that all the average Americans in the room were wearing

Mandell's new steel helmet brain wave detectors, known by their nickname of Detectabrains. The average citizens stared at the monitors before them, watching endless replays of negative political advertisements, registering their reactions on a scale of one to ten (cold to warm), not by pressing feely counters or expressing themselves verbally but by remaining absolutely motionless while their brain wave reactions were mechanically recorded directly by the Dectabrains. No smiling. No grimacing. No facial reactions. No rolled eyes. No laughter or throwing backwards the head. No nods of approval or disdain. They just sat there and watched, providing the ultimate purification of the voter reaction process.

There they were: two hundred average Americans; 103 women and ninety seven men. Among them, twenty two African Americans, of whom fourteen were women (much larger numbers of African American women voting than men); several Hispanics; a diminishing number of blue collars; lots of suits and ties; a few with fast food hats on; ten gays (seven men, one a Navy Ensign, three women); only sixteen union members; a handful of clergy; one Mormon; five cab drivers; three waitresses; a small group of university students; and four complete family units from the suburbs. Here was America itself expressing its collective opinion in the most rarefied form yet envisioned.

"Just look, gentlemen," Mandell pointed proudly. "The brain waves of America at work. Today's session will last seven hours. During this time, five hundred negative political ads will flash across the screen. By ten o'clock this evening, we will know what America thinks about them. By this time tomorrow, our consultants all over the country will have a complete report on what negatives work and what negatives don't work. But I'll tell you right now that my very personal favorite is the one where the candidate slashes his opponent for running negative ads!"

"Amazing, Hap," Controller noted with genuine admiration. Not one average American looked up. Not one even noticed. "How did you get them here?"

"Transported them in from all over the country on a generous grant from Ronald West at your very own Common Good. They're here for four days in isolation. Yesterday, we brain waved the issues which, as you know, are the least important component of a campaign. Tomorrow, they are broken down into focus groups in which we will attempt to determine their attitudes toward leading politicians and other celebrities. Here's where we really pinpoint the most important group, the negative leaners." "You mean they actually talk?" I asked.

"Well, up to a point. We let them talk but warn them that it's much more scientific if they just squeeze the feely counters in reaction to spoken statements. If they must talk, we let them but we don't think it's very reliable. Finally, on the fourth day, it's back to the detectabrains for one final shot at their feelings about the future of their country and the world. When they leave, America will be in our computer. There isn't a candidate who wants to win who will be able to move without our input. From here we take them down for a weekend of mindless fun at Daisyland."

"What are you finding out?" I asked.

"Well, of course we're not sure yet about every detail but there's a clear desire for real change."

"Real change, huh? Gotta remember that," Controller observed. "Write it down, Charlie. Real change. Not just change?"

"No, Doctor," Hap replied emphatically. "Real change. Very real change. In fact, very very real change, social security and Medicare in a lock box lined with prescription drugs, instant education for all and they want some of their money back."

"Gotta give that to Aiken," Controller observed. "This Stephenson woman ran on the need for change. Aiken can get a leg up by being for real change, right?"

"Right," Mandell assured him. "Very very real change," he pointedly hastened to add.

"Hap," Controller changed the subject, "I came over here to introduce you to your next great challenge, the next Junior Senator from Vermont, Ethan Allen Aiken. He's going to stop by in a few minutes and I'd like you to join us."

"Son of a bitch, he didn't even tell me," I whispered to Mandell.

In the din of negative advertising, surrounded by two hundred average expressionless Americans, Mandell was reluctant to leave his project. This initiative by the Doctor was clearly something he wanted to avoid. But there was no resisting Ludwig

Controller so out the door we went into the sunlit parking lot. And there he was.

"Hap, Charlie, meet Ethan Allen Aiken!" announced Controller.

Aiken leapt out of the car, standing tall at 6'2", smiled broadly, tossed back his rusty locks from his rugged but handsome mountain face and with earnestness in his eyes proceeded to squeeze my hand unmercifully while letting out a bellowing "HI YEW!"

I flinched and rolled my eyes. Hap pulled in his stomach (watch those buttons), stood tall and, realizing that HI YEW had now left the South to become the universal political greeting, bellowed back, "Hey, Hi Yew tooo!" I nodded and gave him a limp handshake. How's that, creep.

And there we stood, looking awkward and gawky until Controller broke the spell with "Boys, let's go inside and chat a bit. I want this fella to get to know you guys and to learn at the feet of the experts."

Once inside Hap's executive suite (having skillfully avoided the All American Robots), Aiken blurted out: "boy, is it good to meet you, Mr. Coons. And you too, Mr. Mandell. I've read so much about you. I'd like to take your autograph home to my kids. They've seen you on the TV!"

"I'd be glad to before you go," Hap replied. "But first, tell me something about yourself. Why do you want to run for the Senate?"

"Because I've got the fire in my belly!" Aiken replied resoundingly. "I stood there that night Senator Stephenson won the election and said that it should have been me, a true Vermonter, a Mountain boy, a struggling lawyer in the cause of the people. Fine family, right image, and honest."

"Then what are you doing here?" Hap blurted out before he could stop himself. "I mean, what do you think we can do for you?"

Controller just sat back, letting the conversation flow in a get acquainted mode.

"Money for one," Aiken replied, getting quite serious and changing his tone to a carefully articulated and precise recitation of his ambition. "We will need a great deal of money to take on Senator Stephenson and we will have to start now to build the kind of war chest than can win. Polls. Must have polls to stay in touch with the people. TV ads. Must hike up positive name recognition and build up her negatives. Define her before she defines herself. Neat slogans on billboards. The whole nine yards! Isn't that how you guys put it? I mean, I don't know much about politics but that's what the Doctor here tells me. We're going to need lots of fund raisers down here in Washington. Drag in all those lobbyists you guys have connections with."

"But don't you think that will hurt you in the independent state of Vermont?" I inquired.

"Nah, they know me. Think I'm a good old Green Mountain boy. Besides, whatever I can do for those lobbyists doesn't matter much in Vermont. It's one thing to sell your vote at home. Never do that. But on things that don't affect my constituents, no problem." Then his eyes shifted eagerly back to Hap. Clearly, I didn't rate around here.

"Seems to me you've got it all down pat," Hap observed. "I don't know why you'd need us. Unless, of course, you've taken the Doctor's course in political self esteem."

"Not yet," Controller quickly interjected. "But we'll get there. He's come a long way without it, don't you think? A few tranquilizers and it'll all be complete."

"Indeed," Hap quickly interrupted, barely controlling his growing discomfort with this new wave candidate. "In the meantime, how do you intend to conduct yourself if confirmed as Federal Attorney?"

"I intend to be the most honest, most aggressive, most determined, most righteous and most indicting federal attorney the Justice Department ever saw," Aiken answered forthrightly.

"With a few exceptions," Controller interrupted.

"Yes, with a few exceptions," Aiken quickly added. "You see, there's them and there's us. They're the baddies and we're the goodies. The guys in the white hat. I don't go after white hats."

"Mr. Aiken," Hap concluded, winding down this predictable dialogue, "I think you'll be a great success as Federal Attorney and, with a little help from your friends, an outstanding Senator from the Green Mountain State of Vermont."

Smiles all around. The connection had been made. The confrontation was about to begin. And I was about to throw up. As I left the meeting, I recalled something an old political boss once told me about election to office when I once had the mad and foolish thought of running myself. "Don't do it," he said. "As soon as you're elected, you're indictable." On the way back to the office, I picked up a copy of The Post. And, wouldn't you know it, there on the front page was a screaming headline about the recent indictment of a new young Congressman from Maryland. Apparently, he was accused of the appearance of an appearance of a conflict of interest. Watch out, Charlie, I said to myself. Don't get too courageous. Find a fallout shelter. It's an ugly time to be in this business.

CHAPTER 19

STALEMATE

The beginning of Jo Stephenson's second year in the United States Senate was not a happy time.

Exhibiting a great need to get the family together for the holidays, she and George had arranged for a skiing trip to Aspen. Henry went along with his parents and, miraculously, Raymond appeared from Los Angeles, looking and acting none the worse.

After two days of relative relaxation, however, the inevitable intrusions began to set in. She was spotted on the slopes by a staffer to Senator Bushey who promptly leaked her presence to the local press. That relatively insignificant item was noticed by the Associated Press night editor in Denver who, having nothing better to send out over the wire, turned the visit into a story with a twist and a hook. He actually snickered as he wrote the lead: "despite the Aspen skiing boycott mandated by Hollywood celebrities due to the rejection of a gay rights referendum by Colorado voters, Independent Vermont Senator Josephine Stephenson, an occasional advocate of liberal causes, is vacationing in Aspen this week with her family." (The twist). "Observers also took note of the fact that Stephenson was in Colorado at the very time when Vermont was promoting its own undeniable attractions as a Mecca for skiers." (The hook). "Stephenson was unavailable for comment but other Washington based visitors also in Aspen, who insisted on anonymity, greeted Stephenson's presence there with raised eyebrows. One prominent Senate staffer observed that Stephenson was having enough trouble getting needed federal assistance for Vermont without leaving her state and promoting the tourism values of a leading competitor."

Needless to say, the Vermont media picked up the story with glee. The University of Vermont Cynic, for example, ran a front page picture of Page Coster, the Editor, shouting from the top of Stowe Mountain: "Hey Jo, come back!"

"It never fails," Jo commented wearily on the phone. "You go away, Charlie, the roof falls in. I knew when we got on that plane that we wouldn't get through this week without a fiasco. It's so stupid of me, I guess. I just wasn't thinking."

"What does George think?" I asked cautiously.

"He doesn't give a damn," Jo retorted. "I told him he might have said something for a change. My head was so scrambled, it didn't occur to me. Why does it never occur to him?"

"Didn't you tell Pete and Maureen?" I asked.

"I guess I told them. They certainly know where to reach me. But nobody's been thinking straight. We just didn't catch it. And I so wanted to just get a little quiet time with George, Raymond and Henry. Now it will be nothing but calls demanding reaction. Reaction! That's all I do lately, react!"

"The hell with it, Jo." George had picked up the extension. "You know what? I was looking at the books the other day and I'm going to rake in half a million this year alone. At this pace, after next year, we'll be millionaires and you can say goodbye to the goddam Senate and goddam politics. Frankly, I'm up to here with it."

"I'm not, George. I can't be. People believe in me. Trust me. Want things to change." Jo was giving her speech. And I was in the awkward, to say the least, position of having to listen.

"Nonsense," George shot back. "Nothing's ever going to change. Just settle down, do your job for the state and think about us. Look at Ray. I don't know, and you don't know, how he's really doing. We think we do but we don't. And we never discuss it. Don't want to. Maybe, if we did, it would take us away from this preoccupation with every two bit item in the press. And you know Henry misses you. Even when you're there, you're not there. The other night, before we left, I sat there talking to you about all of this and you didn't even hear me. You just sat there, a million miles away, consumed with all this bullshit. Sorry, Charlie, that you have to listen to this but, what are you doing on the goddam phone anyway?" George asked in exasperation.

Jo answered. "Had to reach Pete. Find out what's going on. Get a statement together. Maybe I should go back early. Charlie, find Pete and Maureen. We'll just have to do something." And return she did the following day, New Year's Day, to Washington as George stayed in Aspen with Henry and Ray.

I never could figure out exactly what George thought of me. I suspect he suspected an affair. At the very least he perceived me as an annoyance. But one which had its plusses in the murky world of the Beltway.   It was, if nothing else, the lingering discomfort all spouses feel about aides and advisors who just seem to displace the normal relationships of family with the expedient relationships of the job. In any event, he made me as uneasy as he was so I guess you could say it was a standoff.

....

It was not a happy time.

There was no way that Bushey, Bagot and Green were going to vote to reconvene subcommittee hearings and there wasn't much to convene about. Jo's reform bills remained bottled up in committee, endlessly wrangled over by the wimp, the wonk and the windbag.   At each moment, however, that it appeared they were dead and that the lobbyist momentum was dying down, they gave them just enough of a jolt toward passage that the lobbying machine became refueled as the interests once again became nervous.

Every attempt she made to revive the McAdams bribe incident reached a dead end. Gregory Marshall, the Global Cleanliness insider, could offer no more. He had produced a million in cash and gave it to McAdams.   Period!   Other leads and other possible scandals became shrouded in rumor, innuendo and suspicion.   Try as he would, Pete and his investigatory team couldn't get a handle on any of them.

Common Good and the New GOP flourished, ironically fueled by fear of the very movement designed to curb its activities. The economy went sideways, security issues overwhelmed the Congress, the moral tone went down, nothing moved, the President more frequently said "oh shit." Finally Ethan Allen Aiken was unanimously confirmed as Federal Attorney for the Northeastern District with Senator Stephenson enthusiastically seconding the nomination by her senior partner, James Webster. I warned about this but nobody wanted to believe me. And the treachery had even escaped Pete O'Connor who, like so many of his colleagues, was dangerously close to losing touch.

But in the midst of it all, the parties went on. Openings at the National Gallery. Dinners in Georgetown. Fund raisers for distinguished members of Congress. Testimonials and gridirons celebrating the gridlock. And fund raisers. More fund raisers and extra fund raisers.

By now, even Jo, with all her independence and supposed maverick tendencies, got invited to some of the best parties in town. Through the McAdams affair, her Chairmanship and her reform posture, she had become a celebrity, qualified at last to break bread with Bobby Berry, premier lobbyist, Willa Schramm, Floyd B. Green, Chris Livengood, former Speaker Righter, Waldo Kleppinger, numerous indicted and pardoned patriots and charter members of Common Good and Alcoholics Unanimous.

At one particularly posh assemblage at the French Embassy that I attended, where guests rent their garments in dismay at worldwide ethnic conflicts, while picking away at a buffet of seafood salad, beef tenderloin, wild rice and tri-color sorbet, Jo showed up on her own and was confronted immediately by Floyd B. Green and his celebrity wife, Mary Agnes, familiarly known as M.A. Jo flinched. She hadn't forgotten and she hadn't forgiven. She stared at Green with a cold smile which he chose to ignore.

"Why Josephine, my dear," intoned the Senator. "How wonderful to see you here. Yes sir, real nice." Then the side glance and whisper, so that everyone else in the room would suspect something confidential was going on: "good you're here. Shows you're part of the crowd. You watch, you'll get more comfortable with this as time goes on. Nobody gets compromised by a free drink. It's the American way. Free lunch, free dinners. Nothing like a few drinks with Willa and M.A. to improve the chemistry."

M.A. gave this big grin and blurted out how good it was to see this famous and courageous woman. "I'm a libber at heart myself, you know," she confided to Jo. "But old Floyd here has to watch what he does back in Texas. Always listen to the constituents, he always says and, let me tell you honey, our constituents don't like libbers." Jo said absolutely nothing. Just smiled her cold smile. One of these days, she thought. One of these days.

Over in a corner, surprisingly unnoticed, and carefully watching the movements of the Junior Senator from Vermont, was Ludwig Controller. He sized her up. He sized her down. He stared intently, motionless, utterly preoccupied with his first real-life view of his nemesis. A settled and sullen hatred was evident in his eyes. But he didn't move a muscle. When Willa turned toward him, with Jo on her arm, and it appeared that they would walk his way, he slipped behind a curtain and caught a brief smattering of their conversation. Unknown to me at the time, Controller paled as he thought he heard Jo make one telling comment: "Willa," she apparently said, "I'll weather this. I have more friends than you know. I've got one of the sharpest guys in Washington, Charlie Coons, working with Pete O'Connor. Charlie's playing both sides for the moment but only to keep me informed on what's going on with these guys. It's only a matter of time before we expose a lot of things in this town."

I was standing at the other side of the room, drink in hand, when, out of the corner of my eye I noticed him staring at me, pale and stone faced. What's his problem? Why the evil look? Something's going on? What's Willa saying? What did Jo say when she took her aside so chummily? Did she talk about me? He knows…he knows. Better check on all this tomorrow. For now, another drink and then out of here.

CHAPTER 20

FRAGMENTS OF A FOCUS GROUP

It was not the first time in my political career that I was concerned but it was the first time I really felt threatened. I woke up at 3.20 in the morning in a cold sweat, imagining in my paranoia what revenge would be taken by Controller for my traitorous conduct. Sprayed with a machine gun at the supermarket. Accidentally run over by a mysterious automobile at DuPont Circle. I now knew that Controller knew and I put nothing past him. In retrospect, it's odd that he didn't catch on before. But sometimes guys in his position don't see the obvious right in front of them as they ponder the subtleties and end up outsmarting themselves. One thing kept going around and around in my mind: "shoot her" he said about Jo Stephenson. I remembered Ronnie West almost fainting as I too squirmed in my chair. If he'd shoot her, he sure as hell would shoot me!

If nothing else, my way of life was in jeopardy. I stared out the window into the bleak Georgetown night. It looked just like the foggy street scene in The Exorcist. Would that some sainted cleric would exorcise Ludwig Controller from the body politic. Dawn, where are you when I need you? I staggered over to the liquor cabinet and poured a straight vodka. Hmmmm. Things seemed a little better in no time. I laid my head back on the pillow and, even though I fought it, sleep returned.

I woke with a start as the telephone rang. Oh shit, it's Controller. Or a warning from a mutual friend. Or a threatening phone call. And then the voice message: "Charlie, Hap Mandell here. Come on over today. I'm putting together some new commercials for a candidate for Governor of Florida and sitting in on a focus group of so called average citizens from Virginia. Would love to have your input."

A chance to hide out! No phone calls. No faxes. No lunches on tangential issues. No Jo Stephenson for a change. And no Ludwig Controller. Clearly, Hap didn't know that Controller knew what I was up to. Leave him in the dark. And get inside his little cocoon where the fate of the American people was really decided. Controller? Think about him later. Jo? Get back to her at the end of the day.

At Mandell's think tank, I slipped into a swivel chair behind the one way mirror, eager to watch the focus group Hap had assembled. Like skipping off to a matinee in the middle of the day. And what a show it was.

Twelve average Americans from the nearby suburbs of Virginia, not Beltway types but real Americans, were gathered in the adjoining room to provide a crossectional view of what the country was currently thinking about its President, its government and its politics.

What entices the rank and file into these almost star chamber proceedings is the fee and the food. They rush in, gobble up the buffet lunch and wait in line for their cash compensation, usually $150 for an afternoon or evening of blowing off steam. And we voyeurs, the manipulators of the public arena, hide behind that one way mirror, peering out at the attendees, monitoring not just their words but their so called body language, the inflection, the nuances, the emphasis, the dynamics taking place in this microcosm of America. To preserve their privacy, each participant received the name of a famous celebrity by which they were called for the balance of the focus group. Today, among others, we had Harrison Ford, Madonna, Denzel Washington, Brad Pitt and Rosie O'Donnell.

The soft spoken, reassuring, medium-like woman moderating the discussion had opened by asking opinions of the First Lady.

"SAPPY!" said Harrison.

"Sappy? Did you say…sappy?"

She was taken aback but Harrison held his ground. For a moment, putting down his tuna fish sandwich and allowing the potato chips to be lubricated with diet coke, he repeated himself. "Yeah," he reiterated. "You asked me what I thought of her and I said I thought she was sappy."

"The First Lady…sappy?" asked the Moderator again. She was an intelligent and experienced woman, trained in the art of gently drawing people out on their innermost opinions about public life but "sappy" was hard for her to accept.

After hesitating for a moment, she recovered her poise and directed the question to the other panel members in the room.

"Harrison here thinks the First Lady is sappy. What about the rest of you?" she asked gingerly. "is there anyone else who thinks the First Lady is…hmm…sappy?"

They all sat there solemnly contemplating the question and finally Rosie, the fat one in the corner, spoke up.

"Well," she said slowly in her nasal drawl, "I kinda like think she's a little bit sappy. Like the way she talks and all that."

The Moderator stared, dumbstruck again, for a moment and then ventured forth one more time. "Let's see now," she said with a forced smile on her face. "How many others?"

Silence.

"Well, let me put it this way," she pushed onward. "Do you think she's a little sappy, somewhat sappy, very sappy or not sappy at all?"

"VERY snappy," interjected Harrison, once again stealing the thunder and causing the dynamics of the room to veer in his direction.

And then, suddenly, Madonna, a mod fringie, and stylish brunette spoke up vehemently. "Now wait just a minute!!!!" she declared. Our always responsive moderator, relieved to have the dynamics shifted by another forceful individual, eagerly tossed the ball to her. "Yes, yes, Madonna, do you have something to say?"

"I certainly do," said Madonna, bracelets dangling. "I don't think it's right to call her sappy. After all, she is the First Lady, and while I don't have any time for that lady business, I think she's doing a great job and I'd like to ask Harrison Ford just why he said that."

Before Harrison could respond, the moderator intervened. "Harrison," she said, "perhaps you could define sappy."

"Can't define it," Harrison quickly replied. "Just know it when I see it."

Then all hell broke loose.

"Look, I didn't come here to talk about saps," commented one middle aged male executive type with the Denzel Washington designation. "I'm more concerned about the Muslims than the saps."

"Me too," seconded Brad Pitt, a younger steelworker. "My reserve unit may get called up because of those bastards." It struck me that this attitude was just a little dated.

"Do you distrust the President on that issue?" demanded Elizabeth Taylor in another corner.

"I don't trust nobody," hollered Oprah Winfrey in the back of the room.

"Crime in the streets! Let's talk about that!" shouted an elderly gentleman whose place card designated him Clint Eastwood. "It's gotten so I can't walk outside anymore."

"Families are breaking up. That's why there's so much crime. Return to family values," volunteered Harrison, having abandoned the sap syndrome.

"Well, it's like, I guess, crime maybe is the big issue," commented Rosie. "Like maybe it's kinda scary walking the streets and like getting in the car at night at the shopping center. Things like that."

"You sound like some stupid replay of a daytime talk show," hollered Clint. "And besides, this whole goddam process is corrupt. All those politicians say one thing and do another. It's stressful."

"Yes, say one thing, do another!" shouted Paul Newman in the back of the room.

"Very stressful, very stressful."

Very sappy or very stressful or both? What indeed were we to believe? Amidst the chaos and cacophony, I stopped laughing and glanced over at Hap. "Hap, this is incredible," I commented. "Is it always like this lately?"

"You're really slipping, Charlie," Hap replied. "There are significant things going on here. Sappy, for example, is a profound departure from mere untrustworthiness. It indicates a level of scorn not before seen in focus group sessions. It contains irreverent implications reaching deep into the American psyche. The fact that no one except the fringie spoke up in defense of the First Lady is disturbing indeed. This whole session is trending toward the complete breakdown of authority and respect. And the voters are getting so high strung that they're getting awfully stressed out. I've seen it elsewhere. It's forcing us to reshape our commercials. In fact, I'm already thinking of a slogan for my candidate in Florida. SMART, NOT SAPPY. That should do it. Or maybe SINCERE AND SENSIBLE, NOT SAPPY OR STRESSFUL. Oh well, something like that will occur to me as I analyze this stuff more closely."

As we peered out into the focus session, Harrison was now crushing his diet coke can as Madonna, with considerable vehemence, was pointing her finger right at him. Brad Pitt had grabbed five of the dozen cookies on the table, diverting the attention and inviting the disgust of at least half a dozen other participants. The Moderator was pleading for a semblance of order when Oprah shouted: "tell those bastards behind that phony mirror to come out here and be identified! We will not be manipulated any further."

At that moment, almost as if by some irresistible collective momentum, the group surged toward the mirror, beating against it, scratching and banging bracelets against the glass.

"More cookies!" Brad hollered.

"Bring us more chips!" demanded Madonna.

"We will not be used!" declared Clint Eastwood.

"Money! We want our money!" cried Elizabeth Taylor.

"I want my free parking pass stamped now!" insisted Paul Newman.

"Let us out of here!" hollered Harrison Ford.

Instantly, Hap scrambled for the door, calling for me to follow him as the Moderator was insisting to the group that "no one's watching, I can assure you. Please, please sit down. We'll get more cookies and chips!"

We raced for the hallway, turned a corner and hopped on an elevator that would take us to the commercial production studio.

"My God, Hap, what's going on?" I asked in astonished terror. I had been in this business for a long time and thought I had seen and experienced just about everything. But the latent resentment and grasping anger of these so called average citizens was frightening, a new and ominous development in the body politic.

Apparently Hap had become more accustomed to such outbursts. "Calm down, Charlie," he said nervously. "Calm down. Everything will be okay."

"Are you okay?"

"Yes, yes, I'm okay."

"We'd better talk."

"No, it's okay. Everything's gonna be okay."

The banality of moviespeak, I thought.

In any event, we were soon far from the madding focus crowd, once again ensconced in comfy swivel chairs, watching the production of Hap's latest senior citizen commercial for his candidate in Florida.

"This guy's an asshole," Hap began. "Not much of a chance. But big bucks. Really big bucks. One thing we can do with him is the old fart bit. The incumbent Senator voted for a less costly Medicare program to cover the cost of prescription drugs. The Retirees Association almost shit themselves. That old bag with the white hair down there on the stage is the President of the Silver Foxes Association. Name's Granny Gooch. Perfect. Wait'll you hear here go after the Senator."

Hap waved at Granny and blew her a kiss. Granny stared back. Didn't seem to think much of Hap.

"Let's give it our all today, Granny," Hap called out.

"Just you wait, Hap," Granny assured him. "I've got my lines memorized and I'm ready to go!"

In a few minutes, the cameras were rolling, Granny in her rocking chair, cup of tea on the serving table, fire crackling in the fireplace, Whistler's Mother in the background.

"Got that Whistler's Mother at CVS," Hap proclaimed proudly. "Two bucks and two more for the frame. Fitting, don't you think?"

"We'll see," I said.

And the commercial began, Granny looking pained and deprived, speaking right into the camera with a combination of hurt and indignation.

"Hello, my name is Elivra Gooch. Old timers in Florida just call me Granny. I'm gettin' old but I'm still chipper enough to fight for the things us seenyrs need and want.

"Six years ago, us seenyurs helped Senator Green get elected. But we've been betrayed.

"Dickie Green voted against our Medicare prescription drug bill so now we don't get all the benefits we're entitled to.

"This year, it's gonna be different. The Silver Foxes are comin' out in force to help Judd Childress beat that two timer.

"And we need you to join us. Let's show that turncoat he can't do that to us seenyurs. I'll sure be looking for all of you to stand up and be counted in November. Let's show that traitor that our memories aren't failing yet. And be sure to vote for Judd Childress on November 5th."

Cut!

"How's that, Hap?" Granny called out.

"Fine, Granny, just fine," Hap replied. "Next time, let's just put a little more emphasis into the us seenyurs line. Try US SEENYURRS! Just a bit more selfish. You know how to do it."

"Like this Hap?...US SEEEEENYURRS!!!"

"Great Granny, great. A little sneer. Drive it home. Revenge, Granny, revenge. Kick some ass on this one."

Granny rubbed her nose and went into deep thought, assimilating the required inflection to drive the point home. I took the opportunity to ask Hap about the issue.

"How many dollars are involved in their bill Hap?" I asked.

"Oh, I don't know. Probably break the trust fund," he replied.

"That much?"

"Oh, several billion."

"Several billion! Hap, that's catastrophic! Don't you think this is overdoing it?"

"Listen, Charlie, them 'seenuyrs' don't want to spend a penny if they can help it. And besides, who gives a damn about the numbers? It's the treachery that counts."

"But it's really excessive Hap," I persisted. "And besides, what about the voters who do care about the deficit?"

"Just finished a poll in Florida last week. Only 4.5% give a damn about the deficit. Do you know how many seenyurrs are in Florida?"

I did indeed know how many "seennyurs" were in Florida.

As the second take on the commercial was being readied, I slipped out of my swivel chair and said: "look, Hap, I've got to go. We'll talk about this later, okay? See you soon."

He looked around as I briskly headed for the door. He didn't seem that concerned. He knew, as I knew, that Granny would likely produce 75% of the seennyurs vote in the state of Florida. Some years younger than me, the difference was that Hap had grown up on MTV. He would soon experiment with computerized dot messages and wave front technology. Something the founding fathers hadn't thought about.

CHAPTER 21

THE BELTWAY VS. BURLINGTON

They weren't returning my phone calls.

I had reached the nadir, the lowest level of American rejection.

They actually weren't returning my phone calls. Now I know that word was getting around that I wasn't exactly one of the boys anymore but I'd known a lot of these guys for years and didn't think they would desert me altogether. Besides, they had to think that they could learn more from me than I would learn from them.

I called Ronnie West five times in the following two days and he was either out, busy, on another call or in a meeting. Meetings! Meetings! Meetings! Busy! Busy! Busy! Everybody in this country is either on a plane, in a meeting, on a cell phone or surfing the web and communicating by e-mail.

I called Rick Brewster three times and he was answering quorum calls.

I called Hap back but he must not have gotten the message because he didn't call back either.

I called Tommy Ragin and Buddy Dartman. Out of town…Tommy to collect his latest five figure speaking fee and Buddy to collect his six figure consulting bonus for a recent primary victory in California.

257

I even called Floyd B. Green but he couldn't take my call.

But the unkindest cut of all was that Dawn didn't return my phone calls. It was bad enough that I had to be a reformer. But did I have to be a celibate one?

Anyway, it didn't take long for me to get the message even if I didn't get the phone calls. Despite my naïve belief that friends would still be friends, Controller was freezing me out. They dare not be discovered talking to me. I was no longer a player. I was no longer "one of ours." I was being excommunicated from the club. And I had the door shut in my face at Common Greed...er...Good.

And so, there would be no scenes or confrontations. No "you dirty little bastard" shouting matches with the monster. Just the freeze. Like nothing happened. Cut me off. Cease all communication. If they ran into me, they would be polite. Talk about the weather. Move on briskly. Not even a reference to the reality. I would become a nonperson. And he would hope that I'd honor the code at least to the point of not ratting on him.

In a sense, I was relieved. I still had income from the think tank. He apparently didn't intend to take drastic action. Yet, I was free to help Jo without playing double agent.

And boy, did she need it.

Slowly but deliberately, the wheels of the political system began to turn, squeezing the state of Vermont in a relentless effort to destroy Josephine

Stephenson and the independent movement. And all in response to the machinations of a handful of politicians and operators acting under the banner of Ludwig Controller.

It was the Beltway versus Burlington. And the Beltway versus Bennington. The Beltway Buddies against the Green Mountain Boys. That woman was to be blamed. It was she who brought this about. And she whose popular support and effectiveness must be destroyed before she could do further damage.

The much needed highway maintenance funds were denied, causing an uproar in the local media, fueled finally by that other Senator, the Honorable Mr. Webster, accusing Stephenson and her staff of gross incompetence in failing to insure that the required documents were in order. Burlington was then denied its enterprise zone money with Stephenson's local staff held responsible for failure to conform to regulations in supporting the request.

"The American people don't need Senators who can't deliver," solemnly proclaimed the deliverable Senator Bushey.

"The American people want results," intoned the dedicated Senator Bagot.

"The American people need elected representatives who will look after their everyday needs," preached the righteous Senator Green.

"The American people! The American people! What do these guys know about what the American people want?" shouted Pete O'Connor at one particular moment of frustration. "They don't give a shit what the American people want and know what they want even less if, in fact, the American people even know what they want!"

"Be cool," soothed Maureen Sullivan.

"Oh...cool!...cool!...the word of the moment. The word of the millenium. Why does everything have to be cool?" demanded Pete.

It didn't take me long to size up the situation: for Stephenson and her staff, all bets were off. Thrown totally on the defensive, they abandoned activities connected with the Ethics Subcommittee and started to explain why applications for federal money weren't flowing smoothly. And so, in explaining, they were already in trouble. In reality, little had happened. Nothing was really wrong. A few blanks not filled in here and there but what was going on had little to do with staff competence. It had to do with an elaborately constructed plot to do her in.

Astonished at the succession of setbacks, the state's newspapers and other media responded in traditional and predictable fashion, urging their new celebrity Senator to stick to the state's business and bring home the bacon.

Joining in the chorus of Bushey, Bagot and Green, Senator Webster expressed his "shock and dismay" in repeated comments to the press, personally visiting the state to "set things right, find out what's going on and turn this situation around." He would be the ultimate savior and, if all went well, Stephenson would be the ultimate loser. "I'm shocked and appalled" he would say, more in feigned sorrow than genuine anger.

The fiascoes, one after the other, attracted increasing national attention. "Dashed Hopes" headlined Populist Magazine in a cover story featuring the attractive blonde Senator, glass in hand, at the French Embassy being whispered to by Floyd B. Green. "Failed Reformer?" questioned The Times, not yet wishing to abandon its darling and therefore formulating its profile with a question mark. The Post focused on Pete O'Connor, quoting numerous insiders in Washington charging that "he was never any good anyway. Dreamer. Bright but not a go getter. Her Biggest mistake." Even Bernie the Congressman had to admit that it looked pretty bad for his independent ally.

Pete didn't "cool it," but did manage to regain his calm. "Jo," he insisted, "stop explaining and running all over the state. Remember, when you start to explain you're already in trouble. And you're getting yourself in trouble. I'm telling you, this is not our fault. There's something else going on here."

"Then whose fault is it Pete? And why are we getting blamed? Isn't it a fact that there were some errors in those filings?" Jo was sitting at her desk, attempting to remain calm too, but clearly bruised by the unexpected attacks and flailing about trying to plug the holes.

"A few errors, yes. But for Christ's sake, nothing to warrant this. You should have seen some of the stuff I saw when I worked for the Speaker. As for whose fault it is, I really believe we're being set up.

And it's just the beginning." Pete was trying to keep his balance, refusing to be shaken by adversity.

The pressure was beginning to show on the Senator. Suddenly she began looking her age. Overnight she was forty five, going on fifty. Dark rings of sleepless nights on her fair countenance. Sadness in her eyes. Panic in her voice. Frustration in her movements as she would tromp about the office, alternately fuming and complaining. But she wouldn't cry. And hadn't cried but once, that time in the car coming home from the brutal assault. Every once in a while, the memory came back, frightening her again, awakening a vague desire to do something about the cities, about race, about crime and about drugs. Drugs? Crime? Race? Cities? When caught between highway funds and political payoffs? What time was there for such incidentals when there were more cutting political issues out there. The politics of the royal court, not of the street, more like the age of Louis XIV and George 111 than Jo Stephenson, eras when the seeds of collapse were sown by excessive preoccupation with ego, vanity, advancement, petty nuances.

But no time for philosophizing. She walked out the main door of her office. Mistake. A dozen rude microphones shoved in her face, cameras in the background, reporters shouting.

"Aren't you letting your state down?"

"Senator, will there be a meeting of the subcommittee soon?"

"When?"

"Would you care to comment on the statement by Senator Green that it seems you've failed to take command of this situation?"

"Your Governor says he blames you. What's your reaction?"

"Aren't you a disappointment to women everywhere?"

"Is reform dead and did you kill it?"

What question to answer first within this demeaning, humiliating and downright rude avalanche of viciousness?

And then she just closed her eyes, sighed, moved on, waved her hand and left them shouting behind her, pursuing her, down the corridor, to the elevator, onto the street where she finally hailed a cab in desperation as the cameras flashed and the reporters screamed. The headlines would be predictable: "Stephenson Avoids Press;" "Stephenson Ducks;" "Open Government Senator Closes Mouth in Public."

TV news would be no kinder. "LATE BREAKING NEWS! LATE BREAKING NEWS! In a surprising display of collapse under pressure, Vermont's Independent Senator, Josephine Stephenson, ran from the cameras." Barry Queen, Dean of Talk Shows would take endless questions from all over America wondering what happened to their heroine while Floyd Green would sit there across the table smirking and shaking his head in dismay. "Backfire," recently expanded by the addition of two disgraced and discredited politicians to its band of fat and wearisome Alcoholics Unanimous public affairs commentators wired by the Ass Kissinger Society, would bellow at one another about the status of the investigations and the sorry state of the state of Vermont.

Funny thing, though. In his daily polling of the people of Vermont, Hap Mandell, to his astonishment, began to see an increase in favorability ratings for the Senator. And her negatives, which had been on the increase, had not only peaked but begun to slip.

Why? Probably because some people aren't as dumb as the politicians think. I've always said: never rely on the intelligence of the average voter. And never underestimate it. Hey guys, they ain't so dumb up there in the mountains.

And now, re-enter Mary Magdalene, the ultimate talentless rock performer, who had been at that party that night when young Raymond lost his innocence to sex and drugs. It was she who had lifted the tapes and it wasn't long before the National Leerer carried the story. According to that revered scandal sheet, she developed a sullen resentment of the public figure of Josephine Stephenson, whom she thought was getting more TV and magazine coverage than she in, of all things, some starched and priggish Puritanical crusade and started taking swipes at the Senator at fashionable Beverly Hills parties.

"She's no fuckin' good," she was reported as shouting, in her very best display of discernment. "She gets her way, the whole sex business gets regulated. Can't you just see her, in her prissy, self righteous way, looking down her New England nose at me? At us? Bitch!"

Then pretty boy Denny Graves, he of the smarmy smile, who was also present that night, reminded Mary Magdalene that on those tapes was none other than Mrs. Stephenson's little boy Raymond.

The way, from Beverly Hills thru LasVegas to a Mafia den in New Orleans, had led directly to none other than Ludwig Controller himself. And as I had always feared, and warned, from the moment I knew they were in Controller's possession those many months ago, we all awoke one bright snowy weekend morning to that front page expose in The National Leerer which delineated, in clinical detail, the sex and drugs escapades of the son of the Senator from Vermont.

Raymond was not to be found. Jo and George were beside themselves. Now, the political press was augmented by the sensationalist press. There was not a hotel room to be had in Burlington. Even Will Sawyer, the kind, calm, thoughtful and insightful interpreter of the era, sensing a buck, arrived with camera crew, "trying to make sense of this thing." It was the first time he had been back to the state since he had been charged with driving under the influence.

And I too flew to Vermont to assist in any way I could.

Jo, then George, made twenty calls in the space of a few hours. Every time, the dull monotone of the answering machine. "Hi, this is Ray. I'm not here right now but if you'll leave a message after the beep, I'll get back to you as soon as possible." And then the beep and the futility of leaving a message. Just the disembodied voice. Was the kid still alive?

Each time the phone rang, Jo leapt for the receiver. Awful. In her desperate need to be in contact with Raymond, everyone but Raymond was calling: the curious neighbor, the concerned constituent, the outraged citizen, the well meaning friend, and most of the time, the calls would be interrupted by the damnable call waiting. Not once but twice during a single call. The perversity of things. But what could she do but hold and hold and take the next one, hoping desperately that it would be him. Finally, the call waiting interruption that mattered. The FBI in Washington. The Los Angeles office had information that may be of interest to the Senator.

May be of interest! May be of interest! What is it? Of course, it's of interest.

"Senator, we thought you would want to know that we have been informed by LAPD that your son, Raymond, was picked up by the Highway Patrol this morning speeding at 110 miles an hour on the Pacific Coast Highway. He appeared to be out of control, driving under the influence, extremely high state of nervous tension. He is in the Cedars of Lebanon Hospital and has been receiving sedatives to calm him down. As far as we know, he is physically alright. Please stand by. We will get back to you as the situation clarifies."

What is this, she wondered? A Sit Rep? This coldly analytical, matter of fact commentary about her own flesh and blood.

"But is he alright? Can I talk to him? Please let me know how I can reach him. I must talk to him. Should we go to Los Angeles?" She was desperate, out of control herself, with George standing by the phone, catching words and phrases in fragments. Nothing else mattered now but their dear son. Oh God, let everything be okay.

"You can do what you want, Senator," said the voice, coldly. "Our only role in this is to keep you informed. We will call back with additional information."

Then the click. And Jo, burying her head in her hands, looked up to tell me. "I heard it," I said. "No need to go through it again. I'll make the arrangements to go to Los Angeles as quickly as possible."

CHAPTER 22

HOLLYWOOD VILLAINS

I waited outside the hospital room as Jo and George went in to see Raymond. I never did find out what happened but George did make arrangements for Raymond to return to Burlington and stay with him at Stowe until a hearing would take place in Los Angeles. In ninety days.

I helped Jo fend off the press in the main lobby of the hospital. "You get Ray," I said to George, "and go out the back way and hail a cab. I'll go out with Jo and hold them at bay, return to the fifth floor and act as if we're staying here. That way, they won't get pictures of you and Ray. Then we can slip out the back and we can be on our way."

How many times, in how many political situations, had I done this sort of thing before.

"Senator! Senator!" screamed the reporters, microphones obscenely shoved in her face, cameras going.

"Senator, is it true your son attempted suicide?"

"Not true," she deadpanned.

"Senator, doesn't this say something questionable about your adherence to family values?" shouted another?

"It has nothing to do with family values," she shot back.

"Senator, Mary Magdalene says this proves you and your son are just like the rest," came the question.

"I don't respond to vulgar people," Jo replied haughtily, wondering if she had said the wrong thing. How will that look in print, I wondered.

"Senator, Denny Graves says that, despite it all he still admires you. How do you respond to that?"

"What an insane question!" Jo retorted. "He admires me! I don't need his admiration. What did he do to my son?"

"Senator, Senator Floyd B. Green said today that this won't help your efforts to clean up Washington if you can't clean up your own family."

We've been out here now for several minutes. Does anyone care about my son's condition?"

"We're here to evaluate this scandal in light of your public position, not to determine the status of a drunken driver," came a rude retort. "But now that you mention it, how is the drunken driver?"

"You people are really obscene," Jo began to lecture and then stopped. "But, for the record, let me tell any of you who care about the life of a human being, that he is in satisfactory condition. He will leave the hospital shortly and return with us to Burlington pending a hearing on the charges in ninety days."

"What's that," came a shout. "Preferential treatment for the powerful? How can they let him leave the state?"

"You'll have to talk to the LAPD," Jo replied, honestly not knowing how George arranged the deal.

"Why's he in the hospital anyway? He's not hurt. Is it a nervous breakdown?"

"I would say he suffered a temporary emotional setback after the story broke," Jo replied carefully. "But we believe he will be alright with some rest."

"Coddling the criminal?" came a question.

Jo shuddered. "I won't dignify that one," she replied.

"What was he doing with the Teen Team anyway?...Does this tarnish your reformer image?... Isn't your whole posture hypocritical?...Senator... Senator...isn't this embarrassing to you?...doesn't it embarrass your state?...isn't your husband embarrassed?...is that son of yours embarrassed?"...a chorus of cacophonous voices, bodies shoving each other, ramming the microphones into her face, cameras flashing.

"That's all for now," I interjected, seeing that Jo was internally shaken and dismayed but maintaining her outward composure. I caught sight of the side entrance to the emergency room and ushered her inside the door where they could not follow but continued to bellow and herd around the narrow corridor. Walking through the emergency room, before we could be stopped for inappropriately using this exit, we caught sight of George and Raymond slipping quietly into the cab outside the window. We ran and continued to run until we just barely jumped in the back as the cameras and the reporters came rushing around the building on a tip from a hospital official.

And the cab didn't stop until we reached the airport. And we were on the plane before the maddening herd could again jam those microphones in her face, get Raymond on tape or take flashbulb pictures for tomorrow's early editions.

And with a short stopover in Pittsburgh, where I changed planes for Washington, they once again were home in Vermont where, to their enormous relief and amazement, no members of the media were at the airport to greet them.

....

In the nation's Capital that day, Floyd B. Green exploded with fury.

By now, he did, as they say, "hate her with a passion." Going ballistic, as the staff always described it, he picked up the phone to the outer office, piercing the hearts of his many aides with dread. "Jackman, get in here," he shouted to his Press Secretary. And Jackman timidly entered the inner sanctum, never venturing closer to the Senator's desk than the great seal of the Lone Star State of Texas. He and the other aides had measured the distance that Green could throw the phone at them and it never reached past the seal. This time, it reached past the seal and almost caught poor Jackman on the chin.

....

To make things worse, I was tipped off that, in the quiet of his office, the Honorable Ethan Allen Aiken was reading, with eye popping interest, the recent publicly disclosed 1040 Form of Josephine and George Stephenson.

"Half million dollars in legal fees!" he shouted aloud. "There's got to be something there. Conflict of interest. Absolutely! Conflict of interest! I'll find it and send the sonofabitch to jail and that wife of his down to defeat. Let the world get ready for United States Senator Ethan Allen Aiken of the sovereign state of Vermont!"

....

As Floyd Green's telephone flew past the great seal of Texas, four more families, two each in Denton and Rockwell Counties, outside of his hometown of Dallas, tried to sign on for welfare as we used to know it.

As Mary Magdalene extolled her venomous vulgarity to Ludwig Controller, Jefferson County, Colorado, opened its twelfth homeless shelter as two more kidnappings of young girls were reported in Southern California.

And as Ethan Allen Aiken peered lasciviously at the Stephenson's tax return, two families in Middlebury saw the bank foreclose on their home mortgages.

But we are assured by President and Congress alike that the economy has never been better and we're all more well off than we were eight years ago. Reassuring.

Inside the Beltway, Stratton, Berry and Snow picked up its first $200,000 retainer from the nervous cable industry association as the game of "Put in the Bill, Scare the Interests and Pay the Lobbyists" continued its unrelenting march to the bank.

And the distinguished Mr. Berry called me as I returned to my office, trying to get Jo's private telephone number in Stowe.

"What do you want that for?" I demanded.

"The kid's a celebrity case. High profile. Certain I can get him off," Berry replied.

"She can't afford you," I replied.

"Sure she can," Berry answered confidently. "Just $475 an hour, the usual celebrity Beltway rate. What's so bad about that?"

"FUCK YOU!!!" I shouted and slammed down the phone.

There was nothing, however, to match the passivity of the organized women's movement. "Just because she wears a skirt doesn't mean she's one of us," declared Wanda Guzguz, icon of the crusade. "Well," more demurely commented Jeanne Engels, President of Women United, "we had such hopes and expectations for her. But you know, really, she has chosen to chart her own course, not ours. And we can hardly be blamed for not screaming in support of someone who has not seen fit to unreservedly support us on our agenda before anything else."

CHAPTER 23

THE FALL OF THE HOUSE OF CARDS

R. Wentworth Brewster's Administrative Assistant was screaming into the telephone, fighting the age old battle of "Who Gets the Credit" in a conference call with the Administrative Assistants of California's two United States Senators.

"We're putting this release out!" he shouted. "Because we deserve the credit because we did all the work, you bastards!."

"The hell you are," came one reply. "My Senator gets the credit because he introduced the original bill."

"We're taking the credit for this one, big time" came the authoritative voice of the third administrative assistant, "because my Senator's the Senior Senator and nobody would have moved this thing without us."

But now I couldn't stay away. I spent hours at Jo's office. I guess I really was secretly in love with her but that wasn't the whole story. For a groupie like me, this was the most incredible political situation I had ever been in. And, as I walked into Brewster's Office, overhearing this 'who gets the credit' battle, more common than the weather report on Capitol Hill, I was reminded of the sign sitting on the desk of the head of Catholic Relief Services many years before: "imagine how much good could be done if no one cared who got the credit."

The argument got hotter. Tim McMillan, Brewster's A.A. finally shouted into the phone, "if you people insist on doing this to us, we'll accuse you both of…of…flip-flopping!"

"Flip-flopping!" came the screams from the other end of the receiver. "Flip-flopping! You dare to accuse my Senator of flip-flopping!" "You're the flip-floppers," came the other voice. "You're the ones who put in that resolution about cutting defense spending. Flip-floppers my ass!"

"No," shouted McMillan. "Fuck you guys. Both your Senators actually voted to cut the defense budget and then the both of you voted for the final appropriation. We'll accuse you not only of flip-flopping but hypocrisy. And we're putting out the goddamn release now! We'll say we're shocked and amazed! Shocked and appalled that you endangered this project and then flip-flopped in order to take the credit!" McMillan slammed the phone down.

"What's that all about," I asked, with a trace of a smirk on my face. "Who's flip-flopping on what?"

"Oh, I don't know," McMillan replied with a huge amount of exasperation in his voice. "The repair of some submarine at San Diego Naval Base. But it's 200 jobs, goddamnit and they're all ours! And $250 million into the local economy and a precedent for more submarine work. Rick's the main man on Defense Appropriations. And you know he's running for Governor. Now these guys are flip-flopping. The both of them did a reversal on defense spending to please the Hollywood and San Francisco crowd and then turned around and muscled the Defense

Department to approve the work after we put the money in the Appropriations Bill. To me, that's a flip-flop. But what do they do? They accuse us of flip-flopping because Rick had a meeting with some peace lobbyists and put in a resolution to cut defense spending. But he really didn't flip-flop because he never tried to stop the money. And nobody believes Rick's a peacenik anyway. Between you and me, he hates the both of them with a passion. Big time. I don't have to tell you, Charlie. You know the game."

No, he didn't have to tell me. And I didn't want to listen either. Prior to leaving Jo's office for Brewster's, I had just cast aside The Washington Post where a story on the President's "A" White House guest list was juxtaposed with a story on the crack epidemic in Southeast Capitol.

"Apres nous, le deluge," I murmured as I went down the hall. "Tuchman on the British preoccupation with the affairs of the court while losing the Revolutionary War. Next Stop, Washington, DC, The Beltway, USA. Folly will be our downfall. Thank you Laocoon. And Cassandra."

"Anyway," McMillan continued nervously, "if we don't get the credit for this and avoid that flip-flopping charge, I might as well send my resume to the nearest defense think tank. What do you want anyway, Charlie? Christ, you've got real problems with that whacko Senator of yours. It must really be embarrassing. And you're a traitor to boot!"

"Embarrassing? Far from it." I wasn't going to fall into the embarrassment trap. "The Senator would like the Congressman to use his influence to report out the Political Campaign Reform Act," I announced as we walked into the inner office and closed the door.

"Then why doesn't the Senator call the Congressman herself," asked McMillan, feigning formality.

"She did. But the Congressman doesn't return her phone calls," I replied directly.

"Doesn't return her phone calls?" McMillan asked innocently. "My, I've never heard that complaint before about the Congressman." He began to smile.

"Yes, doesn't return her phone calls. Come on, Tim," I insisted. "You know what that means. When someone in this town doesn't return your phone calls, you have a real problem. Big time. I suspect that the Congressman doesn't intend to return her phone calls. I believe the Congressman is trying to send the Senator a message in not returning her phone calls."

"A message?" McMillan asked. "What possible message could that be? Could it be that the Congressman thinks that the Senator is off her rocker? Far out? Cuckoo? Self destructing with her lecherous little offspring? An embarrassment to herself and Vermont? Screwing up projects for her state? We may be whores, Charlie, but we're smart enough to bring home the submarines. Besides, over here in the House our members are getting pretty fed up with the Senate. They're always asking our people to vote on things they don't want to vote on and we're not going to do it anymore. We won't vote if they don't vote!"

"Bullshit," I quickly retorted. "You know what's going on and so do I. She's being set up and shot down. And all these little games are being played as this whole goddamn place is falling apart."

"I don't see it that way," McMillan replied, getting more uncomfortable. "Anyway, we've got our own problems. Those bills of hers are bullshit and you know it, Charlie. Just a way to embarrass the rest of us. Going fucking nowhere. Let's face it Charlie. Rick doesn't want to see her, talk to her, have anything to do with her. He's got two fund raisers this week for the Governorship and the New GOP crowd is coming out in force. All we have to do is really get behind that bill and we're dead. Common Gree...er...Good would kill us. It's bad enough that he pissed off Controller and the boys by not being able to use his influence with her to block Pete O'Connor. You know that. He won't say anything. But that old relationship with Josephine Stephenson is all over. In fact, Charlie, just like our relationship with you."

I avoided the personal bit and concentrated on Jo. "Blood's thicker than water, Tim," I observed. "And the two of them go back a long way."

"Yeah, well, this time the blood's on the floor. And if you're gonna throw club member lines at me, I'll throw one at you. Sometimes personal loyalty asks too much." Tim was proud of himself for that one.

"Okay," I responded as he went for the door. "Okay. But don't ask our help in that campaign of yours. How would you like the nation's only independent Senator coming out to California to accuse your boy of being against reform?"

"Don't mean shit," Tim shot back. "By the time the campaign begins, she'll look so ridiculous, we'll pay her way out to campaign against us. Don't you get it? It's not the issues. It's the money, stupid! And besides, she has her own campaign to run."

I, of all people, knew there was some truth to that. I shrugged my shoulders, gave Tim one last look and left the office.

"Better get back to political consulting while there's time, Charlie," Tim McMillan announced as the door closed. He then got back on the phone. "Listen, you shit, we're taking the credit for this goddamn submarine and you keep your big deal Senator out of it!"

A dismal situation, I thought as I returned to the Senate side of The Capitol.

Who gets the credit?

Somebody's flip-flopping.

Phone calls not returned.

Politicians embarrassed.

Elected officials shocked and appalled.

Hypocrisy in high office.

Loyalties overturned.

Not to even begin to think about a stagnating economy, corporate felons, falling stock prices, decaying cities or terrorists everywhere.

"He's not going to play, Jo," I deadpanned.

"Tell me something I don't already know," Jo retorted.

It was difficult to determine the exact state of mind of the Junior Senator from Vermont after the shattering events of the recent past. It was as if she had withdrawn from the ordinary activities of everyday life. Distant and distracted, she went through the motions mechanically, neither strengthened by adversity nor caving in to its painful psychic pressures. At times she seemed philosophical; at other times depressed. At one moment she was counting her blessings ("how lucky we really are despite it all") and at another, she seemed to be turning dangerously cynical, insular and robotic. She didn't look particularly well, too heavy makeup masking lack of sleep, that pasty face look of someone in trouble. More indifferent than ever to what she wore, her hairstyle. At times, Pete swore she was hitting the bottle, odorless vodka in that glass of orange juice on her desk in the morning that seemed to get paler every day. But he really couldn't tell and besides, wouldn't have blamed her.

She found it painful and difficult to call Stowe, almost wanting to put the Raymond thing out of her head. Sturdy George was handling that and at that point she found it difficult to adjust to the intimacy of family matters. She avoided newspapers and talk shows, wrapped in an official cocoon. All the shows talked about Raymond. Mary Magdalene started shooting off her mouth to the tabloid press. The proper people of Vermont were tolerant but eyebrows started to rise as the media poured it on.

The thing that really frustrated her was the inability to get something done. She believed deep inside that, given time, Raymond would survive. The boy had grit after all. She could handle that if only she wasn't being attacked from all sides for failure to deliver for the state, failure to move her reform bills, failure to promote women's issues, failure to keep The Times and the Post happy, failure to attend endless academic conferences and give lofty speeches to cerebral congregations. Failure, in short, to play the game and not play the game at one and the same time. Phone calls from the state and to her local offices were heavy, running 2-1 against her for all of the above reasons. Constituents complaining about the service they weren't getting on their social security checks, Medicare billings, veterans benefits and passport applications. But Hap Mandell continued to poll the voters, not the callers and the voters were holding firm. Only Jo didn't know it. All she knew was the reality of the phone call and the phone call was from the voter most likely to bitch and complain.

"But I have to get to Europe tomorrow and you said you would help me get my passport in 48 hours!"

"My direct deposit didn't come on time and I want you to demand an answer from Social Security."

Her off the cuff remarks were becoming clipped, curt and cynical. She was tense and testy, prickly and on edge. But through it all Pete and I detected some inner strength, felt she still was keeping a steady hand beneath the turmoil. Who knows about this game, Pete would muse. This whole house of cards could collapse tomorrow. It's so goddamn artificial that one little crack could bring the decline and fall of the Beltway empire.

And so we stared at one another in one of those frozen moments in time when neither quite knew what to do next except, maybe, have a drink and forget about it. Except that, deep down, I knew that a major confrontation was coming. I wasn't sure yet quite what it would be or how it would play out but I knew something had to give. And then Maureen buzzed from the outer office.

"Jo, someone on the phone says she has to speak to you, somebody named Marita Johnson-Smith."

"I don't know anybody named Marita Johnson-Smith," Jo said with irritation in her voice.

"Well, she says you do," Maureen insisted. "Says she's a Senate staffer you met not long ago."

"Maureen, I've met a thousand Senate staffers. Tell her I'm not here. Or find out what she wants."

"Okay," Maureen replied, somewhat offended at the dismissive tone of her sometime best friend, now boss. "I'm just trying to get this call off my back since we're getting so many from constituents complaining about everything that's going on."

Jo didn't appreciate the dig but Maureen, feeling left out, just had to get her knife in. Pay attention to me too, Jo, she was really saying.

Jo looked over at Pete and me, shaking her head in feigned weariness at the constant interruptions and irrelevancies of this ridiculously public life.

"Marita Johnson-Smith," I said aloud. "Marita Johnson-Smith. I think I know her. African American woman. Worked for Wilson McAdams. Before that for Floyd B. Green, better known as the Windbag. I wonder why she's calling you."

The buzzer again. "Jo," Maureen advised (as noted, Maureen never liked it when she wasn't invited into the inner sanctum for Pete and Charlie talks and her voice showed it), "this woman says that she drove you home one night?" Maureen seemed puzzled and suspicious. "Says she dropped you off at your apartment and you would remember?"

And then it suddenly hit her. "Oh God, yes, of course. The one who…" She didn't finish, not wanting to broadcast what really happened that night. "Maureen, Maureen," she said excitedly, "did she leave a number?"

"No she didn't," Maureen replied offhandedly. "Said she'll try to call back. I didn't give her any encouragement." Poor Maureen, now a full fledged staffer, insecure like all the rest, instantly suspecting that there was competition on the horizon from another woman, with skill and experience on the Hill. "If she gets in here to see Jo, what does that mean for me? She wants my job! Gotta cut her off at the pass" was the thought that went buzzing through her mind, the thought that haunted them all on the Hill as they systematically finessed and kept at arm's length all those other bright people with all those nice little resumes.

"Maureen, we've got to find her," Jo almost shouted in the phone. She was on her feet, exhibiting the first signs of life in days. "She helped me so much and I didn't even get her name. I have to thank her and there I went and did some stupid thing like not take her phone call!"

"I think I know where to find her," Pete said casually.

Maureen grimaced on the other end of the phone. Goddamn Pete to the rescue again. Knows everything.

"Where Pete?" Jo asked anxiously as she put down the phone, causing Maureen even greater position anxiety.

"When McAdams died I think she left the staff and went to one of the subcommittees," he replied.

"One of the subcommittees," she replied, frustration in her voice. "Which one Pete? There are so many subcommittees that it would take us a year to get through them all!"

"No, no, let me think. Yeah, I remember. They put her down in the basement. Like they did with me. The subcommittee on Independent Agencies of the Senate Foreign Relations Committee. She handles visas, green cards, things like that. Don't ask me why she's there. Maybe they wanted to bury her but not eliminate her."

Jo was already looking through the Capitol directory and found it. "Extension 4221," she announced triumphantly as she dialed the phone.

"Yes, hello, this is Senator Stephenson," she proclaimed authoritatively. "I want to speak with Marita Johnson-Smith."

And so they finally made contact and after the niceties, Marita said, "Senator, I really can't talk now but I think I can be of assistance to you at this difficult time. Could we perhaps meet early this evening?"

Jo had no idea what was coming, hesitated, thought she had done her duty with effusive thanks and apologies, thought the better of it and said: "why yes, of course. Could you come to my office at 5?"

And so the revelations began.

Maureen's insecurities aside, formalities out of the way, and with Pete and me sitting to the side providing a bridge of acquaintance with Marita Johnson-Smith, they got down to business. She was an extremely attractive woman, I reminded myself. "Classy dame," Pete whispered. Well dressed. Great hairdo. Poised. Serious. And articulate.

"Senator," Marita began, cooly, precisely and deliberately, "I admire what you're trying to do and I've watched with sympathy the difficulties they've got you in. So I just made up my mind that I must come forward and share with you some material which may help you in your efforts."

Jo wasn't expecting this. Her interest heightened. Suddenly it became clear that this woman knew something. Of course, the thought raced through Jo's mind, she worked for Wilson McAdams! And Floyd Green! Why didn't I put two and two together! She's got the goods on them!

"Senator, you were on the right track about Wilson McAdams. I hate to say this because I once admired the man and I know you did too. He wasn't all bad, let's get that straight."

"Yes, yes, I agree with you," Jo hastened to reassure. "I campaigned for him in New Hampshire. He really was for all the right things."

Reluctantly Marita agreed. "That's right, Senator. Up to a point. But when it came to the kind of things that go on around here, he very much became part of the system. He began to depend on heavy lobbyist support and even heavier contributions from people connected with groups like Common Good and the New GOP. At any rate, to get to the point, I have documented evidence that I believe will hold up in a Senate hearing, and in court, that will not only verify Senator McAdams' acceptance of that money you alleged he took. I have in his own handwriting a note which indicates that half of that money went to a Dr. Ludwig Controller. You know who he is, Senator, he's the mastermind behind Common Good and the New GOP."

Hardly believing our ears, Jo and Pete and I were astonished and tried not to show it. I was less surprised since I had gotten the McAdams letter from Controller but could never connect it to him. It was his word against mine. For years, Pete had wanted to get Controller. But it all seemed so legal. Despicable but legal. And Jo despised everything she had heard about him, frustrated in her inability to get to the core of his racket.

Very carefully and very precisely, I took over:

"Marita...I hope you don't mind if I call you Marita...but let's get this straight. You say you have documented proof that McAdams accepted the money. I will tell you here – and not for attribution or I'll deny I ever said it – that we knew he took it. We were told directly by an insider at the IRS that he actually claimed it on his income tax return. My suspicion is that he knew I knew it. Or at least that Controller knew it. And that knowledge led to McAdams' erratic behavior and subsequent death that night at the Gala.

My question is this: is your documented proof the same as ours? And if it is, won't it be impossible to get an old tax return of a dead and honored former Senator whom, we suspect, shredded his own copy of that return?"

Marita looked at me directly. She didn't exactly like the inquisitorial tone and convoluted question but she answered it directly. "The Senator and I were very close. Let's just leave it at that. Yes, I know about the tax return. It was exactly the kind of thing that the innocent and naive side of Wilson would do when confronted with the guilty and cunning side. But no, that's not what I'm talking about. To be very specific, since I had the only other key to Wilson's apartment in The Watergate, I went there late that night, after hearing of Wilson's being rushed to the hospital, and took his personal diary. In that document, he details a lot of things that should never have been done or said. Nevertheless he did them and he wrote about them. One of the things he wrote about was the acceptance of that money and the fact that he split it up with Dr. Controller. It's in his handwriting."

We were amazed. God, what else is in that diary?

"Won't you be charged with burglary if this comes out?" Jo asked anxiously.

"Maybe. I've thought about that," Marita answered matter of factly. "But I've just weighed it against my concern about what's going on here and concluded that I had no choice. When I followed what has been happening to you, it made me even more determined. Look, I'm in that Diary too. So are a lot of other people. I'm willing to take that risk. Besides, I don't think I'm liable. I shared that apartment with him and I can prove it. I had the key. I had regular access to his diary and everything else. My taking it may have been unauthorized but I don't know that it's burglary. But if it is, I'll just have to live with that and take the consequences. Senator, for me this conversation is not off the record. I consider it an official reporting to you, as subcommittee chairman, of the existence of a serious documented record of highly irregular activities involving some major personages in this city. I am a Senate employee. You are a Senator. This is now your responsibility."

"You know they'll charge that you're defaming a dead man. They'll call you a woman scorned," I interjected. "They'll say you fabricated it. Or they'll certainly move to block it as evidence. Are you prepared for what may come of this?"

"I've thought about all of that," Marita replied coolly. "It doesn't bother me. If I have a price to pay for my own actions, so be it. And if I give you the document, I believe you can reveal it regardless of subsequent legal actions. By then it will be too late for them to stop it."

Jo was still catching up, taking notes, now very much aware of how official this revelation was. "What's the next step?" she asked. "Where is it?"

"In my briefcase over there," Marita replied, gesturing to the conference table.

None of us dared touch it. We stared at it as if we had just seen the original ten commandments tablets or the Grail. "Pete," Jo said quickly, "get the lawyers. No, don't get the lawyers. Get George on the phone. No, don't talk to George on the phone. Get him to come down here as quickly as possible. I don't trust anybody on that subcommittee staff. But we must get immediate legal help. And there's not a lawyer in this town I would trust any more than I trust the people on the staff. Don't tell him anything. Just ask him to come. And to bring Ray and Henry if he has to."

She then turned to Marita. "I guess I have to thank you a second time," she said. "What an amazing world where things like this can happen so incidentally. I suppose I should say that I don't know how to thank you enough. But I don't think you would want to hear that."

Marita smiled slightly in agreement.

"Pete, Charlie, this will require all your ingenuity," Jo continued. "With or without a subcommittee vote, I intend to subpoena Controller. This thing must be made public. It's the first time in years that we have the tools to crack this system. Once we get our ducks in a row, I'll call Floyd Green and demand a public hearing."

"I could tell you a lot about him too," Marita concluded.

"Anybody for a good drink?" Pete asked.

"Not in public," Marita and Jo said simultaneously.

"Let's all go separately to my place," Jo suggested. "Marita, this time you have to come up and it won't be a cup of tea."

The time had come. All of my past broken resolutions had to be repaired. I could see the coming of some strange, new and possibly terrible conclusion. Call it melodramatic if you will but by then I had just about been shaken to my roots. And so I spoke.

"Just one more thing," I interjected. All three looked at me expectantly. "Marita, if you're willing to stick your neck out on this thing, I'll join you. If you have the documented evidence, I am now free to corroborate it with my own conversation with Controller. It will no longer be hearsay, his word against mine."

Jo and Pete looked at me as if I had just announced jointly my freedom and execution.

"I was wondering what you were doing here, and worried," Marita said. "Now I know why you're here and I thank you."

"Okay," Pete concluded in his businesslike fashion, "let's go!!"

CHAPTER 24

THE BIG DECISION

As Jo was preparing her opening statement for the Subcommittee hearing, Maureen burst in unannounced. "Chris Livengood is dead," she announced matter of factly. "Died in his sleep in Iowa. No more both sides of the street from the Chairman."

"I'm sorry to hear that," Jo said. "I really am. I think he meant well even though, in the end, he couldn't take it all the way. I've got to go to the funeral."

"Save your plane ticket," Maureen said. "They're gonna lie him in state in the Capital. Can you believe that?"

"At this point, I'll believe anything,' Pete commented offhandedly.

"I know this sounds terribly dumb but who's the Chairman now?" Jo asked.

"Are you ready?" Pete inquired. "Floyd B. Green. Good old seniority system."

"Oh no!" Jo exclaimed. "He'll abolish the subcommittee and Controller will get away! Pete, get out a press release demanding the subcommittee be continued."

"Press releases won't do the trick now,' Pete replied glumly. "We're going straight to the Department of Justice demanding an indictment of that son of a bitch for tax evasion."

291

"Tax evasion? Is that all?" she asked.

"There's a lot more but tax evasion's simpler. It's how they got Capone in the end," I replied. "But before we just go, Pete, I think Marita and I should hold a joint press conference and publicly detail what we've got."

"You'd be willing to do that, you old bastard?" Pete smiled.

"What's to lose?" I asked. "I got fired by my think tank this morning so now you guys can hire me."

"For ninety thousand?" Jo asked.

"Everybody should be so lucky to make ninety thousand," I answered.

"Plus benefits!" Pete chimed in.

"But of course," I replied.

Our decision to go to the Justice Department was the only route left. Green ordered that, in view of Livengood's passing, all investigations would be suspended. Predictably, Controller celebrated with a New GOP dinner at the Congressional County Club with featured speaker, Floyd B. Green. Another golf outing was planned as fund raisers continued at a frenetic pace.

Marita Johnson-Smith meanwhile was getting cold feet. Leerer Magazine alleged her to be a lesbian who had, in her former life, consorted with Islamic fundamentalists. Gossip had it that she had had a sex change operation.

"Senator, I can't take it," Marita Johnson Smith told Josephine Stephenson in a brief phone call. "I'm getting out of town. My life has been threatened, my reputation destroyed and my career ended. I know it's not your fault. All I have told you is true. I just want to be left alone."

I grabbed the phone, told her of my own plans but it didn't work. She was gone. She disappeared. And with her went the diary.

This was almost too much for Jo. Without Marita and that document there was no plausible case against Controller. She could order investigators or the FBI to track her down but it would take time and priority, two things she, of all people, couldn't count on. As she, Pete, Maureen and I met at her apartment later that night, she went to the cabinet, poured a double vodka on the rocks, sat down and heaved a deep sigh, She too had her threats. Evil faces lately in the crowds surrounding the Capitol. Rude pushing and shoving. They'll get her, she thought. Whoever they are, they'll get her before this is over. If they hated what she was doing they'd get her. If they didn't hate what she was doing, they would get her because she was trying to change things in a way that they did not want things to change. She switched from vodka to tea and suddenly she stood up, looked out that contemplative window and said:

"I'm not going to run for re-election."

We all looked around in astonishment.

"It's a little late for that, don't you think?" I finally replied. "When you ran last year to fill the unexpired term, you promised the people of Vermont you would run for a full term. You promised them you would continue to be an independent and fight for their interests. This will look like – not just look like – but BE – a complete betrayal."

"Yes, but the people I'm betraying right now are me and my family. Our lives have been turned upside down. And besides, I can't win. They'll throw millions into the campaign. Talk about my failure to deliver. Run those negative ads about how I've been jousting at windmills at the expense of the state. And they're already talking about running the same guy on both Republican and Democratic tickets. And the guy is, of all people, the man I supported for federal attorney with a name that's synonymous with Vermont, Ethan Allen Aiken."

Silence.

And then it dawned on me, the way to make this campaign the living symbol of all that was wrong with the system.

"Run," I said, firmly and unequivocally. "I will go to Vermont and run the campaign. I have an idea about how to do it. It won't cost big money but it will turn the political system upside down. And it will win. Don't ask me how. Just do it. If you really believe in the things you say you believe in, then believe in me. Announce that you are running as an independent to continue the fight. They will come after you with everything they've got but, in the end, you will win."

Silence again. Everybody looking around the room at each other.

"Let me think about it," she said. "What makes you think you're so smart, so right?"

"You'll find out soon enough," I said. "What do you think I've been doing all these years? You just campaign as you always did and leave the mechanics to me. But you must decide and you must run. Trust me."

"Trust you?" she asked with incredulity. "Why should I trust you? You've always been one of them."

"Yes, and it takes one to know one," I shot back.

"How do we know you're not a double agent?" demanded Maureen. "You'll run the campaign to make sure she loses."

"Maureen, for God's sake, I just got fired!" I retorted.

It was Pete's turn.

"I don't believe that," he said. "I don't know what Charlie's got in mind but I believe he means what he says. And Jo, you don't have any choice. If you don't run, you're going to set back the cause of reform politics a half century or more. You've got to do it and, if you do, you'll have all of us doing everything we can to win."

"And if I don't?" she persisted.

"But you will," Pete said, avoiding a direct answer.

Silence once more.

"Let me think about it" she said again.

"No, you can't think about it," I replied. "There's no time to think about it. You know what you have to do and we know what we have to do. If you don't go right up there and announce, I know an attractive woman in her mid-forties with stylish blonde hair and a professional demeanor in Burlington who looks just like you and she'll do it."

295

Laughter all around.

"Okay, okay. But nothing irrevocable until I talk to George and the kids."

The election was still six months away but the race was on.

CHAPTER 25

THE CAMPAIGN

Now I figured that the only way to beat those bastards was to turn their tools and their money against them.

As soon as Jo announced her candidacy, with the usual pitch for campaign reform and economic justice, the boys began to mobilize the opposition. Aiken resigned as federal attorney and announced he was running to, of all things, "restore sanity and responsibility to the position of junior Senator from Vermont," a convoluted theme false on its face and followed by the predictable issues litany of social security, prescription drugs, health care, education, choice and the environment for Democrats and tax cuts, defense spending and pro life for Republicans.

In no time, armed with the power and promise of money, and maneuvered by the master Controller, he had locked up both the Republican and Democratic nominations, rationalized by the "deep disappointment" of officials of both parties in the performance of their incumbent Senator and, of course, their reverent and abiding respect for this young man who embodied Vermont's finest traditions of Ethan Allen and George Aiken.

Meanwhile, in Washington, Controller and company began raising millions to mount the most massive media campaign in the state's history

297

underpinned by highly sophisticated polling, opposition research and focus group probing.

And Aiken proved to be an aggressive campaigner.

"Hellllooooo everybody," he would bellow as he barnstormed the state with carefully documented background on every town and rural community like a latter day version of the Music Man. He had a packaged answer for every problem and a commitment to deliver where Stephenson failed. Media outlets and editorialists were impressed and overwhelmed by his vigor, enthusiasm and promise of leadership. They listened in amazement as he ticked off the needs of one region after another. "This big bear of a man," one columnist wrote, "has the vision, idealism and leadership qualities to bring this backward state into the 21st Century." Followed dutifully by his trophy wife and two kids, he hired a van, toured the state and began to make progress.

As I watched him once on cable, he was asked what he thought the future held for the state's economy. "Great things! We have three unmatchable assets," he pronounced authoritatively. Before he could list them, I mumbled: location, work force and educational institutions. "Location, work force and educational institutions," he intoned to the satisfaction of his listeners.

Winning this thing could never be done the traditional way, I suspected. And so, I would do it the untraditional way.

One evening early in the campaign, I asked Maureen to assemble the key coordinators for a strategy session outside of Burlington and laid it out.

"This could be a tough campaign," I began. "We could lose. And that will happen if we just sit by and play their game. But you know, and I know, that we can't. We are not going to raise the money they can command. We can't afford extensive polling, opposition research and attack ads. And furthermore, we wouldn't do it even if we could. So here's what we're going to do. First, Jo is going to quietly tour the state as often as she can, meeting people, discussing the issues, disdaining the current state of politics and talking about her battle against the Washington establishment. In the meantime, we are going to conduct the most far reaching and clandestine operation in the history of American politics.

"Now listen to me and let's see if we can make this work. This may be the most independent state in the union. It's exercised the politics of perversity since the days of the American Revolution. Any state that can declare war on Nazi Germany three months before Pearl Harbor and seriously debate secession from the union in the 1990s has something going for it. The way I figure it, Aiken, even with his Republican and Democratic endorsements, probably has, at this time, little more than 30% of the vote. He and his manipulators in Washington are going to spend millions on polling, focus groups and negative advertising to paint Jo into a corner and put together a campaign that they think will appeal to the voters.

"The other thing we have to keep in mind is the fact that there are only 423,000 voters in this state and only 300,000 actually go to the polls. That figure is high but this is also a Presidential election year so you can expect a higher turnout. As I said, we don't have the money to play their game and we wouldn't play it even if we did. So we're going to play our game and it's a game of beating them at their own game."

Everybody in the room began to look puzzled.

"Now stay with me on this. I want everyone here, in strict confidence, to begin spreading the word to Stephenson voters from Burlington to Brattleboro – and I suspect that's about 50% of all likely voters right now – to lie."

"Lie?" Maureen interrupted. "What are you talking about?"

"Lie to the pollsters. Mislead the focus groups. If they're voting for Jo, tell them to say they're voting for Aiken. If they're asked about how they feel about her, tell them to say they really don't like her and are disappointed. If they're asked about campaign reform, tell them to say they don't care about it. If they're questioned about prescription drugs, tell them Vermont's seniors don't want any more federal handouts. Tomorrow, I'll have a whole list of questions to lie about."

"That's incredible," someone hollered from the back of the room. "What good will that do?"

"Don't you see?" I replied. "Every campaign takes the data from the polls and the focus groups and turns it into television ads and speeches. That idiot will end up saying exactly the wrong thing and his ads will deliver exactly the wrong message. In the meantime, Jo keeps pushing hard on her issues and the opposition will think she's crazy since they know – they KNOW – that she's going in the wrong direction."

"But it's impossible," Maureen commented. "We can't possibly reach a couple of hundred thousand people."

"In this state, yes you can," I retorted. "And in this state, you don't need to do it all yourselves. In this state, I know, I just know, that others will start spreading the word because, if there's one thing they're fed up with, it's the system they elected Jo to fight to change."

"This guy's crazy," someone observed.

"Yeah, crazy right," shouted another.

Then a pause as it all sank in.

"You know," the Montpelier coordinator said, "we may just turn the whole political system upside down. And what a place to begin…Vermont."

Suddenly, the enthusiasm began to spread and the fervor caught on. By the end of the evening, everyone knew that something totally different could happen to American politics.

"I get it."

"Ingenious."

"Crazy but, you know, it just may work."

"Okay, let's go," concluded Maureen. I smiled and watched as they began to leave the meeting room.

"Time for a beer," I said to her. "There's a lot to do starting tomorrow."

In all my life, and especially in all my political life, I had never felt so exhilirated. No matter how it turned out, and I was pretty sure it would turn out favorably, I would look back on that time as the rare moment when a clever, cautious and careful slave of the system turned into a free spirit.

CHAPTER 26

UNCHARTED TERRAIN

An old Vermonter I met in the town of Chester told me a story about the gods of the hills and how, in the end, they would protect the citizens of the Republic of Vermont from the evils perpetrated by the rest of the world.

Well, it seemed at the beginning that the gods of the hills were with us. In a bar one night in Bennington, I observed one of our coordinators going from person to person spreading the word about the campaign. And the listeners would nod and smile. They would understand. They would get it. And a look of determination would appear on their faces. This was their exquisite opportunity to screw the system, a delicious stratagem whereby they would strike the ultimate blow at the artificiality, phoniness and emptiness of political campaigning. They winked as they drank, enjoying their mischief amidst the microbrewery pints of the Green Mountain state.

"Now you don't think I'd do a thing like that, do you?" asked the bartender with a grin on his face?

"What?," asked a thirtyish woman waitress. "You know my mama taught me never to lie!"

"Screw the system? Not us!" proclaimed a rugged mountaineer on his fifth beer, guffawing all the way.

"I'm shocked that you would suggest such a thing," feigned one middle aged woman. "I'm going to tell all my neighbors."

And the message spread from town to town, up the hills and down the valleys. No muskets were needed this time. No rebellion had to be declared. The ultimate stealth campaign had begun and the guerilla insurgency would be conducted without firing a shot, issuing a single press release or producing even one negative television commercial.

When I arrived in Burlington, I arranged to meet with my old contact Willie Welsh who had been the first to analyze the Stephenson phenomenon for me two years ago when Dawn and I visited the state to check things out. He was working closely with the Aiken campaign but had a big mouth that he employed foolishly to let everyone know how smart he was.

As he finished his second scotch on the rocks at the Radisson bar, he started to talk.

"Charlie, you know that Hap Mandell's up here running the campaign for Aiken," he said.

"Really!" I replied, feigning surprise.

"And they know you're up here helping the Senator," telling me again something I already knew.

"Ethan's going to win," he stated flatly. "They've got a new poll that says he's ahead 52-27. He's got more than a majority now, Charlie and we've got more than two months to go. Stephenson's negatives are approaching 50%. When people were asked whether they were more likely, less likely or not likely to vote for her, only 20% said they were likely at all. And it's all age groups, men and women, marrieds, singles, all ethnicities and all sexual preferences and ideologies. Why don't you get out of here and save you reputation?"

"I can't Willie. I've made a commitment. I know she'll probably lose but it won't be the first time I've been on the losing side. Seems you've got those poll results down flat. Very impressive numbers."

"Especially among the young," Willie revealed. "And that was supposed to be her base."

I tried to look dejected and hoped it would work but inwardly I was about to burst out laughing. The stratagem was working and all we had to do was maintain it.

"Funny thing though," Willie continued and I began to get apprehensive. "The damndest attitudes are showing up in the survey. The people of this state really don't like her. They don't give a damn about campaign finance reform. They're not worried about big money or negative ads. They're not even that concerned about social security, homeland security or even Medicare and you know we've got a lot of seniors up here. Strikes me as odd."

"Well Willie, that's Vermont. You never know what they're thinking," I hastened to reassure him. We didn't need any suspicious campaign people beginning to doubt the numbers. "I suspect that their opposition to campaign reform and support of big money is just another way of standing up for independence. Everybody's got a constitutional right to do as he or she pleases, money or otherwise. And on the domestic security issues, I guess we're just a long way from downtown Manhattan."

"Yeah," Willie replied. "It's so lopsided right now that I told Controller and the boys in Washington that they ought to let up on the ads and the money. But they're gonna pour it on and not take any chances."

"I wouldn't either if I were them," I advised. "You never know, Willie. Can't let up. They have to keep pouring it on. Me, I don't have much to do. No money. No consultants. Not much staff. Not much enthusiasm. I'll just ride it out and hope for the best."

"First wave of ads is already in the can and on the way to the stations," Willie continued to blabber in his whiskey. "Tomorrow, Hap's bringing up that old buzzard Granny Gooch from Florida to do a seniors commercial. And he's got a Montpelier focus group set up. He's even using those feely counters and may even introduce the detectabrains. And Ethan's doing his own ad slamming Stephenson softly but subliminally. They're not going to stop until they bury her."

"Maybe," I replied as I carefully backed away. "Let's keep in touch."

That night as I stood by my hotel window looking out on Lake Champlain, I began to get apprehensive. It's a dangerous game you're playing Charlie, I said to myself. A dangerous game.

And I thought about that quotation from Jefferson that spread through many Vermont towns, places so small they don't even have a zip code, like Searsberg and towns like Whittingham and Plymouth when they decided a few years ago to withhold their state taxes to protest an unjust new tax provision. "I hold it," proclaimed the third President of the United States, "that a little rebellion, now and then, is a good thing, and as necessary in the political world as storms in the physical."

The storms were coming and I was in the middle of them. May this sly new form of rebellion prevail. Uncharted terrain. Is that what the cable commentators will label this when it's over? I hoped so.

CHAPTER 27

UNNAVIGATED WATERS

Or maybe it will be their other favorite newspeak, unnavigated waters amidst breaking news and developing stories.

It certainly seemed that way to me as I woke to the rays of a brilliant morning covering the lake. Mid-August was here and the leaves were already turning. I was to meet at Jo's house for a strategy session with the Senator, Maureen and George. Pete was staying in Washington, minding the store.

"I'm tired," she said as she opened the door without saying hello or good morning. And she didn't look happy. "The Free Press is publishing a poll saying Allen's 51 to 29. They're saying it's all over and I suspect they're going to endorse him."

"That's interesting," I said as I poured my own coffee. "In their poll you have two more points than you get in the inside poll of the Allen campaign. And he's got one less. I guess we're making some progress."

Nobody laughed. Maureen and George sat by impassively. Oh ye of little faith, I thought to myself.

"Where are you going today Jo?" I asked.

"They've got me scheduled to shake hands in Saint Alban's and give a luncheon speech to the local Rotary. Tonight there's a small rally here in town. Seems useless to me."

I listened patiently, stared at by the trio, not one of whom had confidence in my strategy.

"Not really," I said. "Sounds like a nice way to connect with the voters. Stick to your issues and get some free radio and TV time."

"Charlie," Maureen interrupted in her usual exasperated tone, "we have no money, no ads, no polls and no endorsements. Fifteen Senators are coming to the state to campaign for that guy. They've already poured $5 million into this little state and will probably double it. The whole world is against us and you're acting as if everything's just fine. Well, it isn't."

I ignored her. She should have known better. Weeks ago she stood there listening to the campaign plan and agreed with it. She helped me to get Jo to buy in. So I addressed Jo directly.

"How is it out there? Getting a good reception?"

"As a matter of fact yes," she said. "And I don't get it. Everybody is really warm and positive and then I see these polls."

"Oh for God's sake Jo, of course they're warm," I interjected. "They're for you. You know what's happening with the polls. They're lying and it's working. Don't you understand that?"

Sober lawyer George put in his two cents: "how do we know Charlie? How can you measure it? Why don't we take our own poll?"

"We can't. They'd lie to us too" I answered. "So we can't be sure. And don't you think that bothers me too? But I suspect it's working. Jo, be upbeat, be charming, be appealing and, above all, be aggressive.

You're the lonely crusader, put upon by the interests, battered by the big boys. But that doesn't mean you can't be the happy warrior. If this thing is to work, it won't be because of my strategy alone. If you falter, you could affect turnout. People are for you but, in the final analysis, they'll vote for you if they believe in you and are inspired by you. If you go around with that cloud over your head, the whole strategy will be depressed. And the message couldn't be clearer. The political preoccupation with money, ads, polls and negatives is holding most of your distinguished robotic Congressional colleagues hostage to a system which is fundamentally flawed. No wonder we get nowhere on the economy, domestic security and the like. No time to focus on the substance. How can they be held accountable when the outcome of every crucial election is determined by the bucks and the ads? And the bucks are coming from so many sides that they cancel each other out and nothing happens. Talk about disconnect. You stay on that message and you win. Big time."

"Do you really believe that?" she asked. "And do you really think their consultants are so stupid as to blindly follow polls that are obviously inaccurate?"

"Don't take my word for it. Before coming over here, I had delivered to me a cassette of their most recent ads. Don't ask me how I got it. I got it. Can we look at them now, Madame Gloom?"

All three looked surprised and impressed. Jo took the tape and put it in the machine. In a matter of seconds, it began to roll, the first thirty second ad designed to introduce the charismatic candidate, Ethan

Allen Aiken, walking the streets of Montpelier in jeans and checkered shirt, just one of the folks:

"HELLOOO EVERYBODY! IT'S ETHAN ALLEN AIKEN HERE. I GUESS THOSE ARE FAMILIAR NAMES TO ALL YOU FELLOW VERMONTERS. HA HA (a little laugh and a knowing wink ingratiating him with voters). BEEN A GREEN MOUNTAIN BOY ALL MY LIFE (as he scoops up a baby from its mother's arms) AND NOW I'M RUNNING FOR THE YEWNITED STATES SENATE (shaking hands). I'VE BEEN YOUR FIGHTIN' FEDERAL ATTORNEY FOR THE LAST TWO YEARS (now on the steps of the state capitol) AND I THINK IT'S TIME FOR VERY REAL CHANGE IN WHO REPRESENTS US IN WASHINGTON. MY OPPONENT'S A NICE LADY BUT WE NEED SOMEONE WHO WILL GET THE JOB DONE. AND LET ME TELL YOU STRAIGHT OUT, I KNOW HOW TO GET THE JOB DONE! JUST LIKE THIS (puts a basketball in the net from twenty feet to the astonished admiration of a group of high school kids). And the announcement comes: WITH AIKEN IN THE SENATE, VERMONT WON'T BE ACHIN ANYMORE.

"Awful," Maureen said. "Stupidity oozes from his eyes. And he's fat."

"Yes," I observed. "Not fat. Stocky, they say. But happy. Get that Jo?"

"I get it," Jo replied. "But that's pretty bad. That phrase at the end is ridiculous."

"You may think so," I said. "And I may think so. But that's what they're getting from the polls. When people are asked if the state's doing okay with you in the Senate, more than 50% are saying NO. They're saying the state is hurting and that they're hurting. And what's reported from the polls goes right into the ad."

But how can anybody believe that?" George asked. "Surely the pros know that that's pretty bad stuff."

"They probably do," I explained. "But they began with the premise that the voters are stupid and they believe religiously that the polls are accurate. And that's what you get and that's what they believe…no, that's what they KNOW…will work."

"How will they know?" Maureen asked.

"Because, in the next focus group, they'll ask people whether they like that commercial and more than half of them will say they love it. And those are the people, Maureen, that your coordinators and hundreds of other volunteers are spreading the message to. LIE. How can you not see it?" I demanded.

The one who began to see it was the candidate herself. She smiled. She actually brightened up. Like those people in the bar at Brattleboro, she was beginning to understand. "Let's see the next one," she said and turned it on.

If ever there was a dismal countenance displayed in ominous black and white, it was the grainy and badly shot footage of Jo Stephenson that now came on the screen. It must have been taken clandestinely after that Senate hearing that was terminated when she was standing by complaining to Pete and me about how her colleagues had acted.

"Oh my God, I look awful," she blurted out. "Where did they ever get that?"

"Just listen," I ordered. And the tape continued to roll and the solemn, dark and forbidding voice intoned:

"WHAT GREAT PROMISE WE HAD FOR SENATE STEPHENSON WHEN SHE WAS ELECTED. AND WHAT FAILURE HAS FOLLOWED. HER FANATICAL CRUSADE FOR CAMPAIGN SPENDING REFORM HAS COLLAPSED AND WE ARE THE ONES WHO ARE SUFFERING. HAVING ALIENATED THE ENTIRE WASHINGTON POWER STRUCTURE, SHE CANNOT DELIVER FOR THE STATE OF VERMONT. CALL SENATOR STEPHENSON AND TELL HER WE VERMONTERS AREN'T INTERESTED IN HER SO CALLED REFORM. WHAT WE WANT IS THE FEDERAL MONEY FOR OUR ROADS, HOUSING AND ECONOMIC DEVELOPMENT. (Then the tape shifts from the dismal representation of Jo to the sunny disposition of Ethan). AIKEN FOR SENATE. HE'LL RESTORE US TO REALITY."

"Not bad," George observed. "Except for that pompous sanctimonious voice."

"No, not bad," I agreed. "That is, if you think the message reflects voter sentiment. Schmoozing

313

with the Washington power structure? Is that Vermont? I'd say it's just a bit out of touch."

"And how!" Jo chimed in with a renewed sense of enthusiasm. "Charlie, write down that comment you made about tying the money culture to the failure on substance. He's running on both tickets and they're all the same guys, feeding off the same money and responding to the same pressures, Republican and Democrat. It's absolutely on target. Let's get it clear and simple. And from now on, I promise to smile like a salesman, campaign like I love it and stick to the strategy. You know, I think we can win this thing."

It's about time, I thought. "Go to it, Senator," I urged.

"And just what do you intend to do while I'm out shaking hands and being gracious? Especially since we have no money." Jo stared directly at me.

"This afternoon, there's a focus group Mandell's conducting for the Aiken campaign. I've arranged with the research company to watch it from another room. So I'll just sneak in and see how it's all working. And I intend to have fun."

At that minute the phone rang and George put it on speaker: "helloooo, this is Ethan Allen Aiken calling and do I need your help!" And we all broke up as George disconnected.

"Don't do that!" I shouted too late. "I want to hear the whole script."

"Too late," he replied. "But you'll have plenty of opportunities to catch it later."

No sooner had he slammed down the phone than it rang again. "Hi," came over a charming computerized voice. "Ethan needs your help! Sign up now to help him unseat Jo Stephenson, the woman who can't deliver." Again the phone was slammed.

"They're really pulling out all the stops. It's bound to have an effect, Charlie," Maureen said.

"Maybe," I observed. "Tell you what we'll do, Maureen. Instruct your coordinators that, when they get that volunteer call, to return the call and sign up. Tell them to get enough of their campaign literature to canvass a hundred houses. Then tell them to dump it in the trash."

"Dirty tricks, dirty tricks,!" proclaimed Maureen. "That's not us."

"Oh, alright," I replied. "Then they can wrap the fish in it."

Maureen smiled mischievously. Jo started pacing the floor, anxious to get going. And I was off to the focus group. Only George continued to observe the scene impassively.

315

CHAPTER 28

FRAGMENTS OF A FOCUS GROUP, PART TWO

Stealthily I slipped in the back door of Upper New England Market Research. I had used them a hundred times in past campaigns in New Hampshire and Massachusetts and the owner, Bob Kelly, was undyingly grateful. Clearly, he was taking a chance letting me snoop on the group but I knew how to handle it and not get caught. I had to be sure that the strategy was working and I would risk anything to find out.

"Hey Charlie, how ya doing?" he asked, a little nervously as I walked down the corridor. "Here, quick, in this room. It's not being used and I'll switch the screen on so you can watch. But if you ever tell anybody, I'll…"

"Forget it kid, forget it," I reassured him. "I know what I'm doing. Don't worry."

About ten minutes later, Hap Mandell and Tommy Ragin appeared on the screen, setting up the room for the focus group. But I was taking no chances. When they hired Kelly, I asked him to put together a cross section of Vermonters, most of whom he knew would play the game. Shortly thereafter, those two experts disappeared behind the mirror and the kindly woman moderator took over. One by one the group members began to file into their seats, grabbing their tuna sandwiches and potato chips on the way. It was an interesting group indeed, twelve middle American average citizens, urban and rural, all age groups, geographically spaced around the northern tier of the state. If there was ever a slice of Americana, this was it.

As they devoured their free meal and sodas, the moderator began.

"So nice of you all to be here," she began. "And for such an important purpose. We're going to really put our attitudes to the test today! Please, eat! There's plenty of food. So…for the next hour and a half, we want you solid citizens to let us know how you honestly feel about politics nationally and here in the state of Vermont."

"It stinks," called out one wise guy at the end of the table.

Embarrassed chuckles all around and our moderator giggled and said, "well, we're certainly in for some candid discussion. And that's JUST what we want. And to protect your anonymity, we have a practice of calling you by some very famous names. Sometimes it's Hollywood movie stars or sports figures. Today, we're all going to be famous writers." And so they introduced themselves, placing their name cards in front of them: Ernest Hemingway, Scott Fitzgerald, J.D. Salinger, Virginia Woolf, James Joyce, Anna Quindlen, Stephen King, Tom Clancy, Anne Rice, Emily Dickinson, J.K. Rowling, Patrick O'Brian.

"Well now, we're ready to go. So let's start with the first topic for discussion. Some people think there's too much money in politics. Do you agree?"

317

"No," said Ernest Hemingway. "Everybody's got a right to do what he wants with his money and if he wants to spend it to buy politicians, that's the first amendment to the Constitution."

"Right there in the Bill of Rights," added Stephen King. "We Vermonters are rugged individualists. Bred in the mountains. Except for them outsiders who've been coming up here lately."

"But," asked the Moderator, "how do you reconcile that thinking with support of your Senator Stephenson who's made a crusade about campaign reform?"

"Well, I don't support her," volunteered Anna Quindlen. "Not enough of a feminist for me. If she's gonna be for us women, she ought to go out and get their asses."

"Whose asses?" demanded Hemingway.

"Your asses," she shot back. "Men!"

"Now now, let's get back on the issue here," the moderator hastened to interrupt. "Let's all be on the same page. The Stephenson discussion?"

"Single issue Senator," said J.D. Salinger. "And to have a little fun, I'll pretend I live nearby in New Hampshire like the real Salinger, ho ho. I think I can speak for all of New England."

"And who are you all supporting in this election?" asked the Moderator.

"Aiken," many shouted.

"One of us," said James Joyce.

"Green Mountain boy," said Emily Dickinson.

"Courageous prosecutor," intoned Tom Clancy, although it was doubtful that, in less than two years, he had put anybody in jail.

"Aiken will work with the powers that be," declared Anne Rice. "He'll bring home the bacon. He'll fight for us."

"And he's for early childhood education too," added J.K. Rowling.

"What's this bull shit about fight for us?" demanded Hemingway. "I may vote for him but none of these assholes fights for us."

"Well, well, isn't this interesting." quickly interrupted the Moderator. "Can we have a show of hands? How many for Aiken?"

Oh God, I thought, I hope they all don't overdo it. Let's have a few for Jo.

Eight raised their hands for Aiken.

"Very impressive," said the Moderator. "And for Stephenson?"

Thank heavens. Three raised their hands.

"Eight to three. That leaves one undecided. Are you leaning one way or another, Mr. King? Are you an undecided lean or simply undecided?" asked the Moderator.

"Undecided," answered Stephen King.

"Is that very undecided, a little undecided or moderately undecided?"

"Just plain undecided," he replied.

"And those of you for Aiken. That's a very surprising total. Are all of you very much for Aiken, leaning to Aiken or could you change your minds about Aiken?"

"Relatively for Aiken," said Salinger.

"Very much," declared Quindlen with Hemingway and Anne Rice chiming in, followed by Fitzgerald.

"Well, I guess if Anna says very much, I'll agree," said Rowling and she was joined by Dickinson and Woolf.

"Just a little bit," volunteered Clancy. "I don't follow nobody."

"Neither do I," proclaimed James Joyce.

"Now Patrick, you haven't said anything," she observed, addressing O'Brian. "But you raised your hand for Aiken."

"I'm with Joyce and Clancy," said Patrick. "And I'll just wait and finally decide on election day."

"Could we go on now and discuss some issues? So let's start with Medicare. Any of you have strong feelings about it?"

"We can get along without it," declared Patrick O'Brian. "All this talk about prescription drugs. I don't even take prescription drugs."

"Neither do I, straight liquor," said Hemingway and several ventured positive opinions about aspirin, ibuprofen and generics.

"I want to talk about middle class family values," said James Joyce.

"Yes, family values. Middle class values," added Fitzgerald.

"But before we tackle middle class values, can we have a break so I can go to the bathroom and get some cookies?" asked Quindlen. And so they did and the cookies were being devoured as I slipped out the door. It's working, I thought. It's really working. Not all but most of these people are smirking and winking at each other. Did they ever earn their $150 in cash. Hap and Tommy will be overjoyed. What's going on here today goes directly into their next batch of ads.

Bob Kelly suggested I hang around in the area and he'd get me a copy of the Granny Gooch ad they were going to shoot immediately after the focus group.

I couldn't believe it.

There was Granny, that old Aunt Edna, sitting in her rocker looking like Norman Bates' mother with that same Whistler's Mother print behind her. And she had the gall to say she was from Vermont.

"Hi everybody, Granny Gooch here. Come all the way down from the northeast kingdom to put in a kindly word for Ethan Allen Aiken.

"I don't know Ethan but my daddy knew George Aiken and my great great geat grandaddy fought with Ethan Allen and the Green Mountain Boys in the good old American revolution.

"I swear, this young man is as American as apple pie and as Vermont as maple syrup. He knows we're a rugged bunch and that's why he's not gonna give away the country store on prescription drugs for us SEENYURS...Heck, we've got enough aspirin and home remedies to take care of us the rest of our lives.

"And that woman he's runnin' against. She can't deliver the bacon for us Vermonters and for us SEENYURS. And you know, if you can't deliver the bacon you're in big trouble big time up here in Vermont cause there's nothin' like bacon to go with the syrup and pancakes.

"Call that woman up – what's here name? Josephine? Not this time Josephine! Call her up and tell her you don't like the fact that she ain't deliverin' for Vermont and for us SEENYURS! And tell her old Granny Gooch said so!"

Well, at least they can turn a phrase once in a while, I thought. But it won't work. Won't work. I don't think it'll work. Hope I'm right. Hmmmm.

If you are wondering at this point how we who play this game bear with the pressures and tension, the answer partly is that we don't. We too wake up startled in the middle of the night either because some incident or stratagem invades our restless sleep causing us to turn it around mentally a hundred times or because, in attempting to dull the senses and knock ourselves out, we have one drink too many too late.

Notice that I said 'partly.' The other side of the coin is that we've become so steeled against the loathesome nature of the campaign trail that we often feel nothing but numbness. That night, after mulling over again and again the grotesque Granny ad and the mischievous focus group, let's just say that I experienced a certain level of numb satisfaction. I was no longer just hoping I was right. I knew it.

CHAPTER 29

VILLAINS IN VERMONT

But I didn't necessarily know it in the cold light of day. By mid October, according to all calculations, the Aiken campaign had already spent $10 million. Rumor had it that Controller was still having a fit, demanding more money and doing it at the expense of other campaigns. It had become for him an obsession, going ballistic on the phone to Hap and Tommy, trusting no one, reaching out for whatever Common Greed or New GOP member he could get to go to Vermont and independently check things out.

In addition, hundreds of political operatives, so-called "volunteers," were recruited from other states and especially from Congressional offices inside the Beltway to jump on a plane and get to Vermont to go door to door in a massive 'get out the vote' drive. Starched and ambitious little yuppies smiled their way from town to town, claiming to be idealistic students concerned about the future of the republic. Leaflets were dropped from airplanes and posters with the big fat face of Ethan Allen Aiken smiling in color decorated the highways and byways. The old son of a bitch was leaving nothing to chance and no device was overlooked.

Repeatedly, the answer was the same: the polls were holding at roughly 53-29. The ads, said his spies, were having an effect. Focus groups continued to confirm what the polls reported. Aiken traveled tirelessly around the state, promising the moon, a federal program for every town and hamlet and still inveighing against campaign reform and the failed tenure of Senator Stephenson. Fifteen Senators did indeed make visits, extolling the integrity and ability of the candidate. Democrats and Republicans alike came to his aid. Anything to exorcise the ghost of Stephenson from the body politic.

Finally, with two weeks to go, the pros and the pundits were ready to concede that this race was over. Tommy Ragin, Democrat triumphantly appeared on Curveball, together with his Republican counterpart Tyler Bancroft, to declare the winner.

"Well, I don't know what the hell's gonna happen with the Presidency or control of the Congress," Ragin boomed. "But one race I do know is over and that's the Senate race in Vermont. Our boy's gonna win. Ethan Allen Aiken will take the state in a landslide."

"Oh, I agree," added Tyler. "And what a refreshing change that will be from the dismal performance of the ineffectual reformer, Jo Stephenson. And you know, Tommy, he's proved to be a great campaigner. He's being greeted around the state like a rock star."

"Them Vermonters have always been known for spottin' a phony when they see one and they saw one up there for the last two years," Ragin pontificated.

"There's only one problem Tommy and here we do disagree. With the Senate likely to be evenly split, and with Aiken running on both tickets, the big time question is what party will our boy caucus with? His decision could very well determine who controls the agenda for the next several years."

"I don't know," Tommy replied. "Statesman that he is, he's keeping his own counsel on that. But the party leaders sure have opinions and we've invited both of them here tonight to give us some idea of what'll happen. Ladies and Gentlemen, please welcome Republican leader Floyd B. Green and Democratic leader Alvin Bushey."

Applause from the university audience dutifully follows the cue from the director off camera. Why, as I'm watching this, I asked myself, why do these otherwise intelligent people warmly welcome such posturers?

"Senator Green," Bancroft intoned, "you've been reported as claiming Aiken as one of your own and that he'll be a voting member of your caucus. Could you tell us right now, before this audience and the Amurrican people, if, in fact, you have such a commitment?"

"Now now Tyler," Green cautioned. "We can't be demanding commitments from a candidate of Mr. Aiken's stature before he is duly elected. But his whole outlook is rooted in the political philosophy of the Republican Party."

"What do you think of that, Senator Bushey?" Tyler asked.

"He's obviously a populist, one of us. And I say that with all due respect to my friend and colleague, Senator Green," Bushey replied.

"Well, he's going to be ours," Green stated flatly.

"He's mine," Bushey retorted.

"One of us my good friend," Green reassured.

"Ours," Bushey insisted.

Then the truth from Tommy Ragin: "frankly, gentlemen, I don't know if it makes a dime's worth of difference who he caucuses with!"

"Careful, careful, Tommy my boy," Green interrupted. "We don't want the public out there to think this is a one party system."

"Ours," reiterated Bushey.

"Mine," Green shouted.

At that point, I threw the tuner at the TV and almost smashed it.

To tell the truth, I was getting worried. Lies or no lies, conspiracy or no conspiracy by the people, this stuff was bound to have an effect. I still believed Vermonters were happily playing the game. Liars! Liars! Constant clandestine reports were reaffirming my belief. Jo was working hard, travelling the state and talking with people in her candid, straightforward way. But she was all but blanked out on television. Only an occasional and routine news roundup even featured her. And the Aiken ads were everywhere while those little monster volunteers continued to ring doorbells. Maybe, just maybe, this thing could backfire.

With ten days to go, it was clearly time for one last strategy session in Jo's Burlington kitchen.

"You've got to go on television," I insisted.

"Oh great," Maureen retorted. "Weren't you the genius who said we didn't need all that? Where's the money coming from and what do we do when we get on television?"

"Let him finish," Jo said calmly.

"I don't mean ads and I don't mean sound bites. I don't mean negatives and I don't mean panic. I mean a speech."

"A speech?" George asked. "When's the last time you heard a candidate actually give a speech on television? Talking head, that's what she'll be called. Boring."

"No, absolutely not," I replied. "In fifteen minutes, she can lay this whole thing out. Hell, it took Jack Kennedy less than a half hour to explain the Cuban Missile Crisis. The simple message: clean it up."

I glanced over at Jo. She had changed in the last few weeks of the campaign. Out there on the trail, she was growing in stature and strength, courage and conviction. Worn out but indefatigable, she was truly the woman with a mission. But she didn't wear that mission on her sleeve. She encompassed it naturally with grace and poise. The problem was that the larger audience, beyond the occasional Rotary Lunch or town rally wasn't seeing or hearing her. In their own contrary Vermont way, the voters clearly had an attachment to her but this would put the icing on the cake. I knew she'd make a great impression.

"I like it," she said. "But who's going to write it and who's going to pay for it?"

"Cable and radio are cheap enough," I observed. "We'll put the money up ourselves if necessary. And you and I will write it. It's no big deal. It's what you've been saying all along spread across a larger screen."

"Can you buy the time at this late date?" Maureen asked.

"Already reserved it. Monday, 7 PM across the board on local, cable and radio. No Boston. Too expensive. Then we'll reprint it with newspaper ads in the major dailies. That's just eight days before the election."

"Doesn't that give them too much time to respond?" Jo asked.

"Shouldn't matter," I said. "Too little, too late and, besides, we're already probably leading this race by the exact number they think they are if the people of this state are doing their solemn duty and misleading those jerks."

Jo smiled. That lovely smile of hers. I knew she'd like it. Knew she'd do it. And that would be the end of it.

Monday Night 7 PM: "Ladies and Gentlemen, we interrupt our regular programming to bring you a paid political presentation by Vermont's Junior United States Senator, Josephine Stephenson."

And there she was, looking great (I took her off the road for the prior two days and told her to get some sleep and practice). I had written a draft and she had revised it beautifully. Words and Music. Kennedy and Sorensen.

"Good evening, my fellow citizens of Vermont. In just eight days you will go to the polls to participate in the election of the next President of the United States, a Congressman and a member of the United States Senate. I suppose you're wondering what I'm doing on a paid political program when all of you know how opposed I am to big money in politics.

"Don't worry. A few friends and I have put up the money so that I would have the chance to personally talk to all of you, especially those I haven't seen on the campaign trail.

"I'm going to dispense with all the cliches of routine politics and get right to the point.

"My last two years in the United States Senate and this campaign have one simple message: let's clean it up. Let's get the big money out of politics and give all of us elected officials the freedom and independence to display our courage and follow our consciences in the way we vote and for the things we believe in.

"Some people have charged that I've been an ineffective single issue Senator, so obsessed with the issue of money that I can't get anything done for you and for the state of Vermont. I sometimes wonder why, if I'm so ineffective, the entire political establishment is spending more than $10 million to defeat me.

"Well, I guess there's some truth to the charge anyway. But I have a feeling that we'll be able to build our own bridges, maintain our own roads and take care of our own towns all by ourselves if we have to. The federal government's a double edged sword on

329

that sort of thing anyway. You have to play the insider's game to get its help and then you may get something you don't want at all. Maybe a nuclear waste dump like the one they tried to foist on Newbury a few years ago.

"But money's not a single issue by any means. It's an obsession that distorts one's vision on everything else. My colleagues in the Congress don't wake up in the morning thinking about people like you. They wake up in the morning thinking about their next fund raiser and then become hostage to the people who write the big checks. There's one party in Washington and it's the insider commercial party that makes a mockery of our pretensions to democracy.

"That's why they don't wake up thinking about the people who can't afford a home or face foreclosure. That's why they take forever to extend unemployment benefits for the jobless and don't have time to think about the millions of people in the country – and thousands of them right here in Vermont – without health insurance or trapped in wage slave jobs cleaning hotel rooms when their fathers and grandfathers, mothers and grandmothers, went out and made things and worked with their hands for good wages and even better personal satisfaction, many in their own businesses. That's why they don't think about the people who won't graduate from Harvard and become hi tech entrepreneurs but who need and want to find a future in meaningful and stable jobs right here in Burlington or Brattleboro.

"Those concerns get lip service but really don't count in our nation's Capital because, like so many civilizations of the past that collapsed in ruin, the culture, climate and atmosphere are more like royal courts than the repository of the hopes and needs of the people. Like the Versailles of old, the lobbyists are the lords, the campaign consultants are the courtiers and the pollsters are the princes.

"Is it any wonder that, in such an environment, everybody failed to heed the warnings of terrorism or can't fully appreciate the cynicism and sense of futility that permeate the countryside?

"Maybe I'm wrong but I believe there were times in this country when we did respond to real problems. Some of our past leaders made a lot of mistakes but the best of them never lost their focus. I used to think the Democratic Party was the party of FDR, Harry Truman and John F. Kennedy. And I used to think the Republican Party was the party of Teddy Roosevelt and Abraham Lincoln. But I don't think so anymore. What we have is an insider commercial party where both sides feed at the same troth of money and the people who control it. Roosevelt's feel for the average citizen, his ability, as a patrician, to put himself in the shoes of the little guy and identify with his needs and concerns, doesn't motivate today's elected officials because their focus is elsewhere. Deep down they may care. But that's not what drives them. And that's why our civilization is once again in danger of retardation because too large a body of our citizens is falling behind in the political scramble for money.

"So tonight I'm not going to go through the familiar litanies about women's issues, minority issues, senior issues, family values and middle class tax cuts. I'm not going to insult your intelligence with pious and empty commitments to go the distance for working families. I'm not even going to be so presumptuous to tell you what I think you want and what the "American people" want. Don't label me a compassionate conservative or a trendy liberal. Those phrases, those slogans and those promises are hollow receptacles honed by the big time operators, without meaning and without substance. Just remember this: if I am re-elected to the United States Senate, this state will be sending a powerful message to the royal court that resides in the District of Columbia. And that message will be to end the grip of big money and its courtiers on the body politic and replace it with a government serving the common interests of the millions upon millions who don't have a place at that court or a financial stake in its survival.

"If we straighten this system out, the other things that are really important will follow because they won't be superceded by greed, personal ambition and the vicious and negative political measures taken by people who must use those methods for their own survival. And then maybe a few more of them will wake up in the morning thinking about you because there are no more contributors to bleed and fund raisers to attend. Because, if we don't STOP thinking about money, we'll never START thinking about people.

"That's what this election is all about. You know that. You're the most independent and cantankerous people in America. Prove it on election day. Clean it up. Send me back to Washington. Lord knows why I want to do it. But I'm just as stubborn as you are and I won't let you down. Thank you. And good night."

CHAPTER 30

THE AFTERMATH

When it was over I just sat there in the studio staring at the candidate.

I liked it. But I did wonder whether the voters would. I'm not sure that people want to be populist reformers. I'm not sure they have any sense of history. Why would they appreciate a quotation from Franklin Roosevelt? That's ancient history. More than three quarters of them weren't even born when he was President. I recalled a recent poll in which a majority of people interviewed thought we fought Russia in the Second World War. Cynical, self centered and turned off, maybe they think she's just another politician. If they care at all.

But she liked it.

"Words and music," she said, smiling confidently as she came over to shake hands. Maureen seemed delighted. George was subdued but you could tell he was satisfied. Raymond, home from college for the big event, and Henry, gave her hugs. Somehow we knew it had worked. At least we thought it did.

"Best speech I ever wrote," I said jokingly.

"Careful," she warned. "They'll start saying I'm a captive of the campaign consultant."

That made me a little uncomfortable but I decided to overlook it. Could it be possible that we were in fact installing a new version of the old system with me as the next Controller? Enough of that.

This time we all headed for Maureen's house in downtown Burlington for a drink and an assessment of the situation. While there, her mother got a phone call.

"SSSHHHH," she said as she covered the receiver. "It's a pollster wanting to know my reaction to the speech. I'll put it on the speaker."

"Maam, my name is Roger calling for Non Partisan Opinion Research. Do you have a few moments?"

"Sure do," Mrs. Sullivan replied.

"Did you watch tonight's presentation by Senator Stephenson?"

"Sure did," she stated firmly.

"What was your opinion of the Senator's speech?"

"Awful, perfectly awful. Who does she think she is, the know it all?"

We could hardly contain ourselves. Mrs. Sullivan practically had to bite her lip.

"Really?" Roger seemed surprised. "What did you think was so awful?"

"Her up there puttin' down us seenyurs and not wanting to talk about women's issues. Bein' a know it all with all the answers."

"Then I take it you're not voting for her?"

"Well, I was goin' to until now. But now I'm votin' for Ethan Allen Aiken."

"Is there any particular reason why you're voting for Aiken?"

"He's one of us, a good old Green Mountain boy. Don't know why I was thinkin' of votin' for her anyway."

"On a scale of one to ten, where would you put your favorability rating for Mr. Aiken?"

"Oh, maybe eight or nine."

"And Senator Stephenson?"

"Hmmm, maybe three or four. She's done some things good."

"But you've definitely changed your mind, correct?"

"Yes sir, I changed my mind. No more leanin' to her or undecided or whatever you guys call it. Now I gotta go back to my family. And don't ask me none of those income and background questions. We're just a good old average middle class American family with good old middle class family values."

"Thank you very much, Ma'am. Your time and opinions are deeply appreciated…"

We laughed so hard we practically fell on the floor.

"A masterpiece," I declaimed.

"Terrific," said Jo.

"Mother, I didn't know you were such a good actress," Maureen commented with amazement.

Mrs. Sullivan smiled and waved her hand dismissively.

"Best part I've had since I played Emily in Our Town fifty years ago."

And we were all feeling pretty good about things.

The next day, I couldn't resist. Decided to place a call to Hap and Tommy to see how they thought it went.

"Aiken for Senate Headquarters, may I help you?" answered the cheery woman's voice with the Midwest accent.

"Yeah, hi, this is Charlie Coons. Is Hap there?"

Silence.

"Hello, can you hear me?" I asked.

A cough, followed by a clearing of the throat. "Did you say Charlie Coons?"

"Yes, that's my name. Charlie Coons. An old friend of Mr. Mandell's. Is he there?"

"May I ask what this is in reference to, Mr. Coons?"

"No, you may not ask what this is in reference to. Tell Mr. Mandell that I want to talk to him."

Hesitation again, then a reluctant "just a moment, Mr. Coons."

After a few moments I was on the speaker phone.

"Charlie, what the fuck do you want?" It was Tommy but I knew that Hap was in the room.

"Just thought I'd check in guys. Wondering what you thought of the Senator's speech last night."

"I didn't think shit of the Senator's so called speech last night," Tommy shouted. "Doesn't mean a goddam thing. She's a nut case and nobody but an idiot would vote for her."

"Counterproductive Charlie, counterproductive," intoned Hal, playing statesman to

Tommy's hack. "The overnights indicate that she's actually lost support. Here, let me read you one interview. A senior middle class woman in Burlington said she was awful, came over like a know it all. And this particular voter was going to vote for her."

"That's not very nice, is it?" I observed.

"Not very nice for you maybe, but damn nice for us, you traitor," Tommy replied.

"Sorry you feel that way," I calmly replied.

"Yeah, well you're dead, you're finished," Tommy shot back. "This game made you, you son of a bitch. And you betrayed us."

"Just a moment, Tommy," Hap interrupted. "My secretary tells me the Doctor is on the line. She told him we were talking to Charlie and he wanted to be patched in. Okay with you Charlie?"

My stomach churned momentarily and I got this little electric shock in the hand holding the receiver but quickly got myself together and said, "fine, okay, haven't talked to him in ages." I could imagine what was coming but was rather surprised at the calm of that familiar voice.

"Good morning Charlie," he intoned. "Haven't spoken to you in a while. How's it going?"

"Fine Doctor. And how are you?"

"Fine Charlie. Just fine. I must say that we miss you. You've been such a part of the family. And while I can't imagine what ever made you do this – only love or money they say can trump loyalty – I wish you the best personally. After we win this thing big time next Tuesday, you must give me a call. We'll talk about your future. With so many of your old friends out there with their long knives, you're going to need a friend in Washington. Who knows? We may be together again."

"Well, thank you Doctor. I appreciate that. Nice to talk to you."

"You too my boy. Now I've got some last minute business to talk over with Tommy and Hal and, since you're not exactly on our side in this situation, I'd appreciate it if we could continue this communication in confidence."

"Of course, Doctor. Of course. I'll hang up and say goodbye. And thanks again for the offer. I may need it."

"You will need it indeed, my boy. Need it indeed."

But I didn't hang up and those stupid bastards didn't check to make sure. Then, Controller's real personality revealed itself.

"Tommy, Hap, what the fuck were you doing talking to that no good traitor?"

"He called here, Doc, we didn't call him. And we didn't want to talk to him but thought maybe we'd learn something." Tommy was anxious to placate the madman.

"Don't ever do that again, do you understand? That boy is dead. He's going down the fucking tube with his girlfriend. Five minutes after the polls close, the word goes out to the entire fraternity: you don't hire him, you don't talk to him, you don't acknowledge his existence. Hell, we don't even send him a fund raising letter. He becomes a non-person, do you understand?" Controller was getting more agitated with every sentence.

"Doctor, if I may," Hap sanctimoniously interrupted. "You were the one who told him to call and that you'd take care of him."

"I'll take care of him alright," Controller screamed. "It'll be slow torture. He'll get nowhere and I'll have the great satisfaction of letting him dangle in the wind, all the time thinking I'm his friend. Exquisite torture, Hap. Exquisite torture." Then, calming down, he shifted gears. "Now to the campaign. Everything in place? Need more money?"

At that point I quietly hung up the phone with mixed feelings of apprehension and satisfaction. I had no need to listen in on their strategy. It was dead. And I was now convinced they were going to lose. Big time.

CHAPTER 31

THE LAMPPOST

"The lamppost," I said out loud as I sat at my desk contemplating the waning days of the campaign.

"The WHAT?" asked Maureen with a quizzical look on her face.

"The lamppost," I repeated. "When will it happen and what will it be?"

"What will what be?" she demanded, looking as if she suspected I was losing it.

"The lamppost. The last minute piece of shit. Get it? L-A-M-P-P-O-S-T!!" I explained. "Every campaign has one in the last few days, Some sleazy, mean, lousy, stealth piece of propaganda gets circulated about the candidate. I call it the last minute piece of shit and we have to know about it. It's usually ten times worse than the rotten negative political television ad. It's a piece of direct mail or a circular slipped in mail boxes, often unsigned or falsely attributed to somebody. The opposition solemnly denies it had anything to do with it and by the time the damage is done and the campaign is over nobody cares and lets it go. But we've got to be heads up on it."

"What do you want us to do?" Maureen asked, now comprehending what I was saying.

"An e-mail alert to all coordinators. Be on the lookout, especially in outlying areas where it's more likely to go unnoticed by the media or by our people until it's too late. Tell them to keep an eye out for blank envelopes, folded flyers, stuff on doorsteps or anonymous mailings. I want to know as soon as possible. It's Thursday. That's typically the day of the last minute piece of shit. Enough time to have impact. Not enough time for us to react. Let's go."

With that, Maureen raced to the computer and simultaneously picked up the phone.

"I'll talk personally with our best people," she said. "And e-mail the rest right now."

It wasn't long before the lamppost surfaced. And what a last minute piece of shit it was. Picked up by one of our volunteers off a doorstep in St. Alban's, it was folded inside a plain white unsealed envelope. Addressed to "Concerned Voters of Vermont," it was allegedly sent by the "Rev. Joshua Rouse, Jesse Jackson Boulevard, Harlem, The Bronx, New York." And here's how it read:

"As the election campaign comes to a close, I am writing to concerned voters in Vermont urging them to re-elect Senator Josephine Stephenson. Senator Stephenson's support for federally subsidized housing for minorities in rural and suburban communities is an outstanding example of the kind of enlightened leadership this nation needs in the United States Senate. Your vote for Senator Stephenson will be a message to the nation that the civil rights movement is alive and well in the towns, hills and valleys of the Green Mountain state."

It was signed off by "Your friend and ally, Joshua Rouse."

"This would be ludicrous if it weren't so outrageous," Maureen said.

"Besides," I added, "Harlem is not in the Bronx. It's in Manhattan. I guess Manhattan's not as scary as The Bronx. And there is no Jesse Jackson Boulevard in the Bronx or Harlem."

"And whoever the idiot is who concocted this piece of filth doesn't even know that Jesse Jackson carried Vermont in the 1988 Democratic Presidential Primary," Maureen noted.

"Well, there's not much we can do about it except wait for it to backfire," I observed. "But let's get to the media and expose this stuff and ask Pete in Washington to try and track down the source of this thing. What a deplorably racist thing to do. Classic Controller."

"And stupid at that," Maureen said.

At that point, Jo walked into the office, took one look at the letter and practically exploded.

"Goddammit," she exclaimed. "Get the lawyers, get the authorities. Somebody's going to jail for this one."

"Cool it," I said. "It's bound to backfire. By the way, what's the issue?"

"Of course I voted for subsidized housing for poor people, minorities and everybody else. And of course, if I'm going to be for it, I'm going to be for it everywhere. What do they want me to do? Say I'm only for decent housing in certain places like inner city neighborhoods? This thing is a blatant racist attempt to scare the hell out of people. And who the hell is Joshua Rouse?"

343

"Probably doesn't exist," I replied. "The best we can do is force a denial from the Aiken camp. I hate to stoop to this stuff and I know the voters won't be fooled. If anything they'll be outraged. But we can't let it go unanswered."

By the 11 'clock news, Aiken himself was sanctimoniously deploring and disowning the letter, its contents and its origins in the typical hollow rhetoric of the programmed politician. Pete's attempts to track it down all led to dead ends although he swore that Controller was behind it. Just the sort of trashy thing he would do, Pete said. In the meantime, our people were reporting outrage in those towns, hills and valleys. But the media tracking poll showed the liars were still standing firm: Aiken 57%, Stephenson 29%

I was still in the office watching the reports when Jo walked in unannounced.

"Hi Senator," I said offhandedly. "Settled down?"

"I guess so," she said. "But it's the kind of thing that makes you want to quit this game and go back to real life. Things still holding?"

"I suppose," I said. "You never know in this game. But I suspect that, come election night, the liars of Vermont will send the country the most truthful message they've heard in a long time."

"Charlie, do me a favor. Cancel that hotel ballroom on election night. I don't want any of that hoopla, loud bellowing, drinking and bravura. And I don't want to have to stand in front of a bunch of local and national media thanking everybody from the family to you to the volunteers to Maureen. You know, the traditional ritual stuff. And I especially don't want to be on that podium if I lose."

"You're not going to lose, Jo," I said firmly. "And what do you intend to do on election night? Go skiing?"

"Just stay home. Have a few friends and family over. You, of course. Maybe, if we win, go out on the porch and thank the people of Vermont for the television cameras. But not answer any shouting questions from the press about what now, what next, how did you do it and all that. You tell the story. Besides, I'm tired and feeling very untraditional. And I really don't know what's next."

"Okay. If you say so. But you better have plenty of beer. That gesture will be the last slap at the campaign business. In fact, I rather like it."

"I'm going home," she said as she stood and turned around. She looked at me for a long moment, hesitated and said: "Charlie, I don't know how to thank you."

"Don't," I said. "Thank yourself for the guts to go through with this."

She continued to look at me and sat down again.

"You know," she said, "I still can't figure you out. You've just about destroyed your career. You're up here running the most unlikely campaign imaginable. You have no history of caring the least about campaign reform." She paused for a moment, hesitating and finally said it: "is it me?"

I really didn't want to go there at all. I started doodling with a pencil on a yellow legal pad. I looked down and became pensive. Then I looked her straight in the eye.

"Little bit," I said nervously.

"Then why not say so?" she asked.

Now I really didn't want to get into this. But I took a deep breath and responded, "because it's too complicated. Let's just leave it at that."

"Are you sure about that?" she persisted.

"No, Jo, I'm not sure about that. But I'm convinced enough to realize that a lot of lives would be hurt and a lot of hopes by a lot of people out there could be dimmed. So there it is. And I think it's best we leave it there." By now I was on the brink of stuttering. Never in my life had I felt so uncomfortable.

"We could have made such beautiful music together," she said, calmly but with feeling as she stood up, turned for the door and turned around again.

I barely kept my poise but painfully held my ground.

"Yes," I said matter of factly. "It would be nice to think so."

CHAPTER 32

ELECTION DAY

Twas the night before the Election and all through the state the people kept lying to pollsters they hate. Thus did I spend the waning moments of the campaign composing doggerel and drinking beer with a group of volunteers we had invited to a pre-election party at The Other Place (OP;s), one of Burlington's offbeat brew bars. At one point, our attention was drawn to the fatuous figure of candidate Aiken, still smiling and still intruding himself upon the body politic with a last minute rally a few blocks away at the Radisson.

"Are we gonna have a great victory tomorrow?" he bellowed.

"Yeah! Ethan! Ethan! Ethan!" the crowd bellowed in return.

"Are we gonna show that woman that us Vermonters don't buy her act?" he bellowed again.

"Yeah, Ethan! Ethan! Ethan!" they again bellowed in return.

"Are we gonna return that Yewnited States Senate seat to a real Green mountain boy who'll bring home the bacon?" he bellowed for the third time.

"Yeah, yeah, yeah! Ethan! Ethan! Ethan!" they bellowed back for the third time.

End of sound bite and a quick shift to Jo walking the main drag in Montpelier, quietly shaking hands and telling the cameras she was hoping for the best.

"Well," said the anchor man, "looks like it's all over, doesn't it? And here to give us his own analysis is our political pro and professional election analyst, Willie Welsh. What's your take Willie?"

"Thanks, Jim. Yes. It does indeed look like it's all over. I've been fortunate, because of my insider connections, to get the latest poll numbers from inside the campaign itself. You know, we professionals never rely on the published polls. The only ones we really trust are those we take ourselves. Well, anyway, the latest Aiken Campaign poll, done by the nation's top pollster, Hap Mandell, shows Aiken with a 57-29 lead. That leaves only 14% undecided so even if Stephenson got them all, she loses in a landslide." Old Willie was really impressed with himself.

"Wow, that's even bigger than the published polls and they had Ethan at 53%. What happened?" I took one look at that pompous anchor man with his old buddy Ethan reference and could have thrown up.

"It was her presentation last week that essentially put the final nail in the coffin," Willie pontificated. "Undecideds, undecided leans and even some Stephenson voters moved into the Aiken camp. Her negatives went sky high. That arrogant speech was enough for most Vermonters. And no doubt Ethan's strong ad campaign is having a devastating effect. That Granny Gooch one really hit home with Vermonters."

"Well, thanks a lot Willie. We'll be here tomorrow night to bring you the full coverage but now it's on to the sports and weather."

That day there was only one final stratagem to firm up. All our volunteer coordinators had to continue spreading the word that election day interviewers who conducted the infamous so called exit polling were to be lied to just like all the others. No sense in spoiling the game at this point.

Election Day dawned cold and damp. And all the media and political gossip was about the usual: "turnout." If it snows, will that hold down turnout? And even if it doesn't snow, will the increasingly cold weather hold down turnout? Or will it be a record turnout because of the Senate election on top of the Presidential? Or will indifference deter turnout? Or will the heated up race motivate turnout?

Stupid non-think, you guys. Hell, this is Vermont! Nothing deters turnout! And whatever the turnout, the results will be the same. Low, moderate or medium, the percentages will be in the same proportion.

In fact, it did look like a record turnout and I spent most of the day restlessly meandering around Burlington, checking into the headquarters on my cell, talking occasionally to Jo (she decided not to run around the length and breadth of the state for a media op but her opponent was everywhere with his big bombastic persona splashed all over the mid day news). I drove over to Mad River Glen, tempted to do a little skiing but was too nervous and preoccupied. Back to Burlington, checking on messages but nothing of importance. There was an eerie silence that day but there were also lines at the polling places I passed on the way.

We were due at the Stephenson residence at 8 PM, the moment the polls closed. Prior to that, I stopped in the Radisson bar for a couple of drinks and ran into Willie Welsh.

"Well Charlie," he said pompously, "how long, just how long will it take you to get out of town after the returns come in?"

"Just as long as it takes for the Senator to declare victory," I replied.

He guffawed and looked at me as if I were demented.

"Charlie, you really made a stupid decision on this one," he admonished. "It will ruin your career if it hasn't already. I just don't understand. Don't understand."

"You don't have to say it twice Willie," I replied in slight exasperation. "Why don't you just wait until the polls close?"

At that point, Pete walked into the bar. He had just arrived from Washington and decided to join us for decision time. I introduced him to Willie after a big hello and he gave us the news.

"Just ran into the network guy who gets the exit polling data," Pete said, looking dismal.

"What are they saying? What are they saying?" Willie asked anxiously. He had acquired this irritating habit of repeating himself.

"It's not scientific just yet," Pete replied. "But early indications are that Aiken's ahead by at least 55-45."

"Phew, that's a relief, that's a relief" Willie observed. Smiling cynically, he looked at me and said: "there's a plane bound for Washington at 10 PM, Charlie, 10 PM. Be on it." He chuckled…and chuckled.

"I guess you're right," I said. I felt like saying 'you jackass, you jackass' but wisely refrained. What did surprise me was that Pete appeared to take the exit polls at face value. Didn't he get it?

At 8, we went over to Jo's house where the vote count operation had been set up in the dining room under Maureen's supervision. Her mother, she of the masterful polling interview, was on the phone to key voting divisions. George was sharpening his pencil for the long evening. Jo was in the kitchen cooking up, of all things, scrambled eggs for dinner. Ray and Henry were watching television with some key coordinators.

"Scrambled eggs!" I shouted. "Scrambled eggs!" Too much time spent with Willie. "How about some pizza?"

Jo didn't even look around. "If you want pizza, then order some pizza. Those of us here are having scrambled eggs."

"And beer, where the beer?" Pete demanded.

"Where do you think it is?" she asked impassively. "It's in the refrigerator and there's more cooling out in the back yard."

Just as Pete and I popped open our first of many cans, Maureen came running into the kitchen looking terrible.

"First returns from Bennington," she announced ominously.

"Two voting divisions. Aiken 745, Stephenson 430."

For a moment, Jo stopped scrambling and stood motionless. Then she said: "let me take a look at the locations." She glanced at the addresses as we stood petrified and calmly announced, "that's where he lives. What do you expect?"

Everyone breathed a sigh of relief and then Henry came running into the kitchen. "Mom, Mom, the TV guy just said he would have a report on the Vermont Senate race right after the commercial!"

We all went into the living room, straining to catch a glimpse of what was going on and then Phil Cummings, the mighty national news anchor reappeared.

"And now, ladies and gentlemen, let's take a look at Vermont. The race there has gained national notoriety because of the election reform crusading of the incumbent Senator, independent Josephine Stephenson."

"That's a lousy picture of you Mom," Henry ventured.

"Shut up Henry, let's listen!" said Ray, giving his brother the elbow.

"Ray, don't use that language, shut up," Jo admonished as we zeroed in on the report.

"Earlier this year," Cummings continued, "both parties slated the same candidate to be her opponent. He's a young man with a famous name, Ethan Allen Aiken and he's been considered the favorite throughout the campaign. Now, we've told you, prior to this election, that, because of all the confusion created a few years ago about exit polling, that we wouldn't announce the results of exit polls until the vote tally was completed. But this time we're making an exception. The results in Vermont are so definitive that this is one race where the result is uncontestable. Our exit polling in Vermont indicates an Aiken landslide with better than 65% of the vote. Accordingly, at 8.35 PM, the first big "W" for winner goes up next to Aiken's name and we can return to coverage of the Presidential race and other key contests throughout the country."

Henry and Raymond looked crushed, descending into deep silence. George appeared pensive and slightly defeated. Jo was, as she had been since we got there, impassive. Maureen tossed her pencil in the air as if to say, well, that's it.

Then all turned and looked at me.

"What's the matter?" I asked bravely and nonchalantly. "You don't believe that, do you? You know that the people of this state have been consistently and perversely lying to all these guys. That's been our strategy all along. What makes you think it's changing now?"

"Because we heard it on the TV," Ray complained.

"Yeah, those guys know everything," Henry chimed in.

Even George had his say. "You must admit Charlie, that that's pretty powerful stuff. It's kinda hard watching that 'W' go up on that guy's photo."

"Yes, and it's going to be a lot nicer when they take it down in about two hours,' I said confidently but nervously.

"Let's just hang on and see what happens," Pete counseled as the phone started ringing.

Maureen answered. "No, we don't have any concession statement. No, we don't have one planned. No, the Senator is not going to some downtown hotel. No, we don't intend to start talking about what went wrong." And then she hung up.

"Off the hook," demanded George and Maureen did just that. "They'll be around here soon anyway," he added.

At that point, one of our volunteers rushed in from the dining room with more official totals. Maureen grabbed them and shouted: "Burlington, 50% of the vote counted: Stephenson 4,740, Aiken 1325!!"

Everybody roared. Everybody, that is, except, Jo. "My home town just like Bennington is his," she cautioned.

Suddenly the results began to come in droves. Jo had carried Saint Alban's 2-1, Brattleboro, 3-1, Montpelier, with 63%.

Then, with unexpected speed, just a little after 9.15 PM, local television news carried a report from the state capitol that, with 82% of the vote in the state already reporting, Stephenson had 64% of the vote to Aiken's 36%.

Pandemonium broke out. Ray and Henry were calling their friends to come on over. "Mom's won!!" they shouted victoriously. Maureen collapsed in an easy chair and stared straight ahead, still unbelieving. Jo was dishing out the scrambled eggs and I was paying the pizza deliveryman as the news broke. She ran over and hugged me in a rather formal way, then went into the dining room and embraced George who was getting uncharacteristically teary. Pete popped another can of beer and I just had the silliest, broadest grin on my face.

And once more, Henry was shouting. "Mom, Dad, here's Phil Cummings again!!"

Looking absolutely flabbergasted, the mighty anchor man watched as the 'W' left the Aiken photo and moved to Jo's.

"Ladies and Gentlemen, shortly after the polls closed, we broke our standing rule and told you that exit polling indicated a resounding victory for the challenger in Vermont. We said then that we projected his vote at roughly 65%."

"You said better than 65% you jerk!" interjected Ray.

"Shhhhh," said Jo. "Let's hear him."

"Well, something went wrong with our exit polls. Once in a while, something does go wrong and we're wrong this time and apologize for it. We're not only wrong now but apparently we've been wrong throughout this race because all the polls indicated a consistent and overwhelming lead for the challenger.

It appears from the official count that it is Stephenson who will actually get 65% of the vote, not Aiken. We don't know what happened but we're going to find out and we'll inform you of it as soon as possible. And now on to the Presidential race." If there ever was an uncomfortable performance, that was it.

"Maureen, put the phone back on the hook," George demanded. "We'll answer those bastards now."

"Charlie, you do it," Jo said. "I'll talk to the people but you talk to the media. I'm not sure I could explain it anyway."

Suddenly, the television reporting switched to the Ailken so called victory celebration. With stunned wife and bewildered children in tears, the candidate of the money, the polls, the focus groups, the political organizations and Granny Gooch, made a convoluted concession in which he thanked everybody and ended by saying: "we conducted the great crusade. We fought the great fight. And it's just the beginning. We'll be back because our cause is just and our message is clear." Behind him, ashen faced and funereal stood Hap and Tommy. I was surprised they showed up.

Aiken never did call Jo and that was just fine with her.

Amidst the joy and confusion, mingled with derisive reaction to Aiken's hollow rhetoric, something very different was taking place outside. We rushed to the windows at the sound of a commotion on the street. From every direction, people were quietly moving toward the house in candlelit parades. A few held creative placards proclaiming "Liars for the Truth," "Deceivers for Democracy" and "Prevaricators for Political Reform."

Media cameras and reporters began encircling the Stephenson residence, puzzled by the placards, astonished at the way things had developed and hoping to get some statement from within.

With what could only be described as an enormous sense of relief, Jo opened the door and appeared to the subdued but steady cheers and warm applause of the growing number of Vermonters who had come to her doorstep in a show of victory, solidarity and determination. There was nothing raucous or vulgar about this crowd. No shouting or bellowing. Only a kind of solemn celebration more akin to a religious procession than a political rally.

Flanked by George, Ray and Henry, she moved to the top of the steps. "This is overwhelming," she said. "And I assume that no political operators or advance men planned it."

"You better believe it," someone hollered and those up front started to laugh.

"Well, I don't know how to thank you," she continued. "For everything. For your support, your votes, for staying with me in the good times and bad. I think we taught the country a lesson today, don't you?"

Applause and gestures of agreement.

"And I think we made history today, don't you?"

More applause. More gestures of agreement.

"Now it's too bad that I'm not in some fancy hotel room thanking a thousand big contributors and twenty political consultants. The only people I have to thank are you. Don't you think that's a shame?"

"NOOOOO" they shouted.

"Just a lot of people from Vermont interested in clean politics, good government and elected officials who follow their conscience and not somebody else's opinion polls. I wish I had room enough in my house for all of you but I certainly didn't expect this."

"That's okay," an elderly man with a long beard called out from the back of the crowd. "We got what we came for and we don't need nothin' else."

"Then all I can say is thank you again. I don't know what the future will bring. I'm still only one in a hundred. But what you did here today will echo throughout the land, from here to Minnesota and from Minnesota to California.

"Politics in this country won't be the same because the manipulators of our system will never trust or be trusted again. People all over this country will be getting the message and this country will be the better for it. I'll go back to Washington to continue the fight to change the system but please, remember one thing: I will always be with you. I won't forget who I was before I went there and I'll never forget the people who made it possible. God bless you all."

With that, they applauded again and slowly filed away, candles still burning bright on a chilly November night.

Jo happily refrained from tearing up and, as she walked back into the house, the sainted Senator elect turned realist again, commenting to me, "this time we'll finally get that son of a bitch Controller."

I told her that the networks were screaming for comment and she once again said "you talk to them. I don't want to and I don't want to be on Backfire or Curveball or any of those political talk shows either. We'll just keep our eyes on the real ball."

And so I walked down the steps and faced the cameras.

"Charlie, what was this all about? How did every single poll call it wrong? What did you guys do?"

"We really didn't do anything. It seems that, in their traditionally perverse manner the fine upstanding voters of Vermont decided to turn the mechanical technology of politics against itself. Apparently, they don't like to be manipulated by money, polling, focus groups and negative television ads. So they collectively fashioned a grass roots strategy exquisite in its perversity. They, well, to put it bluntly, they decided to lie and deceive the political system in the interests of a higher goal."

The reporters looked astonished.

"But that's impossible. Hundreds of thousands of people simply don't act in unison."

"Nevertheless, they apparently did," I replied.

"How much money did you spend?" demanded one interrogator.

"Didn't raise any, didn't spend any, aside from the few bucks we put up ourselves to do that speech last week."

"Oh come on, Charlie, that's ridiculous. How many polls did you guys take?"

"None. Except the one that took place today."

"So what happens next? Will campaign reform take center stage in Washington?"

"I'm not sure," I replied. "We have a new President and a lot of new members of Congress. The Senator will go back to Washington and fight for the things she believes in. Hopefully we can systematically dismantle the political apparatus that has, for too long, stood between the people and their elected officials. One thing I do know: as a result of this election in one of the smallest and most independent states in the nation, politics in America will never be the same again."

EPILOGUE

The day after the election, a group of grim and determined citizens of Vermont gathered in front of the Radisson Hotel in Burlington to deliver a message to two of its most prominent guests, Hap Mandell and Tommy Ragin. "Villains, you have two hours to get the last plane to Washington. After that, you get tarred and feathered." Hap and Tommy left for the airport in plenty of time to get through security.

Early that morning, the editors of the nationally prestigious Millenium Magazine rushed to their operations center to erase, with photo editing software, their cover photo of Ethan Allen Aiken captioned "The New Face of American Politics." They quickly substituted a picture of Senator Josephine Stephenson captioned "The Amazing Victory of Reform Politics."

With audiences and viewers laughing in derision at the political commentary of pollsters and consultants, now that the game had been exposed, both Backfire and Curveball were cancelled by their respective cable networks.

In January, the newly elected Vermont state legislature began debating the possibility of a national Constitutional Convention to eliminate any First Amendment protection of political money in the name of free speech. Scholars in Montpelier noted that, in the early 20th Century, when women's suffrage was still being blocked, the nation came within one state of having a new Constitutional Convention and everybody became so terrified of the implications that they rushed to approve the 19th amendment in 1920: Some legislators went even further, reviving the decades old movement for Vermont secession from the union in the event that the conspiracy to "get" Stephenson were to continue. But such a move was deemed by less radical heads to be premature.

In Washington, both "Common Grrrreee…Good" and "The New GOP" quietly went out of business. The Ass Kissinger project was abandoned. Consultants, pollsters and certain lobbyists began to be viewed as suspect, causing no end of economic hardship for the elites of the political establishment. Rumors abounded that the American people were turning into a nation of perverse and deliberate liars when it came to political polling so why should anyone trust these guys? Ronald West, it was reported, applied for unemployment compensation.

Senator Stephenson returned to the Capitol, still an outsider but feared and reluctantly respected by her colleagues. Her ability to attract the media and influence legislation continued to grow and soon thereafter, under enormous public pressure, she was restored to her Chairmanship of the Ethics Subcommittee whereupon she vowed to pursue Ludwig Controller and other malefactors in the Beltway fraternity. Although her reform bills still faced formidable political and constitutional hurdles, a strange thing began to happen: the amount of money raised and spent started diminishing because of the growing distrust by those running for office of the reliability and effectiveness of the consultants, pollsters and media operatives.

As time went on, several Senators and Congressmen were reported wandering the halls in bewildered state, not knowing what to do, how to vote or what positions to espouse, having lost all trust in their pollsters and consultants, and therefore having no support mechanisms to make up their minds for them. But a growing number also began to consult the courage of their own convictions and, to a person, those who were considering retirement because of disillusionment decided to stay on. Gradually, uncertainty and the loss of dependency gave way to an enormous sense of relief as more and more members freed themselves from the shackles of their pollsters, consultants and money men.

Pete and Maureen returned to Jo's staff. George stayed in Burlington, Henry went back to school and Raymond returned to UCLA, having been granted probation for the drunken driving charge.

I, Charlie Coons, took a year off to write this book but I have become increasingly paranoid in my suspicion that, sooner or later, the villains will have their revenge. I must admit that, on occasion, with my reputation as the master consultant of them all restored, I am frequently tempted to go back into the consulting business. In fact, I received some feelers wondering whether I would be willing to accept the award for Cleverest Campaign of the Year at Controller's annual dinner. An acceptance did not seem entirely inappropriate.

And, oh yes, Ludwig Controller received a full Presidential pardon for anything he did or may have done in violation of federal law. The pardon was quietly promulgated on the last day in office of the outgoing President of the United States.

THE END

ABOUT THE AUTHOR

Dick Doran has had thirty years experience in politics and government, including six years of service as Chief of Staff to the governor of Pennsylvania and four years in the cabinet of the mayor of Philadelphia. A veteran of numerous political campaigns, Dick has also been a TV talk show host, a writer and commentator on public affairs and a teacher of English literature. This is Dick's second published book, the first being "Suddenly 65, A Chronicle of the Millennium".

Reform movement ? } shaky
Jo: Charlie

drop focus group — momentum
letter ? — multiple copies
explanation

Printed in the United States
1521000001B/26